IN THE
COMPANY

OF EAGLES

Ernest K. Gann

——— SIMON AND SCHUSTER – NEW YORK

—to Jackie for her research and Dodie for her care . . . my gratitude.

E.K.G.

War is a series of awful mistakes created by both antagonists trying to dominate without full knowledge of the other's mistakes . . . .

Prologue

December 15, 1916
Near Revigny
With Captain Adolphe
Massine—

"SERGEANT CHAMAY, I have asked you to come here directly so that I may have your version of what happened this morning."

". . . we were at a thousand meters just to the south of Vacherauville. The ack-ack was troublesome, but really not too bad—a lot of seventy-seven-millimeter stuff slapping at us from batteries I never really spotted because I was too busy keeping the Caudron right side up and heading for Vacherauville and I knew we were late. Why is it we fly the slowest and clumsiest crocks in the sky? One expects the English to stagger around in relics that must have been designed by Da Vinci, but why should Frenchmen?"

"Never mind, Chamay. Try to stay with the sortie. How many were in your escort? I requested six Nieuports. An infantry officer who witnessed the whole sad affair said he counted only four."

"Well he needs a new pair of eyes. If only four had shown up I would really be raving—but there were six all right. Three of them dropped down so they were about five hundred meters above me and the other three took the same position above Raymonde."

"Sergeant LaFrenier was your friend?"

"Raymonde and I grew up together. We sat side by side at Stanislas and entered the École Polytechnique together."

"Please continue only if you feel like it. Otherwise we can wait until tonight or tomorrow morning."

"No. I prefer to get it over with. I would say the escort did what they could although certainly some of them were looking down when they should have been looking up. I'm trying not to blame them entirely for what happened—maybe if Sevier hadn't been hit on the Boche's first pass Raymonde would have had someone to shoot for him and with the escort snapping at the Boche's tail, maybe he would have run for home."

"How many Boche were there?"

"Only one. That's just it! What kind of an escort is it when one Boche can pass through the whole lot not once, but three times?"

"Are you certain there were no other German aircraft about?"

"I am positive."

"Would you object if I passed on your statement to the commandant of the providing escadrille? I believe it was the Twelfth."

"I certainly would not object. They deserve—"

"Now just take a moment to cool down a bit. I'm not going to give you some pap about how we've all lost dear friends, but if I pass on your remarks—even if I soften them a bit—it's going to sound as if we are accusing the escort of cowardice before the enemy, and that is—"

"I am not accusing them of cowardice, but of ineptness. The Boche not only caught them asleep, but when they finally realized he had already made his first pass and killed Sevier they did everything wrong. The Boche was up when they were down and down when they were up. He made monkeys out of them and I doubt if he took a bullet hole."

"What was he flying?"

"An Albatros. I believe it was a D-II, because I don't recall any V-strut configuration."

"Color?"

"The usual motley green—lozenge pattern—and purple spots—"

"Not quite so fast. This part I want to write down. Would you say his camouflage was successful?"

"It was perhaps more difficult to see him against the ground, since the earth is almost the same color except where there are patches of snow left, but the fancy paint work doesn't help him against the sky, in fact it makes him easier to see, which leaves even less excuse for the escort—"

"You believe he was an experienced pilot?"

"No question. He was also a bastard."

"Anything else remarkable about his flying, or his airplane?"

"He had a white target painted on his fuselage. A bull's-eye just

3

forward of the tail. Dutoit sighted on it but thought we were much too far away for deflection shooting."

"Dutoit is your observer?"

"Yes."

"Did you know Sevier?"

"Casually. He's only been here a week or so."

"Did he fire on the Boche?"

"No. I doubt if he saw anything—never knew what hit him. I saw a shadow pass between us and the sun and thought it was one of our own Nieuports above. I was just about to wave to Raymonde because I was feeling good about our job being done when I heard a quick burst and I saw Sevier slump down in his cockpit. He never moved again. I am sure he was killed instantly and suffered no pain. You can tell his parents that. I only wish that Raymonde—"

"Then you saw the Boche pass?"

"Yes. He dove down to about three hundred meters and pulled up for a second pass from beneath Raymonde. That time he hit the fuel and set him on fire."

"Was his Caudron damaged during the first pass?"

"I don't think so. Raymonde immediately took violent evading action, so his controls were certainly intact. I could see the German, but I doubt if Raymonde could because the bastard was clever enough to stay directly below him."

"And where was the escort at the end of the first pass?"

"Scattered all over the sky in a panic."

"You are making an assumption and I can't throw that at them. Please stay with what you actually know."

"They were certainly scattered around. When they woke up, the German was already lined up for his second pass from beneath Raymonde. He was coming up while they were diving and all six of them nearly collided at the place where he had been. They never seemed to consider that in thirty seconds he would be elsewhere. Tell me, Captain, were those pilots graduated from Pau yesterday?"

"Recriminations will do little good now. Let us simply state the facts and be done with it. Go on."

"I'm not so interested in recrimination as in seeing that it doesn't happen again. Supposing there had been another Boche around or even two or three more. Can you imagine how long we would have lasted with the entire escort sucked down below us?"

4

"You may be sure I will ask that question of the Twelfth's commandant. Now you and Dutoit were to photograph the effect of the barrage and the other Caudron was to drop smoke fuses on the enemy positions around Vacherauville. Did you accomplish your mission?"

"Yes. Our photos are in the lab wagon now if you want to look them over. Raymonde and Sevier dropped their fuses right down the throats of the Boche infantry, they were so low. The fuses had ample burn time and were still smoking when the artillery began again. It was a miracle Raymonde wasn't hit by our own shellfire. He was a very brave man."

"How long were you over the lines?"

"I cannot say exactly."

"Approximately will do."

"Thirty minutes then."

"And the escort was visible to you all that time?"

"I took them for granted. I was very busy trying to evade the ack-ack and still position Dutoit so he could take his pictures from the right angles. And a Caudron doesn't fly itself you know."

"After approximately thirty minutes you turned for home? Both of you?"

"Raymonde turned first. I assume he was out of fuses. We had to hang about another two or three minutes while Dutoit took a final photo."

"Was the escort with you when you turned back?"

"Yes. I looked up and they were there. It was really the first time I had looked up since we were over the lines."

"How long after you left the lines did the Boche attack?"

"I don't know. We were over the Meuse. There was sunlight on it."

"I thought the weather was abominable."

"It was. But suddenly there was a break—there was the sun and there was the Boche."

"He got Sergeant LaFrenier on his second pass then? From under him?"

"No. On the second pass from beneath he hit Raymonde's fuel tank and there was fire almost immediately. But Raymonde was not hurt—not at all—I'm sure of that. We were no more than four hundred meters high. I feel sure the Caudron would have stayed in one

5

piece until it hit the ground even though Raymonde left his cockpit. He might have been burned and smashed up, but at least there was one chance in a hundred he would be alive now. The Boche deliberately took that last chance away from him."

"I don't quite follow."

"There was fire in Raymonde's cockpit so he crawled out of it and then back until he straddled Sevier. His helmet and flight suit were smoking and burning around his shoulder. There he was standing up in the rear cockpit and I saw him pull off his helmet and then try to get out of his suit. The Caudron was spiraling down by itself. I think it would have hit flat and there were only open fields below."

"This was near Charny?"

"Yes. Raymonde had pulled the suit down to his waist when the Boche came at him from above. He had plenty of time and took it— the escorts were still out of range. He even cut his power for an easy glide and waited until he was only a few meters from the Caudron. I saw Raymonde throw up his arms, he was kneeling in smoke—or standing now, I don't know which—and there was smoke trailing away from his body. But he was very much alive."

"Would you like a brandy, Chamay?"

"No. I want to get this over with and mail the letters he left in the escadrille box and then . . . I don't know what I will do. I've got to find some way to get that Boche. He is the kind of barbarian the propaganda people tell us about. What kind of a human being would do what he did?"

"What did he do?"

"Raymonde's Caudron was obviously finished. The observer was dead. Raymonde was burning enough so it would be a long time before he would ever fly again—he was *absolutely helpless!* The German was quite close enough to see all that, yet he gave Raymonde a full burst from both guns right in his face. I saw his head explode while his arms were still raised. I'll never forget it."

"Then did the Boche come after you?"

"No. He held his glide past Raymonde and went right through the Nieuports, who fired at him—at least they made noise—but they certainly didn't hit anything, because the Boche scurried home a few meters above the ground. He disappeared in some low scud and artillery smoke."

"Did the Nieuports follow him?"

6

"They milled around above me for a minute or so, then two of them took off after the Albatros as if they had even a prayer catching it. The rest of them circled with me watching until Raymonde's Caudron hit. It landed flat all right. He could have walked away from it. That Boche was not a soldier. He was a murderer. I'll get him if it's the last thing I ever do."

"The chances of meeting him again are rather slim I should think, but I wish you luck. Based on your information I will of course write the official letter to LaFrenier's parents and to Sevier's. I will also recommend both men for the Medaille Militaire. Since LaFrenier was your close friend would you be good enough to see after his personal effects?"

"Certainly."

"Chamay, I will have a drop of brandy myself if you don't mind. I have been watching you for some time. You are a good pilot, but not, shall we say, a natural for a reconnaissance escadrille. You are too impetuous, too high strung for this rather dull and thankless job, if I may say so. Believe me, Chamay, I do sympathize with the loss of your friend and I well understand your present state of shock. I will remind you that if the Germans had more than the vaguest notion of honor there would not have been this war. Now I have been watching you and listening to you for the better part of an hour. I must be perfectly frank and say that for the time being at least this unfortunate sortie seems to have rendered you rather difficult for us to employ in the usual way. We most value steadiness, extraordinary placidity in the midst of turmoil, eyes that will view the enemy objectively rather than as a personal antagonist. Now as you stand before me, still bristling with hurt and fury, I find myself wondering if your talents might better serve France employed in a different style. For example, if I were to recommend your transfer to a fighter escadrille would you be willing to go?"

"Captain, I would be forever in your debt."

BOOK ONE

Chapter One

April 1917
Near Sissonne
With Jasta 76—

PRIVATE PILGER EXHALED such great clouds of vapor as he walked across the stubble field that he fancied himself a steam engine. He experimented hopefully with a high-pitched feminine sound which he considered akin to a train whistle, but he soon desisted, for this morning the stubble field was unusually quiet. There was no thumping of the heavies to the west of the surrounding hills and Pilger knew that if anyone here in officer country heard him trying to imitate a steam engine he would order the medics to look inside his head.

For the moment, Pilger turned his simple face toward the graying sky and thanked God that after all he still had a head on his shoulders—particularly when it was one of the largest heads in the German army. Twice when he had been on the Eastern Front, the first time at Grabowic in '15 and the second at the attack near Lake Naroch in '16, Pilger had been witness to the sudden removal of a comrade's head. Both Gutterman and Schneider had been decapitated by shrapnel. The instant incongruity of their quivering trunks still caused Pilger occasionally to raise one of his heavy peasant hands toward the top of his neck—just to make sure.

It was long before the sun, and the crunch of Pilger's boots on the brittle, frozen stubble sounded so much like snare drums he instinctively fell into march cadence. All of the field was white with frost as was the hedgerow from which jutted a line of makeshift corrugated iron shacks. Pilger was shocked that officers of the Imperial Air Force were quartered in such seedy conditions. After all, they were not infantry who had no choice. My own quarters are better, he thought. With eight of us in the same tent we can at least keep warm.

Each of the iron shacks housed one and sometimes two officer pilots of Jasta 76. Pilger was willing to concede that the stink of the latrine on this side of the pasture was quite equal to that of the latrine on his own side and also that there might be something significant about the fact, but the moment he sat down long enough to ponder such matters someone ordered him to perform some silliness and his social meditations were invariably stillborn. And who was it, he had asked himself many times, who was always so clever with words? The men who had never been shot at, of course. Their mouths were forever flapping about men like Sebastian Kupper, who was a far better officer than most soldiers would ever know.

It was as much a German soldier's duty to hate officers as to obey them . . . true. Who would expect anything else? But both the obeying and the hating should be conducted along fixed rules set long ago when uniforms were blue and helmets black and officers carried swords. There was no sense in going about upsetting things.

On his leave of only a month ago Pilger had been distressed by the trend of unrest in his native town of Nienburg. It was, he thought, all very well to complain about the lack of lard, the tea made from blackberry leaves, the difficulty of buying any kind of cheese, and who could truly claim things were going famously when many people were trying to get through the terrible winter in paper clothes and without coal. Yet such miseries were far from unbearable, and it was Pilger's belief that if the profiteers could all be caught and shot there would be enough for everyone. But he could find very few of his acquaintances who would even partly agree with him. Everyone, it seemed, was displeased with the Kaiser and some openly praised the English. It was astonishing. The Kaiser had six sons at the front. People were recommending that at least one of them be killed as a sacrifice to please the public. What kind of madness was this?

Eventually Pilger decided he had been unfortunate on his leave and had met only the wrong people. Yet the general undercurrent of civilian attitude still lingered in his thoughts and it troubled him deeply. Not that people were afraid to talk. Just the reverse. People who should know better seemed anxious to dump their resentment at a third year of war on those who were actually fighting it. All soldiers were guilty by association with the military, and the military

13

was a vague collection of Junkers who drank champagne and ate roast duck all day long and told the Kaiser what to do. Pilger had been at some pains to explain that in his experience, which included a full year on the Russian Front, he had seen officers drinking champagne on the Kaiser's birthday but they did not eat roast duck. They were too busy dodging Russian bullets and scratching Russian lice like everyone else. And furthermore, he told whoever inquired about military evils, he had as yet to see any officer have even the remotest contact with his supreme highness. He had once seen Von Mackensen at a distance and watched him inspect a turnip field full of Russian dead—the idiots were wearing *white* blouses when they charged our machine guns!—but Von Mackensen, in spite of the decorative skull on his shako, looked exactly like Kappel, the Nienburg taxidermist, and Pilger did not believe the Kaiser would pay such attention to him no matter what he said. He held the same opinion of Prince Eitel Friedrich, who had arrived on the Eastern Front accompanied by a huge staff of adjutants and orderly officers. Absolutely nothing happened as a result of his visit, Pilger insisted. Neither the Prince, nor the Grand Duke of Saxe-Coburg-Gotha, nor Mackensen nor Ludendorff himself, could change the basic situation. The Russian soldier was a dumb animal led by fools. And in spite of the unfortunate accidents suffered by the heads of Gutterman and Schneider, the Russians were short of ammunition. How could such verminous beasts hope to survive against the Germany Army? They were too busy scratching to fight. Nine thousand lice on every Russian prisoner according to the men who operated the delousing station.

One evening during Pilger's leave there had been a meeting in the Nienburg florist shop where he had been employed before the call-up of his military year. The proprietor, whom Pilger had never liked very much, but who at least served as a destination for a soldier without any real family of his own, announced that he had invited a few friends in for coffee. He explained how he wanted his friends to meet a soldier so recently come from the front. Pilger had objected. He was not a monkey in a zoo, he said, and he did not like being placed on exhibition. And he tried to make it clear how he had not really come from the front this time, but from quite a pleasant spot some twelve kilometers comfortably to the east of it. Indeed, since the transfer of the 37th Division to the Western Front, life had been like a grand tour of the world—Cracow, Breslau, Dresden, Leipzig, Nuremberg, Karlsruhe. Now, if the proprietor would like his friends to hear about such places it might be interesting even if Pilger's acquaintance with them had been limited to his view from the troop train.

The proprietor had been unenthusiastic. No, his friends wanted to hear about how the troops were suffering in every horrible and conceivable way, while their officers lived like kings. And they would especially like to hear of any signs of mutiny Pilger might have seen and who the brave soldiers were who defied their officers and refused any longer to serve as cannon fodder, and most important of all, since Pilger was a front-line man, had he seen any signs of fraternization between German troops and French or English. There were many reports of this sort of mutual sympathy among all the poor souls who had no choice temporarily but to serve their cruel masters.

"When I was in the front line I never saw anything like *that!*" Pilger swore. "Of course I was only one soldier, but it seemed to me the French were just like the Russians. They did not want to shake my hand in the least. They wanted to kill me. That is why I am so pleased about my transfer to the Luftstreitkraft. It's as if I am suddenly a hero. Two days before Christmas they haul three of us out of the trenches, wipe the mud out of our ears, and give us new uniforms. And now the only possible chance of my being injured is if I am crazy enough to stand outdoors while the flak batteries are potting away at the sky. And I am not that crazy. And I am not an authority on the *Western* Front, because I only spent four days there. The Russian Front, yes. But that was months ago and no one would be interested."

The proprietor had said that his friends would be more than interested in any soldier from the Russian Front and as long as he was a soldier who just didn't drive a field kitchen or do paper work in some headquarters, they wanted to talk to him.

It seemed the florist had a great many friends. About thirty appeared, and until he remembered the lack of soap and the extremely cold winter, Pilger was offended by their smell, which he decided was quite as rancid as the stink of front-line troops during the heat of Russian summer. And he had fancied he saw the few remaining plants droop in their pots when this collection of patriots started expounding their views. Except for two men, one minus a leg and

15

one minus an eye and part of his nose, who had been invalided out of the service, no one seemed genuinely interested in what Pilger had to say.

"I remember July eighteenth," he began. "It was midsummer night and for bonfires we had all of the villages in the area blazing. There was a Russian attack right in the middle of our celebration and for a while everything was confused. But finally the Russians ran away and we found out later they had expected a brigade of Cossacks to come help them, but they didn't come."

Pilger knew he was not a good storyteller and he saw that he was losing his audience when they learned that he was no longer firing a rifle or even wearing a helmet. There were several scraggly-haired women in the group, a few of whom Pilger recognized as locals; but most of the men were strangers to him and he wondered especially about the presence of four men dressed rather better than the others who spoke with marked Berlin accents. It was they who said the war was lost. The declaration infuriated Pilger and for a few moments he nearly gave in to an impulse to reach out with his big paws and knock their heads together. When the same men claimed that America would soon declare war against Germany, Pilger was convinced they were all escapees from the insane asylum. Didn't everyone know there were too many Germans in America to let such a thing happen? Pilger did because some of them were his very own blood relatives.

Later when the beetroot coffee was served, the discussion washed around Pilger like waves against a rock. He was there and yet he was not there. He was a something in a rather grubby uniform, too big across the chest to ignore, yet certainly not deserving to participate in the group discussion. Pilger brooded on their thickening words until he himself became inflamed and stood up to have his say.

"You are idiots!" he began. "You are talking about a revolution and a new world when we are still dying for the old." Pilger had never been noted for his eloquence and now he was astounded when very suddenly all eyes were upon him. He became as thoroughly frightened by their silence as he had been angered before. He opened his mouth, barely avoided an apology, and gasping, launched haltingly into his thoughts. "Consider for example my officer Leutnant Kupper, who is from Mainz. He is not so young as many of the others. In fact, for an aviator he is an old man."

"You are his serf!" someone said. Pilger was so busy hanging on to what he intended to say that the remark sailed past him.

"Leutnant Kupper is thirty-six years old and had a fine education before he put on the uniform—an electrical engineer employed by Siemens he was. He could have stayed right in Berlin at the factory, but he did not. He volunteered to be sent to the flying school at Darmstadt. They taught him to fly and sent him off to Bulgaria and then to the Galician front, where you never saw such flies. Like quail. You could shoot them with a Luger."

Instinctively Pilger brushed a nonexistent fly from his cheek and tried to reassemble what he wanted to tell these people about Sebastian Kupper, who was a remarkable man even if he was an officer.

"Leutnant Kupper already has eighteen victories. He is an ace—very much of an ace. Almost twice an ace!" Pilger added, remembering that when Kupper had twenty victories he would be just that.

Pilger's audience chose to ignore him except for one man who said that Von Richthofen had at least thirty victories and what difference did it make? You couldn't win a war shooting down aviators.

Pilger clung desperately to his theme. It might be cold outside, he thought, but it was stifling in this room and his thoughts were being smothered. "I have heard many others say Kupper will also be one of our greatest aces if he is not killed too soon!"

The woman directly in front of him turned to her companion and snarled quite loud enough for Pilger to hear that he was a true bourgeois, one of those lost slaves who liked their chains and so was more to be feared than pitied.

"Now," Pilger asked of those further removed from him, "can anyone say it is right for me to desert a man like that? Even if I could—is what I really mean."

"You are one body wasted taking care of another which should learn to take care of itself," a man answered in a thin whine. He wore heavy glasses and Pilger had never seen him before, although his accent marked him as a local. Pilger brought his fist down so hard on the plant table, three pots capsized.

"Leutnant Kupper is not an *it!*" he shouted. "He is a human with a lot of nerve and absolute belief in our cause!"

"Your mouth is a sewer for his defecation," the voice whined again.

That had done it. Pilger instantly lost all sense of where he was and why. His only all-consuming desire was to silence that whining voice forever. Dashing his coffee cup at the floor he lunged at the reflection of thick glasses. En route to his objective he capsized the two women who had been sitting in front of him. Their screams were joined by angry shouts as Pilger plowed through the Berlin contingent. There were suddenly many bodies including that of the florist between Pilger and the thick glasses. The man himself was barely visible, cringing behind the blockade. Pilger howled with rage, charged into the human barricade and the melee exploded. Pilger flayed his great paws indiscriminately at men and women alike. For a wonderful instant he had a firm grip on the proprietor's nose, squeezing it as he would a lemon. Finally he actually did make contact with thick glasses long enough to seize him by the neck and spit in his face, but almost simultaneously he was overwhelmed. Even his great bulk was no match for so many. The women bit his hands and his ears, he was held down and kicked nearly senseless by the men and was finally dragged through the street door and left lying on the cobbles. The florist, nursing his nose, stood over him.

"Do not come back here again, Pilger. Not even after the war." The florist turned away and after a moment Pilger's round cap came sailing out the doorway followed by his kit sack, which came sliding to a stop against his knee.

Pilger had picked himself up and was relieved to discover that his uniform was not torn—nor had he suffered any serious injuries except to his dignity and sense of righteousness. His anger faded quickly to contempt. "So much," he muttered, "for returning heroes."

Walking to the railroad station, he even managed a wry smile as he remembered how a corporal of Pioneers whose business it was to tunnel mines under the French trenches had warned him only the week before that the homefront could be exceedingly dangerous.

It was two o'clock in the morning before Pilger had found a train bound for Cologne, where he would change to another and eventually reach Mons. From there it was only some fifty kilometers to his Jasta's new base. Pilger boarded the train without the slightest regret and reported back for duty two days ahead of his schedule.

"Oh, you absolute fool!" croaked Feldwebel Groos, who was also an ex-infantryman. His strange cheek pigmentation was a permanent souvenir of earth blasts at Verdun. The ugly tattoo left him with a secret fear that no woman would ever submit to him willingly, hence he had denied himself their company since 1915. Now the subject of women so haunted him he could only smile when vicariously enjoying the fleshly adventures of another.

"Tell me all the details, Pilger. Begin with how you first met her and omit nothing. Of course, if she gave you a disease you will immediately take thy wang to the medics—that is, after you tell me the details. Begin."

"I do not have a disease."

"Then . . . ?" Feldwebel Groos regarded Pilger with open disapproval. "Don't tell me you couldn't get it up any more. You would be a disgrace to the Jasta."

"I came back because I know what I know," Pilger said simply. "And that isn't easy these days."

On this crisp morning, as he crossed the stubble field with Sebastian Kupper's polished boots dangling from one hand and a pot of hot water from the other, Pilger decided that as far as his contest with the home elements was concerned he had actually been victorious. Not only had he displayed his contempt for their meeting, he had also been correct in one of his major challenges to their predictions. America was *not* in the war.

Pilger stopped before the door of the second hut in line and set the boots and hot water pot on the stoop. He pulled his tunic down as smooth as it would ever go, and cautiously opened the door. At once he was assaulted by a large Alsatian dog. There followed a violent tussling and mutual growling during which Pilger allowed the Alsatian to nibble at both his ears. But their manner was entirely without malice, dog and man thoroughly enjoying the pummeling of each other until a voice called from within. "Pilger!"

The ceremony ended, the Alsatian leaped back into the hut. After straightening his tunic again and picking up the boots and pot, Pilger followed him. The Alsatian went straight to Oberleutnant Sebastian Kupper. He was lying in his bunk staring at the corrugated metal roof.

"Good morning, Pilger."

Pilger managed to click his heels in acknowledgment without actually halting his progress.

"I wish," yawned Leutnant Kupper, "that you and Louie would

have your morning wrestling match at some place farther away from here."

"It is not my idea. Louie is at me the moment I open the door and I can't get away from him."

Kupper kneaded the loose skin beneath the Alsatian's neck and smiled at the apparent trance produced by his manipulations. "Ah, Louie," he sighed, "I wish someone would do the same thing to me every morning."

He continued to massage the Alsatian as he watched Pilger set his boots beneath the crude wooden table, then carefully place a pair of hooks just above them. Setting his boot hooks just so was Pilger's idea of serving him, Kupper knew. He had never used the hooks, but Pilger's self-imposed program was consistent if nothing else. He had set the hooks out that way the first morning he had reported for duty as Kupper's batman and for a very few moments he had succeeded in masquerading as one of those strange yet invaluable men who request such duty for reasons beyond the comprehension of most soldiers. Such men, when conscientious and practiced, often became more than servants. While their official duties were those of valet and housemaid, they often became men of considerable power within their military unit. If their officer was of high enough rank they might even learn of military plans and secrets most officers would not hear about for months. They were a direct link between an officer and his men, a means through which the officer became aware of the latest barracks complaint, and likewise if the batman craved attention he could hold the stage against almost any competition as he related in colorful detail just what the officers were up to.

Unscrupulous batmen made a very good thing of their unique position. For a fee, or some tribute in local kind, they might pass on to the officer concerned that a Private Schmidt was not requesting leave just because he was beginning to squirt semen from his ears. They would make up a credible history concerning Schmidt's ailing father, and how for a few days at least, he sorely needed help on the farm. An enterprising batman could engage in all manner of trade, selling everything from army materiel to medicines guaranteed to simulate kidney disease, ailing heart or whatever was needed to obtain a disability discharge. And a batman's influence usually became even more solid with time until he needed to be obsequious only to regimental sergeant-majors, whose extraordinarily sensitive noses could smell the activities of most batmen from afar. Kupper knew such men could be exceedingly dangerous; the more so when some displeased staff officer discarded them. Then, likely as not, they would slide resentfully down to servicing some hapless Leutnant like himself.

Watching Pilger set out his razor, toothbrush, comb and shaving brush, Kupper thought how fortunate he was. Pilger had been a front-line soldier and his second class Iron Cross should have been first class if even half of what he told was true. He had never asked for the slightest favor and Kupper had never heard him complain about anything—even in a winter which had set all records for bone-chilling. It had taken some time before Sebastian Kupper the man had been able to separate himself from Leutnant Kupper the flying officer and view his batman objectively. At last he was gratified to discover that Pilger was not an oaf or merely a great hulking nonentity in uniform who did uninteresting chores. He was, Kupper had finally concluded, somewhat slow of thought only because he was an innocent. He believed in his superior. This, Kupper knew, was a very great burden on any man's mind if he was part of an army at war, and a soldier with such precepts was likely to be among the first to die. Yet Pilger had survived Tannenberg, Gorlice, Przemysl, the terrible battles on the Stokhod, and finished his combat days with some lively skirmishes on the Somme. He had come away without a scratch, which was miraculous enough no matter what his principles might have been.

Now Pilger was stropping the razor. "I will not pour your water until you get up, Herr Leutnant. It is still very cold outside."

"I think we are involved in a return of the Pleistocene age," Kupper groaned.

"What would that be?" Pilger returned the razor to its place on the towel and Kupper saw that as usual he had placed it ten centimeters west of the soap and five centimeters east of the brush.

"A time when it was much too cold for fighting." Kupper rose from his cot.

"Everywhere in the world?" Pilger asked politely. But Kupper saw he had really not understood.

"Yes, particularly in France and Germany. So there is something good in every age."

21

Though Kupper slept quite naked his feet were encased in a pair of heavy woolen socks. He padded over to Pilger, who held his bathrobe. And as always, Kupper was impressed with the way he held the robe so that it became more of a challenge than an accommodation. He seemed to be saying, "Here! Get into this robe immediately before you take chill. You are valuable property owned by the Luftstreitkraft, and I, Ernest Pilger, have been assigned the duty of making sure you are ready for action at the proper times. And my duty is my duty."

And indeed it was, Kupper thought, slipping into the robe. There was something almost frightening about Pilger's unfailing resolve and placid manner. It was quite impossible to discover if he liked Jasta life or not. It was his duty for the present and that was all there was to it and it was easy to believe he would accept transfer to a submarine or a Zeppelin without grumbling. Pray God there were more German soldiers like him.

"What kind of a day is it besides cold?"

"Clearing."

"Then we'll be flying. Too bad."

There was a long silence between them as Kupper brushed his teeth and then began to shave. Pilger stood by the door, which he had opened just far enough so that he could see across the stubble field. He watched the other batmen of the squadron as they crossed to awaken their officers. Their breaths, like Pilger's, created thick clouds of vapor and the crunch of their boots on the frozen stubble was like the roll of several drummers. Then without looking away from the stubble field, absently, as if he were contemplating a menu, he asked, "Will you be having a Frenchman or an Englishman for breakfast this morning?"

Kupper's razor paused and then moved more slowly across his square jaw. There it was, the special detachment of the common soldier. It was not just callousness—they were capable of existing from day to day as tin soldiers. Their uniform was their license to kill, their urge for survival inspired the immediate action. No more. Your enemy is dead and you are alive. How could it be explained to men like Pilger that killing men you instinctively admired was the ultimate depravity of war? How explain to the Pilgers of Germany, or any other country for that matter, that the iniquity became even more sinister and fierce when so much of the combat advantage was on your side? Who was the true victor and who the vanquished when, as so often lately, the combat had been simple murder. The French planes were inferior, the English planes even worse, the majority of their pilots were clumsy amateurs, and they were usually outnumbered. It was not much of a contest when six hawks leaped on one pigeon, yet that was the new fighting philosophy as conceived originally by Boelcke. The day of a lone man fighting through the sky against another lone man was finished. There were only a few exceptions left alive: Richthofen, who must be insane with his wretched silver cups commemorating each victory, and the incomparable Voss, a child who must also be mad, but in quite a healthier fashion. Yet the rule and style now was to hunt and fight in packs, which made survival extremely unlikely for those who strayed from their friends.

Again Kupper's razor paused and this time he was aware that his hand trembled ever so slightly. It was something new, like the strange hesitation in his speech. It had become almost a stutter although it was not so much a stumbling over syllables as it was a seeking for the right word, which refused to come. The subject seemed to have no influence—it could as well occur over schnapps in the mess as in giving an order to the armorer. Who had noticed it—so far? Probably no one, Kupper decided, and told himself that if he stopped thinking about it, it would go away. Ah, but *thinking* was the most dangerous function of man. It should be forbidden to all soldiers, officers and men alike. For were they not already lost in the wilderness?

By making a special effort Kupper succeeded in forcing depressing thoughts from his mind until he had finished shaving. Then he remembered reading a report in the Paris *Figaro* which came to the mess through Switzerland. It concerned a French pilot named Guynemer of the Stork Escadrille who apparently was quite as bloodthirsty as Richthofen. Well, they were both welcome to the carnage in their souls.

He turned to look down at the Alsatian. He was always there, head up, adoring, a man's dog. "Louie," he said, "something should be done about people."

Only last week Kupper had met two Englishmen who had been shot down trying to attack the observation balloon in the next valley. During the afternoon they were brought to the Jasta mess, where Kupper had personally signed the chit for an extra bottle of wine to ease their first sense of captivity. How he had enjoyed speaking English again and how amusing the British had been with their comic imitations of German officers. There had been a great to-do about finding a monocle for one of them so the show would be better. Then someone remembered that English general officers were also partial to monocles, and by reversing roles the performance was turned into a hilarious game. Certainly there had not been the slightest sign of hostility from any man present from the time the Englishmen arrived until they were hauled away singing drunk to their compound. Yet only a few hours before they would all have tried to kill one another.

Kupper stared for a moment at his blue eyes in the steel mirror and he thought, When my eyes start twitching then I'll ask for leave. He held his gaze, wanting to be absolutely certain about his eyes. Then he spoke again. "Pilger, what would happen to you if some Frenchman or Englishman had *me* for breakfast?"

He glanced at Pilger and at once regretted asking the question. For the supplication behind those eyes, he thought, was exactly that of a hound begging reassurance. He was worse than Louie. How could Pilger know that he was to be envied? He had some means of reassurrance. And *himself?* Who except God and Maria was interested in a weary clown?

He remembered the letter which he must get off this day:

My dearest Maria, When next you see me, expect a clown. The impression is due to my now customary environment and the clothes designed to exist in it. For several hours each day I must wear a leather helmet and fur-edged goggles which are supposed to protect my face from the elements—but only part of my face is covered by the goggles so about my eyes there are two great arcs of dead white flesh which extend halfway down my cheeks. In contrast the lower part of my face is so beaten with wind and oil it is quite like the skin of an ancient beer keg. My chapped lips look as if I have been chewing on them instead of food and are horrible to behold. Certainly you would not wish intimate contact with this ogre who will frighten you out of your wits. But do not, I beg of you, run away too fast. Pause until you can fully appreciate the comic element which is my nose. It is quite unprotected except for grease, and projects outward into a two-hundred-kilometer breeze when I am just hunting and a three-hundred-kilometer gale when I dive. Hence my nose is always a deep cherry color, which taken by itself might be something left cooling on a blacksmith's forge. The total effect is precisely that of a Hegenberger clown—who will cheer up instantly at the sight of you . . .

He wiped the last of the soap from his face and ears, hurrying now as if driven.

"Pilger? You didn't answer my question."

"I am giving it some thought."

"Forget it, Pilger. I am not going to be eaten this morning or any other morning in the foreseeable future. The way things are going I doubt very much if any Frenchman or Englishman has more than one chance in a hundred of potting me, which is better odds than standing in a trench. You of all people should know that."

"I do not know what the odds are up there," Pilger answered as he studied the lightening sky, "but I will give it some thought also."

"By all means do." In his letter today he would write about his clown face and refrain from writing a word about his damned Pilger. It was uncanny how he had become such a complicated figure in their letters. It had begun with a description of Pilger's failure to grow a mustache, which had been only intended to amuse Maria. But his literary effort had sailed back to him all too alive. "Dearest Sebastian, Do tell me *more* about your poor baby-skinned Pilger fellow! He sounds like sort of a propaganda composite—a symbol of our German soldiers everywhere—stolid, brave, patriotic, and strong." Later, as the comments on Pilger became more searching and speculative, Maria had changed her thinking. She had written, "Yes, I suppose he does represent something, and I am not at all sure I like it. I wonder if Pilger might not be something more ominous, the emblem of war—the helpless, confused, fundamentally barbaric creature swept up and carried on by events and evils over which he has not the slightest control."

It was astounding, Kupper mused as he carefully combed his blond hair straight back, how completely this pen-conjured version of Pilger had entered their lives and monopolized their correspondence. The pen version of Pilger was no longer very much like the man standing in the doorway. In the letters he always seemed to be saying something meaty, and the total impression was of Pilger's

25

being a rustic sage. It was simply not so, and his stature as an omniscient figure was becoming irritating. Kupper blamed himself for the original creation. Now here he was, Pilger the soldier, marching again and again along the rolling tops of Maria's nicely controlled script. She had even sent Pilger some Hanoverian cheese for his birthday. If he survived the war would Maria marry him without his bringing Pilger along as a sort of dowry?

. . . I have been thinking about Pilger again [she had written in her last letter] . . . do you think he actually cares whether the war ever stops or not? Or is he inured to it—has it become such a fixed way of life for him that the prospect of its ending would be a sort of dying within him? Isn't it possible that deep within him he knows instinctively that he, a simple peasant, is a part of something tremendous which he will never have the chance to be again? You, my dear Sebastian, will always have high attainments to inspire you. You are still young in spite of your uneasy feeling about being the oldest pilot at the front. That is not so. Have you heard of Jacob Wolff? I have read he is almost fifty! And Boelcke was thirty-five, wasn't he? What difference does it make? The whole world will be available to you once peace has come again—new conquests for your brilliant mind, new and safer adventures as you please. But for Pilger? What for him? Nothing, I should think. A void of potatoes and beer and family into which he must literally disappear without so much as a brass button to distinguish him from any other ex-soldier.

Kupper thought ruefully that the letter had devoted three pages to the affairs of his batman against a mere two for his own.

He smeared his chapped lips with a white cream which further emphasized the clown mask and then slipped on his breeches. Pilger brought his boots out from beneath the table and steadied him against the inevitable struggle.

After the boots Kupper began what he called the first mummification of a German soldier. His heavy underwear formed the primary layer, then his shirt and then his tunic complete with Iron Cross. After his fifteenth victory Kupper had allowed himself to hope that a *Pour le Mérite* might be dangling from his neck any day, but the weeks had passed and three more victories and nothing whatsoever had come of it. By now he had lost interest. He wore his tunic only partly for the added warmth it might afford. It would be bad enough to be shot down and taken prisoner, but to appear before the enemy in anything other than correct uniform somehow horrified Kupper. Perhaps, he thought wryly, my own Teutonic mind also has its rigid limitations.

The tunic was followed by a very heavy high-necked sweater of pure sheep's wool. Kupper had seen it on a Baltic fisherman when he had passed through Lübeck the previous fall. He had immediately bought it from the fisherman, dirt, odor and all, and had been the envy of the Jasta ever since. With such a sweater beneath his leather greatcoat, and with two mufflers wound around his neck, plus a heavy pair of farmer's gloves and a dollop of brandy in his tea just before take-off, he had found it possible to remain reasonably warm for the first half of a flight and avoid rigor mortis for the rest of it. There was, he thought, at least some benefit in a brush with the enemy. The instant an opponent was sighted hot juices were pumped through a man's veins and the temperature in the winter sky ceased to matter.

"Well, here goes the stuffed goose," he sighed, stamping for the door. His leather greatcoat bulged and rumpled with the padding beneath it and he appeared to be as broad and as heavy as Pilger, who followed carrying his helmet and goggles. When they came to the latrine Kupper entered it. Pilger stood outside blowing clouds of vapor at the sky and rubbing the Alsatian's ear with his free hand. When Kupper emerged they continued across the stubble field as if there had been no interruption. The Alsatian trotted alongside his master. He paused to sniff at a thicket. Thank God for you, Kupper thought. You can still think.

Beyond the hedgerow and across the second field stood the line of hangars, which were great black tents supported by a wooden framework. There were ten such hangars and in front of each fires had been built to warm the congealed engine oil. Thirteen Albatros D-III airplanes were aligned parallel with the hangars. Kupper could hear the early morning jollities of the armorers and mechanics as they moved around the machines, and as always he found it strangely reassuring.

These morning patrols were somehow quite different from those which would be made later in the day. There was still zest in the mornings. No one had been killed or nearly killed, yesterday's memory had been softened by the night, and what little survived of Sebastian Kupper's combative instincts became revitalized. There was a heady sense of power in the sights and sounds of his assembled Jasta and he was reminded that it was more than an empty honor, command of such a group.

There were sixteen officers, twelve of whom were pilots. There were thirty-six enlisted men of varying aircraft skills, from riggers to armorers. They were directly concerned with the care and maintenance of the Jasta's twelve new Albatros D-III fighter planes which had recently arrived to replace the older D-II's. The balance of the Jasta's personnel complement was devoted to the innumerable auxiliary services, from supply to communication.

Kupper was pleased that his pilot officers were so keen and his ground officers so conscientious. And the enlisted men were devoted and on the whole a cut above average. Now before the first patrol of this day the entire Jasta, except those confined to the communications hut, would be assembled. It was not a compulsory formation but rather an informal gathering which clearly demonstrated interest and respect for those who were about to seek the enemy.

Kupper found it stimulating, and in spite of his intense desire not to behave like an ass, which in his opinion most flight leaders seemed to consider their duty, he often found himself on such mornings with a much stiffer bearing than he intended.

Yet recently there had been this other thing. It seemed he could touch it.

It was something he had occasionally recognized in others and now to discover it in himself filled him with loathing. Each day had been marked by further weakening of his will to fight, an insidious drawing away of antagonism, which soon must stop or the disaster would be complete. For any fighter pilot who engaged the enemy with hesitation, or for one instant allowed himself to think the enemy might emerge the victor, signed his own doom. Confidence, absolute, as Kupper knew all too well, was imperative. When he had been at Hudova airdrome in southern Serbia it had been possible to be much less severe about self-discipline. Then the neophyte pilot Sebastian Kupper had been flying photo reconnaissance with the 30th Section, and the greatest danger lay in their ponderous L.V.G. machines, which were so slow they presented an almost stationary target to the Russian guns if the wind aloft was against them. Fortunately there was so little ground opposition from the Russians it had been amusing to dwell upon the odd chance of a stray bullet or bit of shell finding some vital part of one's anatomy. The Russian airplanes were so few, chances of encountering more than three at a time were infinitesimal. In his four months on the Eastern Front Kupper had engaged only one. He had fired a short burst, not one bullet of which hit the Russian. The Russian had panicked and attempted a violent dive for safety, and almost at once his machine went to pieces in the air and crashed to its own grave in a marsh. Yet here on the Western Front, brooding upon even slight enemy success was extremely dangerous, as Kupper had told his pilots time and again. Then how dare you, he thought, approaching the table which had been set up at the end of the line of airplanes, how dare you presume to lead the men in this Jasta, especially in the late afternoons when confidence has nearly bled away?

Each fine day the early morning ceremony at the table cheered Kupper. He considered it fitting for a fighter Jasta and immensely valuable in setting everyone up to that degree of keenness so necessary for the next hour or so. As usual a crisp white tablecloth had been spread and two mess orderlies stood alert behind it. There were small cakes spread out for those who liked something solid at this hour and a rank of coffee cups upon which each pilot's name had been boldly painted—Zimmerman, Keim, Kessler, Hochstetter, Mueller, Steilig, Hinkmann, Just, Schröder, and his own. There were two cups without names. These were set out for Haube and Sellerman, who had joined the Jasta only three days ago. There had not been time to paint their cups properly or really know the young men. They stood a little apart from the table now, the first to arrive. They waited rather humbly, as was fitting in view of their relative inexperience. They had made but one patrol since their arrival and had so far not fired a round except to test their guns nor had they been fired at, which was quite another thing. They clicked their heels when he said good morning.

The coffeepot was a battered German Army field type which Kupper considered a disgrace to the mess, but at least it held a vast amount of liquid. Its plebeian effect was overcome by a magnificent samovar donated to the mess by Kessler, who had brought it from his tour of service in Macedonia. The samovar gave an air of elegance to the table, and Kupper was doubly grateful because unlike most of his comrades, who preferred coffee when it was available, he had a passion for tea. After their return from patrol, then of course there would be a full breakfast in the mess, taken leisurely, with time to analyze and reanalyze each action of the morning.

Kupper nodded and managed to smile at Feldwebel Groos, who as sergeant-major was in charge of everything from the temperature of the tea to the posting of furloughs. Kupper did not like Groos. He was efficient enough in his job, but he did no more than he had to, or what regulations specified. A professional in all respects, Kupper thought, including conniving.

Kupper then acknowledged the good mornings of the orderlies, tossed his gloves to Pilger and accepted the teacup held out to him. Brandy? Was it his imagination or was the orderly becoming too heavy-handed with his pouring?

He turned to look at the line of Albatros airplanes through the pleasantly scented steam rising from the cup. All appeared to be in order since now the mechanics and armorers had ceased their clambering about the machines. They had been working since long before dawn and were anxious for the patrol to take off so they could warm themselves and eat.

It always amused Kupper to contemplate the various designs each of his pilots had chosen to have painted on his Albatros. The designs were so characteristic of the men themselves. Schröder, the Jasta champion, with his chessboard, Hochstetter with his monkey sticking its tongue out, Steilig with his flaming sword, and Keim with his beer barrel dripping bullets. There was a Bavarian crest, a witch, a thunderbolt, and a lion. Hinkmann, Kupper decided, had after all been the most original—there was no device on his fuselage.

Kupper was reasonably satisfied with these new Albatros D-III's. This latest type had Mercedes engines with the cylinders in line and enough horsepower to give the machine a speed of more than two hundred kilometers per hour. They could climb better than three hundred meters per minute and the two Spandau machine guns had so far shown little inclination to serious jamming. After more than one hundred and seventy hours of combat flying in the Albatros, Kupper had concluded it might have been a better flying airplane given more aileron control, yet it was overall a most successful design. The Albatros D-III could match the French Nieuports, the

Spad 7, and the English Sopwith Pup. The design had only one distressing weakness—the unfortunate tendency to shed one or more wings in a prolonged dive. Hence the hawklike swoop down on a prey must now be used with due regard for angle and speed. Better, if possible, to borrow something from the plane's appearance, which on first sight had reminded Kupper more of a shark than a bird. Thus he had conceived an alternate to the traditional dive out of the sun—a sharklike approach from below, a swift close and bite, then roll away.

And here comes my school of sharks, he thought, watching the line of figures crossing the stubble field. Not a very fearsome-looking bunch at this hour. More like a parade of sleepy-eyed teddy bears, some of them still yawning and confused. And it struck him as it had so many times lately—how very young they were! Like boys pretending to be men. Yet Steilig, who was only nineteen, had already killed eleven men for certain and probably several more, Zimmerman had killed two on his own twentieth birthday, Kessler and Schröder each had three victories and were almost overeager for more. The oldest of the lot was Keim, who still had seven years advantage over his Jasta leader.

Kupper watched Hochstetter reach out his toe and attempt to trip the man who walked in front of him. There was an explosion of high-pitched laughter from the others as Steilig nearly fell on his face.

No wonder I am so lonely, Kupper thought. How can I, at my age, join in their horseplay? Now Hochstetter was the perfect age and temperament for this business, he was a mischievous fellow, always in or up to something, but his popularity with his comrades was firmly established. Kupper had frequently checked an urge to take a ruler to Hochstetter's backside for some of his childish pranks rather than treat him as a German officer. Yet to be overly severe with Hochstetter might risk his own delicate relation with his fellow officers. By his complete devotion to the welfare of the Jasta in the air and on the ground Kupper was at last certain he had achieved that rare esprit sought by every conscientious leader. His men not only respected him, they obviously liked him. There was no other way to interpret their frequent and open display of approval. Kupper deliberately reminded himself that luck had also cooperated nicely since he had taken over as flight leader. Only one pilot, Hettrich, had been lost to enemy action, and over twenty victories had been con-

31

firmed. The former leader of Jasta 76 had not been so fortunate. In a mere two months he had lost eight men and then had himself been shot down as he attacked a lumbering French bathtub known as a Caudron, which was engaged in artillery spotting. Thus Sebastian Kupper's leadership looked even better than it should have and he forced himself to remember the fact.

He could sense the spirit of his men as they approached him smiling, smiles that persisted and lingered in their eyes even as each one paused the half-second necessary for the heel click and easy salute and then proceeded on his way to the table.

He was pleased. Their good mornings were respectful without being stiff, which gave Kupper a good feeling within himself. For this, he thought, here at sunrise every morning, was the only reward worth tasting in this rotten business. Let the stiff-necked Prussian professional officers go their iron-hard way. In Kupper's opinion they often ruined the chances of winning easy engagements simply because their men feared them to the point of terror, or despised them. And there were the nobles complete with an entourage of servants and orderly officers who stamped about, cleared their throats importantly and wore officer epaulets thanks only to imperial decree. More often than not, the "vons" led their men into trouble from which escape was extremely difficult. And then there were those swine of every army who had no right to their epaulets, divine or otherwise. Those were the clever ones, rarely seen, thank God, anywhere near the front. It had long been Kupper's resolve that nothing would supersede the Jasta in his time or devotion, and these younger men now sipping their coffee knew it.

Kupper glanced at his watch and then at the sun. Five minutes more, perhaps ten, and they must be aloft. As the others blew rising steam from their coffee cups Kupper again glanced down the line of Albatroses. His eyes paused affectionately on his own, particularly where the sun struck the prominent black and white target device painted on the fuselage just midway forward of the tail. He was pleased with the design, which he had chosen because he hoped a distracted enemy might concentrate his attention upon it—for just at that point his bullets would do the least harm.

He turned back to the table and wondered what the journalists who were forever ranting about the Fatherland's dashing aviators would have to say if they could see this squadron now. There was not a complete or regulation uniform among them. Some wore short leather coats, others long ones—Schröder wore a white fur jacket sent to him by a relative in Sweden, and Steilig, who claimed he never became cold, wore only his straight tunic as if he were about to stand inspection. Keim was bundled in a collection of garments that might have been more seemly on a Silesian peasant, and Hochstetter, who was rich and could afford such things, looked like a grand duke in his greatcoat lined and collared with seal. It might be a very good thing if the French or the English could see them now. They would be too busy laughing to be able to shoot.

The sun! It was climbing through the still-barren branches of the elm trees which lined the distant road. It was a pale sun, strangely without warmth for so late in the year, but it was their friend in the mornings. For they could be certain it would rise in the east, which placed it at their backs as they waited for the enemy to appear. The French or English, compelled to fly eastbound if they were to accomplish anything at all, set their course directly into its path. It was a double dagger at their throats. They were blinded to what might descend on them from above, and their wings glistening against the darker background of the earth presented a splendid target.

"Gentlemen," Kupper said, nodding at the sun, "I suggest we drink up."

The lively volleys of conversation ceased as they drank the last of their coffee. One by one, they set their cups down. Then each man, in his way, girded his armor of gloves and leather helmet and buckles, buttons and straps. With their goggles pushed up on their foreheads they walked off to their machines. According to Kupper's most strict instructions each pilot circled his own airplane once, regarding every detail of wings, fuselage, engine and *empennage* with intense concentration. "You must do so," Kupper had cautioned them, "and not because you are likely to find anything wrong. Your mechanic and your armorer will have all as it should be. But as they circle a few paces behind you, bear in mind one thing. If you are not interested in the condition of your machine, they may lost interest—in which event it is *you* who may die."

Now solemnly circling his own Albatros, Louie pressing against his leg every time he paused, and with Webber, his mechanic, and Grubbe, the leading armorer, imitating his inspection, Kupper finally stopped to smile at the painted target device. There was one patch in the fabric next to the outer ring. Two others followed it across the fuselage in a straight line—three bullets only. So far, he mused, no one had won the grand prize by hitting the bull's-eye. When would it be?

Pilger, grim as a pallbearer, handed him his helmet and goggles. Something would have to be done about Pilger in the mornings, Kupper thought. It was bad enough to have one's own misgivings in the afternoon, but to start off each day with this oversized ghoul was more than a man should be asked to tolerate.

He slapped his chest and immediately the Alsatian rose to the invitation. His paws landed just below Kupper's shoulders. His tongue licked out and caught his master under the chin. Laughing, Kupper gave him a hug and spun away. Louie began a torrent of excited barking as Kupper swung into his cockpit. He called out to the next Albatros, where Steilig was already waiting to start his engine.

"Hals und Beinbruch!"

Steilig smiled, waved his hand and shouted to Hochstetter, who was next in line, *"Hals und Beinbruch!"*—Break your neck and leg!— and the magic challenge which had become a custom in many Jastas echoed cheerfully through to Zimmerman, Hochstetter, Steilig, Hinkmann, Just, Schröder, Kessler, Mueller, Keim and the neophytes Haube and Sellerman.

In four minutes they were all climbing swiftly for the sun.

Chapter Two

April 1917
Near Épernay
An inn in the place Faubourg—

A FULL MOON rolled through the wind-torn clouds.

Now, when he was so utterly at peace, it seemed incredible that only a little while before the alternating light and soft shadow in the room had been violated by his agony. Here in their secret oasis little whimperings had first risen in his throat, then suddenly he opened his mouth and achieved a peak of strident shouting. At last, after the seconds which had seemed hours, he became quiet again.

Denise had endured these frightening moments, knowing she could never fully comprehend what he had seen from beyond his closed eyes. And she thought, Even in his torment he is extraordinarily beautiful.

She slipped closer to him, pressing her body against him gently, watching his face in the moonlight which splashed through the elaborately cracked window. She found the window most appropriate to this odd rendezvous with her lover—beyond it yawned a courtyard from which rose a bouquet of manure, slops and wet hay—all as it should be, all symbolizing the decay of that moral pride which she had formerly considered so precious. Let it be dead, she thought. I am the better, healthier woman.

The inn was within the sound of cannon fire. The muffled thunder of the guns could not be heard this night, but the night before when the wind had veered to the northeast their rumbling was plainly audible. Yes, she thought, nothing was incongruous. Monsieur Pinchard, the inn's former proprietor, had been one of the first reservists to die for France. He had been skewered by a German Uhlan before he fully realized he was involved in a war instead of annual maneuvers, and all that remained of his memory was a sister who wept every time she passed his portrait in the hallway. Her husband, Monsieur Michaud, made no pretense of lamenting his late brother-in-law. "A hero's death," was all he would say, although he sometimes added a cynical *"Vive la France."*

By some miraculous oversight the inn had not been chalked for army billets since the spring of 1915, nor had the stables been requisitioned for either horses or troops, so it remained much as it had been before brutality marched everywhere. There was beer for the soup and sauces. There were duckling pies and lark pies in the Flemish tradition and enough of the ash-colored cheeses of the Marne to satisfy those who could afford such indulgences. Monsieur Michaud was very careful about men in uniform who sough admission to his inn. If they passed a strict financial examination, they might sip at a bottle of the local wine which had not been champagnized; and if the cost of it did not cause a noticeable bubbling in their livers, then Monsieur Michaud might blackmail them with a Champenoise eel or fried gudgeon followed by a better than ordinary dandelion and bacon salad. Finally, if his customers had a sou left, he would sell them stale gingerbread or soggy waffles which he insisted were as delicious as any to be found in Reims before the war.

Within ten minutes of meeting Monsieur Michaud Denise had decided she hated him. For the first time in her life the cost of anything became important and she felt exploited. I devoutly wish a Boche shell would land in the middle of his bald head, she thought, even if I must expire with him. Or perhaps I could slit his fat throat with one of his own butcher knives and be decorated as a heroine of France. For a pleasant moment she saw herself standing before a frock-coated delegation in the Louvre as a medal was pinned on her favorite green dress. Yet suppose the ribbon which supported the medal was a clashing green? If she knew that in advance would she still kill Monsieur Michaud?

She smiled at the cracked window, laughing inwardly at herself. You are the silliest woman, she thought. You would build a monument in a barnyard and canonize the bulls. If someone gives you a bit of broken glass it becomes a diamond. And yet you are also at this moment the most spoiled woman in the world, for see who lies beside you.

Hardly breathing, she stared down at the man she loved, as a child might inspect an adult unawares. She honored the hardcut lines of his brow and nose, approved of the slight tilt about his eyes which caused him to appear Slavic at times and she blessed the lips between which she so loved to bury her own.

"Paul," she whispered. "Wake."

But he did not stir and she knew she would have been disappointed if he had. These were such precious moments with the moon illuminating all that had become her treasure.

She touched his straight black hair and found it the perfect complement to the deep olive color of his skin. She regarded the strength and proportion of his neck against the flowing lines of his powerful shoulders, and this union pleased her profoundly because nothing was ill-matched. Then in musing wonder, moving cautiously like a mischievous child, she pulled away the quilt so that his whole body was revealed in the moonlight and she smiled again at herself as she thought, I am already a heroine of France! Am I not relinquishing him to his duty?

"Paul?"

He remained still except for the slow rise and fall of his chest. A noble chest, she thought, admiring the flow of line down to his flat belly. Only his feet appeared incongruous. Absurd! The feet of a Gascon peasant, which was the more ridiculous since the Chamay family came from Loudéac in Brittany and had never been in Gascony. His feet were like paddles! She remembered the first time she had given herself to him—not so long ago really, or was it a thousand years?—and she remembered afterward looking down at his feet and accusing him of sabotage in denying his country the use of such devices for marching through the mud. She had explained how he might stand at a stream and transport an entire battalion to the other side with those two great paddles firmly planted in the mud. The Boche might be outflanked, the Kaiser brought to the guillotine, and with peace in the land some sort of convenient niche might be found for him in one of Augustine's enterprises. Supervisor of the leather works in Grenoble? Director of the potash plant in Toulouse? Augustine, dear, what shall we do with him to show our appreciation? And Augustine *was* a dear husband and so he *would* do something—and life could be enjoyed to full measure instead of only during these fleeting moments.

Augustine was a dear husband, her mind repeated. Augustine was an aristocrat respected throughout Burgundy, and all the great people of Dijon acknowledged his presence at least with a nod of their heads.

Augustine was a porcupine. There was no right way to approach him. He was going insane or he had always been insane—so a second voice told her, a small voice tremulous with fright. Today Augustine would be reasonable, aloof as always, yet in his way treating her as his true and Catholic wife. Tomorrow he might be in the mood for torture, which he could accomplish with words quite as effectively as he had on those rare occasions when he had employed physical force. He was a brilliant man, Augustine, an eloquent monster. In the four years of their marriage his wrath had brought her only two beatings, but her brain had often been left bruised and bleeding. As it had been the first time she met this man who slept beside her.

The war was still young that hot summer afternoon when Augustine cordially welcomed the two aviators. The introductions had been formal enough to please even Augustine. Paul Chamay, Raymonde LaFrenier—air cadets from the aerodrome at Pau. Paul explained that he was the student and Raymonde, who had red hair and was so amusing, said he was the instructor and added that it was the blind leading the blind, since he knew so little of flying himself.

Raymonde—Paul, Paul—Raymonde. The inseparables, the two of them, paired like a perfectly matched set of duelling pistols.

They had not been afraid of Augustine. They were not, then, afraid of anything.

Perhaps she had sinned mentally on that first meeting and Paul had sensed her willingness. What difference did it make now? He had persisted and finally conquered.

"Paul, it is time."

He moved one leg toward her, but his eyes remained closed and his breathing was that of a weary man deep in slumber. She turned on the bed which so loudly protested every movement. As she brought herself to a kneeling position the moon rolled behind a cloud and the resulting shadow caused an illusion of motion about his face so that he seemed to smile.

39

"My dear exhausted Paul," she whispered. Dear, dear Paul, may the moon and stars forgive me if I wake you . . .

Still watching his face, she lowered her head and ever so lightly caressed him with her parted lips. Soon he tensed, then his hand rose to press on her hair.

He groaned and slowly raised himself up until he sat looking at her. "How do you know it is time?"

"A rooster just said so."

"Don't you ever sleep?"

"Yes. When you are not here."

"That's most of the time."

"So I do not care to waste these hours. I can sleep when I am old." Instantly she regretted her words, for the subject of age was a delicate one between them. As it always is, she knew, when the woman is older than the man—and especially if the difference is five years.

"You will never grow old," he said, rolling from the bed, "and I shall never have the opportunity."

"Do not say such things."

"I am simply stating a truth. There is the law of averages." He found the box of wax matches and touched one to the candle which stood atop the commode. Watching him, she shivered, reached for the quilt and wrapped it about her nakedness. Then still kneeling on the bed, she began to laugh.

"What are you laughing at?"

"You. You are formidable!"

"Turn around. Stop staring at me."

"Why?"

"Do as I say."

Pouting, she turned to face the cracked window. She watched the moon while he dragged the pot from beneath the bed and carried it to the opposite side of the room.

"You are often like a little boy," she said.

He did not reply. She heard the clink as he replaced the lid on the pot, then she turned back to him. She watched him as he squirmed into his heavy underwear.

What a strange costume for the son of a diplomat! In her thoughts she had often envisioned Paul's father as the personification of intellectual nobility. A man who had served France in Indochina, in Morocco, in Turkey, and even now in Brazil, a chevalier of the

Legion d'Honneur, a man who spoke six languages and had himself taught his son both English and German, must be a very great man indeed. When Paul had once shown her a photo of his father she had been disappointed. He was a short, bald-headed man. She had concentrated on the rosette in his buttonhole.

She began to chatter, allowing her voice to rise and fall as if there was nothing on her mind except plans for a very ordinary day. She vowed that if the sun shone as it certainly promised to do if one were to judge by the clarity of the moon, she would walk to the stream that is only four kilometers from the village—and perhaps even farther if it was a proper April day, it all depended.

"And where *is* spring?" she asked. "Augustine, who knows about such things, says it has been the longest and coldest winter in history. He has predicted that the spring will come suddenly, when it comes, which will make the situation in his vineyards even more difficult. He also said it will be very difficult at the front because of the mud. But where is the mud? Everything I can see is still frozen stiff."

"You haven't seen anything and don't go back to Dijon and say you have."

He is angry with me, she thought. He is angry because he is tired and he has already left me for his war. "I will most certainly not tell anyone in Dijon that I have been anywhere except to see my sister in Paris. You cannot imagine how hard it was to get here without even passing through Paris."

"I can imagine."

"For you, I will attempt anything."

She spoke so simply that he paused in his dressing and looked at her. He smiled. "I don't know what happened to the spring. Perhaps the Kaiser swallowed it."

Again she sensed a strangeness between them. She sought desperately for something amusing to say lest she contaminate the whole atmosphere of their parting. "I am so *bored* when you are not here! I am not a farmer's wife or his daughter. I cannot cobble shoes or weave flax. I am so utterly useless."

He seemed to ignore her words, for which she was deeply grateful since she wanted them all back. Men did not hurry their return to complaining women.

"Be careful where you walk," he said. "All the roads are streaming with troops—Algerians, Moors, Berbers, Senegalese wild as apes.

I have heard there are even some Russian regiments. Something very big is starting. They have kept us on the ground so there would not be too much visible activity. As usual we are putting our heads in the sand. But the roads are teeming, especially at night. Everyone is moving up. It will be something huge, I think."

Her thoughts almost compelled her to reach for him, and then instantly she knew the gesture would insult his mood.

"I have no idea when the push will come," he said. "Commandant Féquant does not confide in me. Nor does General Nivelle, or even His Excellency."

"Who is this Excellency?"

"A man named Jourdan. He should have been a priest."

"How foolish of them not to make you a general—" She watched him roll his puttee and was pleased at his deft movements. "Why do you wear those? They look like bandages. Why don't you wear boots? You're allowed to wear what you please in the air service. You told me everyone makes up their own uniform."

He laughed. "Boots are expensive and puttees are warmer."

"I would buy you boots."

"You would not. Augustine would. It is one thing to take another man's wife—and quite something else to accept gifts from him at the same time. And I feel very strongly about Augustine. He is one of the most courageous men in the world. The night I met him he had the nerve to tell me war is necessary to mankind, like shitting."

"What did you say?"

"I had never killed a man then. Now I do not think war is necessary."

"Please never forget to laugh. You have the most intriguing laugh I have ever heard in a man. It is utterly disarming."

"Laughing is easy when I am with you."

He completed rolling his puttees, stood up, and moved toward her. "Now listen to me carefully if you really plan to go walking. Some of the Moroccan units can be worse than the Senegalese. Do not wear rouge or paint your lips. If you see men resting, particularly if they are in small groups, give them a wide berth—"

"Why?" she demanded.

"There are many strays and always some deserters. Also there are almost a million men in the Champagne area. I promise you they are all lonely, most of them are frightened and all of them are homesick

42

and restless. Many believe that what they do these next few days will be the last thing they do—ever. They are certain that they are condemned and they are probably right. So why should they not take what is flaunted before them? Rape? Why not if they are going to be shot at anyway?"

"Don't, don't, don't—there are so many things I must *not* do. Where is life?"

"It is hibernating until this thing is over."

"I do not have time for it to hibernate very much longer."

He reached out across the brass bed and she came to him on her knees. He encircled her head in his arms and said, "I tell you these things because I love you. I cannot let anything ugly happen to you. You are my *marraine,* my great fortune. Without you there would be little hope left in me."

"M'sieur," she said mockingly. "Your words transport me. Could it be possible that you need money?" Now, she thought, I have things back on the basis of frivolity, where they should be.

"Nonsense. I am a sergeant and my grateful republic pays me two francs a day." He turned his cuff so that the moonlight fell upon the double red stripe of his rank. She rubbed her cheek across the stripes and with her face turned away from him she found the courage to ask him if he remembered the night.

"If I ever forget it I deserve castration."

"Do you remember shouting?"

She felt his heart quicken and for an instant the pressure of his arms increased until it was painful. Frightened that she might have angered him, she whispered to God for forgiveness.

Slowly he relaxed. "I—I was dreaming of Raymonde again."

"That was months ago. You cannot carry this thing in you forever. You will only destroy yourself."

"When that Boche is destroyed—then I believe it will leave me."

Again she felt him stiffen. Pressed against him it was as if she could hear the rushing of the blood through his veins, as if she could almost touch the animal deep within him. She caught her breath and remained absolutely still.

"I will find the Boche who killed Raymonde. I intend to live until I do. *He* is my war."

"Paul—*please!* Revenge is the first step to madness. You can't go on shouting in the night. You need rest. Can't you ask for a furlough?"

"Of course. Commandant Féquant will be delighted to accommodate my whims. He would treat me exactly as he did the Tonkinese pirates." He drew his hand across his throat and stuck out his tongue.

"But the German is only another fighter pilot, like you. Why should he single out Raymonde and say, 'That man—I want to kill *him!*'"

"He came back at Raymonde while he was still alive. Not once but twice. If I can't find him tomorrow I will meet him the next day or the next, and that is all I am going to say about it until the job is done."

He kissed her on top of the head and she could feel the brute retire within him. He embraced her with finality and then released her. He slipped on his tunic, and as he quickly buttoned the brass buttons she saw a dancing shape behind him which puzzled her until she realized he was leaning slightly forward so that his Croix de Guerre dangled away from his chest. The nearby candle magnified its shadow a hundred times upon the wall. She shuddered.

He reached for his kepi, clapped it on his head at a jaunty angle, gave it a pat and smiled. And that smile, she thought, was enough to warm her heart for the rest of the day.

"Don't your ears freeze?"

"Not if I keep wiggling them."

"I will knit you a *passe-montagne*."

"Do, now that spring has come. I will wear it above three thousand meters."

He sighed, then said mournfully, "I will now mount Celeste."

"I wish you wouldn't say that. It sounds so vulgar even if it is only a motorbike. I'm jealous of the original Celeste. Who is she?"

"My maiden aunt. A very sturdy woman. She has a mustache, a voice like a frog and a tendency to leap into the air on the slightest provocation. In every way she reminds me of my motorbike. Both of them, incidentally, have rusty teeth. *À bientôt.*"

He unlocked the door and opened it cautiously.

"When?" she whispered.

"Who knows? Maybe the next bad weather."

"I'll pray for a deluge."

44

"Do—but don't depend on me. If I come and you are not here I will understand you are either back in Dijon or at your sister's in Paris."

"And I will understand if you do not come. God protect you."

She waved a kiss to him as he slipped out the door. She listened carefully, sensing rather than hearing his footsteps fade down the hallway. She waited to hear him descend the stairs, but there was no sound, nor was there any when he passed out the street door. Only when she heard the rumble of the motorbike's exhaust and waited until the sound dissolved in the darkness was she satisfied that he had gone. Now, she thought, I can pity myself without restriction until the good merciful God brings foul weather.

She turned on the cracked window accusingly and frowned at the moon.

It was only twenty-nine kilometers to the aerodrome near Ressons, where the 322nd Escadrille de la Chasse roosted. Paul Chamay had allowed himself three full hours to travel the distance from the brass bed to the canvas and wood Bessaneau hangars which sheltered the wings of his escadrille. There, even now before it was light, Babarin, who came from Auvergne, would be fretting over the Nieuport which was his difficult child. Babarin was not a very good mechanic, but Chamay deliberately and often reminded himself there must be worse. At least Babarin, with his doelike eyes and grand mustache over which he appeared to be peering, was totally dedicated to his machine. Before joining his regiment in '14 and eventually finding his way to the Service Aeronautique, Babarin had clerked in a cutlery store. And he yearned for the day when he could resume his trade. As a consequence he polished the Nieuport's fabric wistfully until the fabric and metal shone like wedding silverware. Chamay had once even found him burnishing the bronze flying-wire turnbuckles and had not the heart to tell him his time might be better used examining their inner strength.

But now Babarin would be having a fit! Chamay could easily visualize him chewing on his mustache. Where would his pilot be? Not in his bunk. Not in the mess. Where was Sergeant Paul Chamay, who was not to be found anywhere on the aerodrome, and with dawn not long away?

The traffic was such that he had not progressed more than fifteen kilometers since leaving Denise. Even the narrow back roads which twined between the farms were jammed with troops, horses, wagons, chugging trucks and rumbling artillery. Alternate blobs of shadow and moonlight created a dreamlike atmosphere about the ordinary countryside. Small buildings became gigantic ruins, the helmets of the moving troops bobbed up and down like foam bubbles in the pools of light. The 227th Regiment, a good one Chamay remembered, were singing the "Montagnards" when he passed them, but it was not the same lusty singing as he had heard from their brothers on the perilous way from Bar-le-Duc to Verdun. There was an unmistakable discouragement now, a minor note like a unanimous groan.

For a while Chamay skittered his motorbike along a column of Territorials who were chanting the *baa-baa* of sheep being led to slaughter.

Chamay was shocked. Could this be the French Army? What had happened to their *élan?* Then at once he was ashamed. He remembered a vow he had made after his first visit to the trenches. It was at Fleury near Verdun and he had managed to contain his terror long enough to appear as the bold aviator. But once out of their special hell he swore he would never censure a poilu for anything.

If he had not several times been mistaken for a dispatch rider and waved on, his progress would have been even slower. The rural roads, designed for an occasional manure cart, could not contain the flowing mass of men and material bound toward the front which had been fixed for so long. The roads suffered the weight of apparently numberless batteries of 75's, wheel, swing and lead teams jangling harness and snorting steam at the descending moon. The roads were pounded by the heavier 155's and endless columns of troops, their heavy voices rising and falling like waves upon an ocean of weariness. All moved along as best they could through a quagmire of Champagne clay.

For a time Chamay rode along the flank of an Alpine chasseur regiment, then worked his way past it to join a battalion of spahis. Later, he was forced to fall in with a train of trucks carrying Moroccan infantry, their red fezzes black in the moonlight. The Annamite drivers stared down at Chamay unsmiling, and he wondered if they were dreaming of the warm Cambodian rain. When at last he maneuvered past them, he was lost for nearly half an hour amid the 269th Regiment of Grenadiers who had struck such a miserable part of the road that independently they had sought better ground. No one, it seemed, knew where the proper road was supposed to be. The cries of Corsican sergeants trying to restore unity among their wandering men made Chamay laugh in spite of his growing concern with the time.

Just at moonset, when there was the first far-off light to the east, he passed a battalion of the Foreign Legion. He noted that they were marching instead of merely plodding, the bearded ranks almost in perfect step. At the head of the column, the color bearers seemed to carry their staffs proudly though the flags were cased in leather. Chamay was certain they had been marching so all night, and would march all day if commanded. He was uncomfortable among the Legion. They were true fighting men. He wondered how long any of his spoiled comrades of the Service Aeronautique would last in the Legion, and then he remembered how a batch of two hundred pilots had been sent to Verdun. Seventy had been killed within one month. The spoiled airmen who died there were much less menacing in appearance than most Legionnaires, but they had died just the same.

The way became clear for a time, the road more firm. He bent forward into the biting wind. Speeding around a turn concealed by camouflage netting, he nearly collided with the rear of a soup kitchen before he could slow to its pace. Beyond it he passed a regiment of Algerian Tirailleurs and then once more he was free.

Long before daylight he heard a continuous chumping of guns to the east. He thought it more concentrated than usual and it was certain that the Boche had lost another night's sleep.

It was full daylight when he saw the canvas hangars looming above a patch of willows. He turned across the little bridge which led to the aerodrome and bounced full speed along the road bordering the stream.

Babarin was waiting for him. "So! In the name of God, where have you been?"

"Away." Chamay looked down the line of hangars. He saw the lanky Bernhard and Dutoit, who was relatively a dwarf, and Folliet whose passion was fencing with the rapier rather than with airplanes. They were standing at ease near their Nieuports, waiting. There was LeSage from Ugine in the Savoy, a great ox of a man transferred from the Blue Devils after proving to a solemn committee of officers that he could indeed wriggle his bulk into the cockpit of a Nieuport.

There was St. Hilaire from Paris, who was known to be as wealthy as he was handsome, and Claude Mooney, a serious student of music, also from Paris. He had been breveted to the 322nd Escadrille only two days before, replacing Girod, who had been killed while attempting to snap-roll his Nieuport fifty feet above the ground.

There was the gloomy, hard-eyed Delander from Marseilles, also new to the escadrille although not to flying. He was a professional aviator who had flown exhibitions in Farmans and Blériots before the war, and it was rumored that he had almost raced at Reims. Delander was, and had been, a near success and a near corpse so many times that a great weariness had set in about his face that was apparent in his sagging jowls and in his eyes. He accepted his breveting to the 322nd Escadrille as simply another move by fate to divert him from traveling first class. So far in the war, the victory record of the 322nd was anything but inspiring.

Surveying the line of Nieuports, Chamay saw that all was well. If the pilots were still lounging about they were waiting for Captain Jourdan, who commanded them, and no catastrophe or miracle had occurred to upset his iron obedience to the clock. Five years before the war Jourdan had graduated from St. Cyr without distinction. He was remembered only for his formality of manner, which strangers often mistook for haughtiness and he retained it now with the escadrille, which was why his men normally referred to him as "His Excellency."

After his first week of service with the 322nd Chamay could no longer contain his disappointment. He had hoped a chase escadrille would mean frequent combat, yet during the first ten days of following Jourdan through the skies of Champagne he had not fired a single round at the enemy. "How can he behave this way?" he asked those who had been longer with the escadrille. "What is he waiting for? The Boche is going to march right through our front gate if we don't punch him back *now*. We must kill Germans faster than they breed —and Jourdan acts as if we had the rest of our lives! I'm surprised he isn't still wearing a plume in his kepi or carrying a sword in his cockpit. My God—we are being commanded by a turtle!"

The veterans of the 322nd agreed with Chamay, and yet, they pointed out, there was something about him—a something which was difficult if not impossible to identify but which might perhaps be called *savoir faire,* an indestructible dignity which might profitably be imitated by more Frenchmen these days. It was reassuring, was it not?

And after a time Chamay agreed that Jourdan had some attributes which balanced his lusterless record.

Now Babarin came to him grumbling ominously. "You were nearly late. I would not be surprised if His Excellency would order you shot if you missed a sortie."

"I am not a deserter. I am here on time and ready for duty."

"There are great bags under your eyes. When you go up you won't be able to see. The Boche will shoot you."

"You're bound to have me shot one way or the other." Chamay laughed and slipped into the heavy beaver fur coat which Babarin held for him. He turned to Sussote the armorer, who waited at the wing tip. He was a good man, but rather childlike and forgetful. When loading ammunition drums for the Nieuport's Lewis gun, he often lost track of the tracer sequence so that proportions would vary from one in three to one in five and once he had forgotten the sparklers entirely. Yet Chamay loved his foolishly innocent smile.

Chamay said to Sussote, "Our genius Monsieur Babarin scolds like the old woman he is. Right, Sussote?" Enjoying it, Sussote nodded in violent agreement.

"I'm naturally concerned for you," Babarin said.

"Concern yourself with our *bébé*." Chamay patted the Nieuport's fuselage. "Is she ready?"

"More than you are. I suppose you are hungry?"

"Always."

Babarin stood on his toes and reached into the cockpit. He brought up a chunk of coarse gray bread and tore it in three with his greasy fingers. He thrust one piece toward Chamay and one at Sussote. He took a bite out of the third and tucked what remained under his armpit while he chewed thoughtfully. Finally he swallowed and said to Chamay, "Eat while I tell you of important things, O lover of flesh and wine."

"I have been away exactly thirteen hours."

Babarin blew bread crumbs from his mustache and shook his head as if he were being patient with an errant son.

"Important things have occurred since then. Have you noticed that the artillery are having a special spasm?"

"I have."

"There is much preparation everywhere."

"Truly?" Chamay did not wish to mention the troops he had seen lest Babarin guess the direction from which he had come and intrude even vicariously upon his night at the inn.

"You do not know the most important thing. We are to have Spads. It is official, by word of His Excellency himself."

"When they are here, when one is mine to fly, I will believe it."

For a moment, while he studied the spectacle of the first sunrays stabbing the clouds, Chamay considered the plight of his commanding officer. All the fates were apparently in league to thwart him. While his neighbors Fonck, Nungesser, Bourjade, Madon and of course the fabulous Guynemer achieved victory after victory, Captain Jourdan had a mere four. He needed one more to make the ace category by French standards, which among other amenities automatically included a three-day leave and a cash bonus from the Michelin Tire Company. Not that Jourdan would have accepted such vulgar accolades. He *was* the Service Aeronautique, having joined it in the very beginning when almost every ascent became a crisis. Yet God alone seemed to appreciate how faithfully Jourdan had dedicated himself to military flight. He strove to become a skillful pilot and at least a fair shot and he had certain natural talents as an administrator, but of luck, Chamay soon learned, he had not had a spoonful. During the first six months of his command the 322nd had, through one misfortune or another, lost 80 per cent of its flying personnel. Yet no one could fairly say that a single one of the deaths or injuries was due to neglect or malcommand by Captain Jourdan.

Gradually Chamay learned of His Excellency's difficulties with superior officers, particularly those concerned with material. His attempts to obtain more and better equipment for the 322nd were as pathetic as they were persevering. Again no one could exactly explain his continual failures, although it was reasoned that the people in procurement might resent the lofty manner which seemed his sole defense against rebuke and reverses. The grand manner was all the more eccentric in a consciously democratic service in which pilots in the enlisted ranks enjoyed the same status as commissioned officers.

The dreary truth was that no one appreciated Jourdan except his patient wife, who lived in Orléans, and the men of the 322nd. In time they had become fiercely protective about His Excellency. A sort of perverse pride obsessed them so that they bragged of his shortcomings while at the same time defending him to all critics, and they watched with the detachment of predoomed men as their melancholy Don Quixote moved through endless calamities with only his swagger stick for a lance. And they knew in truth that Jourdan's restraint was far from heartless. It was said that in the privacy of his quarters Jourdan wept after the loss of a pilot, even if the man's own stupidity had brought about his end.

As a consequence of Jourdan's abominable luck the 322nd Escadrille was, as everyone secretly admitted, the most hapless orphan in the service. Since January, one crash after another, of which only a few were a result of enemy action, had so reduced the available supply of airplanes that it was impossible to fly at anywhere near full strength. Jourdan had to take what he could get. There were four two-seater Sopwiths borrowed from the British, seven Nieuports which formed the one and two flights, and four fuddy little Morane Parasols, which were nearly useless except for strafing. Sensible maintenance was nearly impossible with such a variety of airplanes. Only the Nieuports were taken seriously by the Germans. The famous Stork Squadron, based only twenty kilometers to the south, naturally flew the new Spads, but the Storks were nearly all celebrated aces whose luck was obviously better than Jourdan's. His Excellency had begged for only five Spads, but the promises he received never turned into airplanes. He had taken his troubles to Ménard, commander of all chase escadrilles, and had even petitioned Major Paul-Fernand du Peuty, commanding the entire French Air Organization. And though he stared longingly at the sky each day, not one Spad had so much as graced his field.

Now leaning comfortably against the fuselage of his Nieuport, Chamay stretched, closed his eyes and smiled. He hummed tunelessly. Babarin eyed him carefully and the bread which formed a lump in his cheek stopped moving up and down. "You are content. What was her name?" he asked solemnly.

"Denise."

"A stranger?"

"No."

The lump behind Babarin's cheek resumed its motion. Again he swept the crumbs from his mustache with a flourish. "Ah," he said. Then looking past Chamay, he nodded.

The tall officer strode toward the line of airplanes. Though he

51

wore a bulky flying suit, which hung loosely on his gaunt frame, some inner regal quality enabled him to appear smart. Chamay glanced at his watch and noted that it was exactly six o'clock. Of course, why had he bothered to look? He ran to join the other pilots before the center Nieuport. His Excellency much appreciated respect, of which he considered promptness the true indication.

When they had quieted, Jourdan looked over their heads at some vague object in the distance and said, *"Bonjour, messieurs."*

It was not so much the greeting as Jourdan's manner when delivering it. He was so courtly that he might as well have swept off his helmet and flourished it across the ground. He was for the moment a nobleman addressing other noblemen of France, which Chamay found particularly amusing in view of a peculiarity of the French Service. Unlike the British and the Germans, the majority of the pilots in the Service Aeronautique were not officers. Hence they officially failed to qualify as gentlemen, let alone noblemen, and hence their word could not be trusted. And hence if they claimed a victory the actual combat and fall of the enemy had to be seen and the facts supported by at least three witnesses. This was often difficult, and because most of the action was over German-held territory it was sometimes impossible to obtain such testimony.

Like the others Chamay had learned to prepare himself for His Excellency's verbal clumsiness, and there were times when his captive audience didn't know whether to laugh or cry. They shuffled silently into a rough semicircle about Jourdan, jostling each other affectionately in the unashamed way of brothers in combat. There was Vincent from Lyon, who looked more like a drummer boy than a sergeant, and De Rose, who was not much older at nineteen. De Rose had only been with the squadron three weeks and had already scored two victories. He had dash and assurance in the air, and if he survived long enough to perfect his technique it was very possible that the greedy Stork Escadrille would reach down and gather him to more illustrious company.

There was Launany from Brive, Andeac from Montmorillon, Tredac from Algeria, and Pleven from Brittany. All were eager to distinguish themselves.

"We are not yet the masters of the air," Jourdan began as usual, "but we shall be."

Chamay glanced at his comrades—Jalicot, Didier, Artaud, Perret.

Their eyes were expressionless, probably, he thought, because they dared not express their true reaction to Jourdan's dreary recitation. Their lips were forced into a properly solemn line.

"We will rendezvous with three Caudrons over Ribecourt at zero seven hours. They will be spotting artillery fire in the Vauxaillon sector. Number one flight will hold at two thousand meters and number two flight will hold at four thousand. . . ."

Chamay listened without really hearing, for unlike the others he knew both sides of an escort sortie. He had often thought it a pity Jourdan had not been leading the Nieuports on the morning Raymonde was killed. He would certainly not have allowed his entire formation to go chasing after a single Boche. And he would never abandon a Caudron to dive after a tempting victory.

Whoever was flying those Caudrons today would be fortunate. At least they could be sure Jourdan would look after them and keep at least half of his fighters so near their altitude that only a very numerous enemy would dare close in for a kill. No tricks—Jourdan would not waste two Nieuports as decoys. He would keep his two formations together, the one above and the one below, and he would want the enemy to see them both. He wanted to discourage rather than to provoke, because in any melee it was unlikely the Caudrons would get away clean. All of which, Chamay thought, did nothing for the escadrille's victory record. Nor did it make aces.

Now watching His Excellency, Chamay sighed. As Jourdan droned on, Chamay concentrated on his long nose. At least it was something to use as a focal point while his commander reviewed something everyone knew—the winds aloft and the compass course to Ribecourt. And suddenly, bouncing right on the tip of Jourdan's nose, Chamay saw the target circle. He closed his eyes. I am having hallucinations, he thought. I have not had enough sleep, or I am going mad.

When he opened his eyes he saw the target circle still perched on Jourdan's nose. Of course—now, as Jourdan turned his head again, the source of the illusion was obvious. The sun was directly behind him. His goggles were pushed just above his eyebrows and the sun struck them so that a miniature explosion of light flashed the spectrum down to his nose.

Chamay shivered. Denise had been right. He must get rid of this obsession. It was not healthy to see such things at this hour.

He concentrated on the distant bombardment until Jourdan

reached his routine conclusion. ". . . after the spotters are well and safely away we will join up and search for the Boche . . ."

Oh, indeed we will, Chamay thought, and by that time our fuel supply will be so low we'll be lucky to make it back here, much less go chasing after Germans. Champions like the Storks did not waste their energies playing nursemaid to Farmans, Caudrons, Voisins, and every other type of aeronautical junk that waddled into the air. They went straight for the enemy, found him and fought. And their record of victories was phenomenal.

". . . good luck, messieurs."

Babarin stood facing the Nieuport, one hand on the propeller. He called to Chamay in the cockpit, and down the line of Nieuports their exchange was repeated as each mechanic and pilot shouted the morning litany.

"Coupez!—plein gaz!"

Chamay repeated the instruction. Babarin swung his leg high, poised an instant to adjust his weight, then heaved down on the propeller. There was a gasping sound as the engine rotated a half turn. Babarin spit on his hands ceremoniously and rubbed them together. Again he stepped to the propeller.

"Contact—reduisez!"

"Contact—reduisez!" Chamay repeated as he turned the small switch above his left hand and closed the throttle.

Again Babarin swung his leg high, glanced at Chamay with a confident smile and heaved on the propeller. An asthmatic gasp from the engine, then silence. Babarin stood back and regarded the engine as he might assess a living creature. Down the line one by one, the engines of the other Nieuports caught and snarled with power.

Babarin patted his mustache thoughtfully. Then he looked at Chamay and blandly shrugged.

Chamay clenched his teeth and tried to contain his temper. Babarin, you donkey! Not again! Hopeless, noodle-fingered Babarin! You are an artist and a philosopher without equal! You are the marrow and the bone of France! You are also the world's worst mechanic!

Babarin spit on his hands again. *"Coupez! . . . plein gaz!"*

They repeated the ceremony. Babarin took a very deep breath and heaved on the propeller. The engine snorted a cloud of light blue smoke and once more became inert. Again Babarin glanced at Chamay, his eyes apologetic, his smile wan. He shook his head ever so slightly.

Chamay understood he was beyond swearing. The engine had defeated Babarin. In his hands it became a mass of metal deliberately assembled to thwart one Babarin who should have been polishing cutlery in Auvergne.

Now Babarin looked at Sussote and shrugged. He is really beyond embarrassment, Chamay thought. He is asking Sussote, who understands next to nothing, to support him in his war, which is not with the Germans at all but with the manufacturers of Le Rhone engines. It had been the same with the guns. When the single Lewis gun on the top wing was reinforced by a Vickers .303 installed to fire through the propeller, the Nieuports took on much sharper teeth—except for the one piloted by Sergeant Paul Chamay. Thanks to Babarin's doubtful genius that project took four days longer than it took any of the others. The British-manufactured interrupter gear was too much for him. The first test had been on the ground, fortunately, because Chamay shot off his own propeller with the first four bullets.

Chamay had forced himself to set aside his misgivings and he pleaded with Sous-Lieutenant Miralle, the squadron armament officer, who had two firm ideas as to what might be done about Babarin. Miralle said he would send Babarin to the infantry, where he could polish his bayonet until it glistened and perhaps the reflection might bring down a shell on his addled head, or perhaps he could be smuggled into the German Air Force, in which case the Kaiser was doomed.

Chamay saw the line of Nieuports, now nose-to-tail and taxiing away from the line. They would soon be in the air and there was no waiting for cripples. He bent around the rim of the cockpit to see if Babarin was doing anything. He had disappeared.

Chamay swore softly. So help me God, he thought, if I miss this sortie I will recommend Babarin to be sent to a soup kitchen bound for Verdun.

Chamay looked at Sussote. He pointed beneath the engine, then Babarin reappeared. Chamay knew there was absolutely nothing he could have done beneath the engine except possibly pet it, yet Babarin had the nerve to pretend he had found the trouble. He was grinning.

55

Vastly pleased with himself, Babarin twisted the ends of his mustache and again shouted the opening line of his personal farce. Chamay responded with even less confidence than before. And again Babarin swung his leg high.

"Contact!"

Babarin grunted mightily as he hauled down on the propeller. The Le Rhone spat and coughed, obscuring the whole fuselage in blue smoke. When it cleared there was Babarin standing in triumph, the palms of his hands turned upward. *"Voila!"* he shouted, as the Le Rhone settled down to a steady rhythm.

Sussote pulled the wheel chocks. Babarin held the left wing tip as pivot until Chamay could turn in line with the hangars. Then he was off down the field. The other Nieuports were already in the air. They would circle the aerodrome once—time enough to catch them if he took off downwind.

The escadrille passed through a layer of broken clouds at one thousand meters and vanished. Chamay, considerably below and still some distance behind the others, was not concerned. He knew the course and point of rendezvous. And there would undoubtedly be a wait for the enemy-shy Caudrons.

Climbing out of the aerodrome, Chamay laughed. The downwind take-off had been a very tight squeeze. If the trees had been one meter higher—there would now be no Nieuport or Chamay. He must accuse Babarin of growing a garden in the landing gear. What other explanation could there be for the leaves that must certainly be pressed into the wheels?

For a moment he wondered why a man should take so much satisfaction in risk. Was it the elation afterward when one had slipped away or merely the pleasant confirmation of what one had known all along—it is not going to happen to me?

Climbing an airplane gave moments when a man picked up his own spirit, passed through an invisible barrier and emerged into a separate environment aloft. Here, Chamay thought, I am a new kind of ruler, in charge of my body yet demanding so little of it— a touch of aileron now, a gentle shove on the rudder to coordinate, a slight tug on the elevators. During a climb the mind prepared itself for what would be found at the heights. It would be ready when altitude was reached for the prospect of combat and willing to face the certain hazards.

56

Now was the time when a man might even sing; the sense of mounting toward infinity placed all other matters in proper perspective, from the ridiculous byplay with Babarin, to the laments of His Excellency, to the very smells of earth. This was the overture to the coming aerial excitement so that a man sat spellbound waiting to see what the skies would offer.

There were wild mornings when the air became so turbulent that the sensuous rhythm of flight was constantly ruined. Yet there was always the compensation of struggle, of lurking danger, which was tonic to some men and torture to others. These were the moments, Chamay decided, when he was most alive.

There would soon be the supreme excitement of the hunt, during which a man sat not upon his rump but upon what seemed like a thin slice of air. So tense did the body become, so taut every muscle and nerve, the whole of a man floated a protective millimeter away from all solid objects until the actual fight was joined. For what wild animal, no matter how vicious or courageous, could shoot back at its hunter with a machine gun?

These days Chamay was willing to concede that the animal within him often ruled.

On his first fighter sorties he had been shocked to discover the difference between being pursued and pursuing. Once the enemy was sighted he seemed to become a stranger controlled alternately by wild bravado and sheer terror. He was certain it was not altogether the memory of Raymonde which brought him to such basic savagery. It was something deeper, it caused the hair on the back of his hands to prickle, his breathing to become a quick gasping and his guts seem to rise and press hard against his chest. He now had three victories; two Aviatiks, and a two-seater Rumpler which had not yet been confirmed. Since his first experience as an attacker he had wondered about the "coolness" of aces like Guynemer, Madon and Fonck. Were they superhuman or did they also return to primitive ferocity?

He remembered an oration Jourdan had delivered one evening in the mess. He had said there were three stages in a fighter pilot's career. There was the beginner who had so much to learn so quickly he was likely to be daring at the wrong time and cautious when he should be daring. The casualty rate among beginners was awful. Yet if God was tolerant and presented a series of miracles so a beginner survived ten or twenty aerial encounters, then a fighter pilot's middle-age would be achieved. It was, according to Jourdan, the best and safest era in a fighter pilot's career. The excitement and fear and visual confusion were still very much at hand but not so overwhelming that it was impossible to think. Casualties were relatively low in the middle stage. Most of the pilots of the 322nd Escadrille had now entered it. Only Jourdan and Delander were at the final stage, whose danger was as much conjecture as fact. Yet it seemed that when a man had been too long in combat flying he became careless; no one knew if so many veterans had been shot down because their nerves had snapped just at the wrong time, or if in their hard-won experience they had become overconfident. It was discouraging to believe that their luck had simply run out, and Jourdan had not elaborated on his own classification.

Chamay looked down at the toy villages which appeared to glisten in the yellow morning light. The red tile roofs were still wet with dew and in the surrounding fields foreshortened peasants only a few millimeters tall were already at work. And they would continue to labor, Chamay knew, though the Boche were just over the horizon. France, he thought. My France—my sky.

This was one of those mornings which caused Chamay to whistle in admiration. He whispered a prayer of gratitude for what he saw and for his ability to see. For now the first sun burnished the towering cumulo-nimbus, transforming their fat protuberances into the ramparts and minarets of distant golden cities. This was the kind of morning when he sat quietly in awe, easing the Nieuport higher and higher, his body nearly motionless except for his eyes, which drank so thirstily of the beauty.

"I must soon cease this dreaming," he said aloud.

For a long spell now, the German pilots had kept to their own domain, rarely venturing west of the lines. A mere ten minutes east of the aerodrome and the situation changed. Every cloud became concealment for a possible ambuscade, and the sun in a pilot's eyes became an evil, frightening thing. There was no longer even a moment to observe or appreciate beauty.

Once above that withered land which stretched from Verdun to Arras, the gigantic bulge of devastation warned all pilots to keep their heads swiveling. There was a saying: "If you can hear a machine gun other than your own don't wait to discover who is shooting at what. The target is almost certainly you."

Now the broken clouds became scattered and through the holes between them Chamay could see the line of demarcation between the dead world and the world which was still living. It was as if a disgusting disease had erupted on the face of the earth so that what had once been green and lush was now pock-marked and scrofulous. Some giant in repulsion had puked along the banks of the Meuse, the Aisne and the Oise until the surrounding landscape was strewn with vomit. The full extent of devastation could only be absorbed in part because the mind refused to accept what thousands of artillery shells could do exploding in the same area in which thousands of shells had gone before.

Now it was spring. Here there should be the brilliant yellow of clustered laburnum, the bloom of chestnuts, pansies, forget-me-nots and sword-lilies. The May bug, that escort of spring so peculiarly French, should certainly have arrived, and that superb aviator, the swallow, should be darting and swooping after its insect prey. And around the villages cuckoos and nightingales should be announcing the blooming lilac. There should be greenfinch flittering everywhere and new stork nests on the house roofs. Pity the storks seeking a roof in this area. Pity all living things including the mud-smeared poilu crawling like a maggot from excrescence to excrescence. Here there was nothing left except torn trees and ooze and the blood and bones and flesh of hundreds of thousands of men.

"Raymonde, my friend," Chamay whispered now to the morning sky, "when I meet him, you may depend on me."

There were said to be six hundred German airplanes along the Western Front. An American in the Lafayette Escadrille had claimed to have seen a target device like that on an Albatros, although not at close range. He was a vague sort and admitted the German was so far away it might have been some other type airplane than the Albatros.

An English pilot Chamay had met in Amiens one evening had been more specific. Yes, he had seen such a painted target on an Albatros. There had been a scrap over St. Quentin and the Englishman had actually had the target in his sights long enough for a short burst. But the target had done an Immelmann and become lost in the general melee.

Where was the target this morning? With what Jasta? Was he on leave? Or dead? Or perhaps he had been promoted to flying a desk and would thus cheat his way to old age.

"Keep him for me!" Chamay asked the sky.

There were the Caudrons just above the fast-thinning clouds. They were waddling around like a pair of fat ducks as they waited for the ascending Nieuports. Chamay caught up with his flight just in time to make a reassuring sweep past the Caudrons.

Then all of the flock, the swift and the plodding alike, turned eastward and settled on course.

Chapter Three

April 1917
To the east and north of the
Chemin des Dames—

VERY HIGH, a milky scum of thin cirrus absorbed all the color from the sky and chilled the climbing sun. In the clear, a thousand meters above the uppermost deck of cloud, Sebastian Kupper cruised with his swarm of Albatroses.

He shivered in the draft-swept cockpit and made his usual attempts to hide from the slip-stream blast while still observing all that he should. They had not been more than ten minutes at altitude before his neck began its customary behavior. Kupper reached back now and prodded the muscles. They turned to stone these days at the mere prospect of sighting the enemy. It was not altogether fear but even more the cumulative fatigue of more than two hundred and fifty combat sorties. He tried to console himself by remembering that some physical wear was inevitable and that an insubordinate neck was less obvious than trembling fingers.

He looked down.

Between St. Quentin and Soissons the lowest cloud level was at one thousand meters. The clouds were widely scattered, stretching to the horizon in long lines like carefully prepared dumplings. Above this deck lingered another layer still heavy with the moisture of yesterday's storm. Here the clouds were soggy, lean and shapeless and dragged long tendrils of dirty white vapor as if trying to establish physical contact with the fat pastries below.

They were flying an inverted V formation with Kupper at the leading point. Behind him on either side, stepped up one above the other, were the veterans Steilig and Zimmerman, ready to take the lead if required, then the neophytes Haube and Sellerman. Just above them as the V spread were Kessler and Keim. Thus Haube and Sellerman were protected as well as could be. If their tensions did not overupset their bowels they were unlikely to suffer serious accident. For above their nearest protectors were Hochstetter and Schröder, Hinkmann, Just, Mueller and Meyer, all arranged to nurse the fledglings through their first few bewildering weeks of combat.

There were other formation patterns, but thirteen airplanes was an unhandy number, for which Kupper preferred the V. He had never favored "line abreast." It left the flight leader relatively safe since the mere task of holding formation required all eyes to be focused in his direction. And if as many as thirteen airplanes flew "line abreast" then number twelve and the end man were left exposed to any experienced attacker.

There was also "line astern," which had advantages for airplanes with restricted upward view. Yet in a single line Kupper had found that each pilot must spend so much time watching the airplane ahead he neglected side vision.

The inverted V pattern was a compromise. It allowed pilots forming the sides of the V to watch each other's flanks while simultaneously using his comrade as an auxiliary guide to speed and separation.

Kupper glanced back at the six Albatroses rising and falling on invisible waves of air, undulating gracefully like a bank of migrating birds. If any wild fowl could be so dreadful, he thought. Including his own pair of Spandaus, these gently dipping birds bristled with twenty-six machine guns, each capable of firing five hundred rounds per minute. They were painted a hodgepodge of color, splotches of green, yellow and black, which according to the camouflage experts would make them nearly invisible on the ground. A pity something hadn't been done about making them invisible in the air, Kupper thought. Then, remembering the target circle which he had caused to be painted on his own Albatros, he smiled. And for a moment he considered the pride of fools.

They were cruising slowly, their Mercedeses throttled well back to conserve fuel. Again Kupper glanced over his tail, this time deliberately to impress the others. In his position at the center of the V and below all the others it was not absolutely mandatory that he keep a sharp lookout behind him, since the rest of the formation served to protect that vital area. The lead airplane at the point of the V should be protected against surprise so that he could concentrate on navigation, the position of the whole formation against sun and clouds, and the early detection of enemy aircraft. Once the enemy was sighted the leader must quickly appraise the situation. Attack? Wait watchfully? What is the balance of power? Run away? By constantly turning his head, even to glance over his tail, Kupper set up a reaction among his pilots. They must not give way to the strangely hypnotic effect of formation flight which often created a state of euphoria. The close proximity of other airplanes persuaded a man that he and not the craft was flying, and the consequence was a dangerous trance. There was a saying that the French fought with *élan,* the English with guts, and the Germans with crafty care. Kupper was willing to accept it. Those who mixed care in the proper proportions lived to fly and fight another day.

From Flanders to the Vosges the German armies had retired behind the Hindenburg line, there to await the Allied offensive. Everyone down to the rawest German recruit knew it was coming, but by some special process of military reasoning, the French and English pretended it was still a secret. The German strategy was now defensive, and philosophy in the air was a duplicate of that held on the ground. Let them throw themselves on the prongs of our armor and when the hosts have been destroyed we will easily crush what is left.

So spoke the German generals.

Meanwhile there were less grandiose problems, Kupper thought. His left foot had gone so numb he could not be sure if his toes responded when he tried to move them. All fingers of his left hand were numb. His goggles bit into his cheeks, yet when he eased the strap the chill air penetrated instantly and caused his eyes to water. And there must be a hole corroded in the Mercedes' exhaust stack. He had never been so conscious of fumes.

He decided there were a few other matters unlikely to concern those generals and nobles preoccupied with the final destiny of Germany.

For one thing, dum-dum bullets—one more proof the English and French were not the angels they proclaimed themselves to be. Intelligence reported they were known as Buckinghams, and as Pomeroys. They had been first designed because sharp-nosed bullets had proven ineffective against observation balloons and something was needed to make bigger holes. Dum-dums were the answer. Now they were used on every target and what they did to the human body was an outrage. In Kupper's opinion the man who used dum-dums was a butcher. Intelligence estimated the enemy had produced twenty-six million such bullets. "Twenty-six million," he mused, "and I am a single assembly of bones, gristle and fluid. Twenty-six million chances divided by how many Germans?"

His eyes swept the horizon. Nothing.

He looked below on both sides. There was a wide gap between the lower clouds. Through it he saw the brilliant sparkling of artillery at work. They were at it again. Pounding the world to pieces at six-forty-five in the morning. The flashing marked the approximate line of combat. Unless a very tempting target offered, there was no reason to proceed farther west.

Kupper signaled for a right turn and the thirteen Albatroses wheeled into a gentle bank back toward the east. He searched the horizon again. Nothing. He glanced aloft and down. Nothing.

He changed course slightly to the south so the sun would not blind him. Slowly, in great loose and wandering curves, he led them along the invisible line which marked the separation between what he thought of as German sky and the sky dominated by her enemies.

The eastern sun was soft on his left wing tips. The far upper cloud and haze cut the intensity of all light, and the farther they proceeded south, the less brilliant was the sun. Kupper became ever more alert. Like an animal prowling new jungles. The tenseness spread down from his neck until his entire body was rigid. On this kind of morning trouble could come fast—too fast. The soft light produced an illusion of being able to see a great distance, a natural deception which had lulled many fighter pilots into false security. The present limit of visibility straight down was fair enough, he thought, but aloft and throughout the horizontal plane it was probably not more than a thousand meters.

Hola! Such a sky could be full of surprises! Very well! Admittedly, during the past month most enemy fighter activity had seemed to be a British concentration against Jasta 11 to the north. They were also quite capable of appearing here. This poor visibility gave everyone a chance for surprise. In seconds hostile airplanes could sweep out of the haze, chew off one or two of the Albatroses and be gone.

Kupper raised his gloved hand for attention. Then, so the others could follow his movements, he very deliberately reached forward and pulled the charging bolt on each Spandau. After a moment, when he was certain the others had done the same, he individually pulled the finger triggers for a quick burst of four shots. He waited and listened.

He counted twelve separate groups of double bursts and was satisfied. Good. According to training and order. According to what he believed—which was not to be caught with your sword stuck in its scabbard.

Good. Steilig, Zimmerman, Haube, Sellerman, Kessler, Just, Schröder, Hinkmann, Mueller, Keim, Hochstetter, and Meyer. You will live if you don't do anything foolish.

He squirmed down into the cockpit. God it was cold! He pulled his feet off the rudder bars for a moment and stamped them hard against the cockpit flooring. His eyes swept the instrument panel— oil pressure, tachometer, altitude and airspeed. His eyes paused on a metal plate and for the hundredth time he read it, although he had vowed never to read it again:

ALBATROS WERKE
g.m.b.h.,
Berlin-Johannisthal
Type E III No. 1440

Why must he read that silly plaque at least once every flight? The compulsion was infuriating.

Now his right foot was numb. So also were the fingers of his right hand, which held the control stick. Until recently the gun triggers had been thumb operated, which had some merit when the rest of the hand was so senseless it could barely be moved. But the triggers had been rerigged so that the forefinger closed them. Richthofen's idea. He was a dedicated game hunter and liked to use his trigger finger when after his own species. Anything to please the great man—thumb triggers had been pulled off and junked and everyone was obliged to use his trigger finger whether he liked it or not. Ah well, these days Richthofen received the credit and the blame for everything.

Watch it, Sebastian! Your thoughts are drifting. If you wish suicide do it properly. Not here. Never for one instant forget this wilderness.

He looked below. Nothing. Perhaps down there? The reconnaissance and spotter planes must be below the clouds. He saw a momentary shimmering of the Canal du Nord, which bisected a tear in the lower deck of cloud. Just to the west, he knew, the canal would join the Somme. And beyond that, to the west—how inviting! When would the day come when a man could journey to Paris again, or return to London? And I want to stroll, not march, he thought. I want to wander in Montparnasse with Maria on my arm and perhaps find a small painting to strike our fancy. I want to stroll for miles in the streets of London, hesitating as I please along the Thames. A start from Tower Bridge, perhaps, and walk all the way to Trafalgar. Perhaps if there is enough money I would take Maria and tour America one day. There's a cousin in St. Louis or is it St. Paul?

Sebastian! Watch yourself! What is happening to you? Daydreaming at four thousand meters! You will soon die.

He searched the sky above, ahead, and to both sides. Nothing. Now an almost solid overcast stretched below. Still nothing but space in between.

Nothing. Or are you deceiving yourself? Are you blinding your own eyes so that you will *not* see—so you will not kill what is really there?

These are empty skies, or are they? You know very well an enemy fighter does not appear conveniently silhouetted against a cloud, or sit waiting for recognition at a handy distance and altitude. If you observe such an offering it is almost certainly a decoy, and you should be more wary than ever.

There—something—or was it? Kupper sighed. How impossibly small was man and his frail little bird against these gigantic dimensions!

In spite of his painful neck he constantly turned his head. He must. Often first discovery of the enemy was realized while the head turned from side to side. Then a sidewise glance to make sure, the head still moving because for some strange optical reason it was possible to detect a half-dozen fly specks with a quick side glance, while simply staring at the same area might reveal nothing at all. And first sight meant the chance to take the initiative. First sight,

67

and the greater the distance the better. Distance gave time for maneuvering into the sun or using an intervening cloud as concealment.

Now—nothing to the east which would be unlikely at this hour. Yet, remember, the unlikely has often killed the finest men. Now to the south. Murky down that way, the leftovers of yesterday's storm still hovering over the area. There were doubtless clear layers at the lower altitudes, but that exploration could wait until later in the day.

To the west. Nothing still. The ground observers had reported greatly increased enemy air activity. Where was it? He glanced over his left shoulder and then his right. He was pleased. The two sides of the V were smartly kept, which meant that his pilots were very alert. If any one of them saw hostile airplanes before the leader, he would drop down immediately and advise.

There is nothing here this morning. We are wasting time and fuel. We should return to the aerodrome, take our breakfast, and wait for reports from the ground observers. And the French aerodromes to the south are probably closed with fog or rain. Yet the French are so unpredictable! They stay on the ground when the weather is dreadful. They are obsessed with trickery as befits a nation of rogues and charlatans.

Kupper looked down to see the overcast breaking again. At the bottom of a cloud chasm he saw the ruins of a village. He thought of the French and the remarkable differences in daring and skill among their flying men. How could a people be so diverse? The majority of French pilots were clumsy and frequently made fatal amateurish mistakes. Apparently the experienced kept their hard-won knowledge to themselves. Someone should warn their eager beginners not to dive immediately on being attacked. They might as well put a Luger to their heads. They should be told to climb in a spiral if they could, and if they could not gain altitude they should at least circle. The erratic French would engage ten airplanes when they had less than half as many. *Élan,* they called it. Nonsense. And there was *sang-froid,* the other element believed by the French to be the most valuable attribute a pilot could have. Well—it was, and it was not. True enough, one must not lose emotional control in battle; but unless the fierce instinct of survival took possession of a man his chances diminished accordingly.

He looked up, searching all the sky surrounding him. The cold was causing his nose to drip. He wiped at it ineffectually with the back of his gloved hand. What are we doing up here? We are buzzing hornets in the whole complex and we accomplish very little except to cheer the morale of the even more miserable ground troops. If we do not appear on schedule our own troops sing, "God punish England, our artillery and our Air Force."

What else do we do up here? We slay each other. And when we are dead others will appear to slay each other. Our marching back and forth up here leaves no ruins, all is gone forever with the very next wind.

So many Frenchmen have died in this sky, Kupper thought, their supply of pilots must be nearing exhaustion. One would think they would change their tactics. Now only the Stork Escadrille need be feared. They are clever and tough—they know what they are doing because most of them have managed to survive their own mistakes. They are nearly all veterans, many of them aces. Avoid them. You are not up here to start fights unless *all* the advantage is on your side.

An empty, melancholy sky. Kupper remembered that it was on such a day that Erwin Bohme had collided with Boelcke. Poor Bohme. When he returned to earth he had to be forcibly restrained from shooting himself for his unforeseen mistake which had killed the great Boelcke, father of the Jagdstaffeln. There it was—the unforeseen again. Who would have thought that the man who changed the whole concept of aerial combat, the great teacher, the "Kanone," would be finished off by one of his own students. It was Boelcke who had taught you one of the most important primaries of survival, the steep turn without loss of altitude. If your antagonist was not equally skillful, you soon had the advantage, even if he pounced on your tail.

But that morning belonged to last year. Boelcke was gone and young Richthofen who had been with him during his fateful flight now ruled in his place. So many things had gone.

Kupper, you aging clown. Keep yourself for Maria and let the Kaiser be damned.

An eerie, thickening sky. Another storm making up in the west. There will be no spring—only winter forever. What has gone wrong, aloft and below? Have we suddenly become the last men alive? If so we are magnificently prepared for nothing. We have dressed

69

for a ball only to discover it postponed and everyone informed except us. Where are the English in their silly packing boxes? Where are the French with their fine new Spads?

He began a slow right turn to the north. It was difficult to be sure of their exact position. Much of the earth was obscured by low scud but through a hole he saw a splotch of ruptured clay against the Oise. Probably the town of Chauny.

Nothing aloft. Nothing to the west. Only the pallid sun in the east. And below—nothing, still nothing—no, wait.

Wait!

There! Almost due north perhaps fifteen kilometers ahead. There, just over the lowest layer of cloud. Minute puffs of black against the gray background. German flak. Successive salvos bursting in groups—quite different from the French *rafale,* which put several hundred rounds in the air at the same time. And German flak meant that the enemy must be within firing range. There were no airplanes visible but somewhere in that region they could be found.

Kupper raised his left hand above the cockpit rim and made a definite forward gesture. He shoved on full power to the Mercedes and set the Albatros in a long shallow dive toward the delicate puffs of smoke. From such a distance they might easily approach unnoticed. Not too steep or too fast. The Albatros' wings must be remembered.

My training, he thought, has taught me to remember and see too much.

Soon he leveled off slightly above the level of the bursting flak. There was no sense in being killed by your own people. He glanced back at his flock. Well done! The formation was excellent, with Sellerman and Haube holding position like veterans. He easily recalled how they must be feeling—their fear of being behind on everything, of making some silly mistake which might endanger the others. He knew they would now have such a grip on the control stick that their fingers would be sore for the rest of the day. And he knew that tonight their backs would ache from a tenseness they had not realized possessed them. Now, whether they liked it or not, they were part of the most horrifying and exhilarating game in the world—the hunt for like creatures of like intelligence.

His eyes swept the horizon. There! Two aircraft jinking through the flak which had suddenly diminished. Two British F.E.2b's plod-

70

ding northwest toward Bapaume. Child's play! Did the English deliberately design their airplanes to fly so slowly? And how in the name of God did they dare go aloft in such antiques? Whoever was responsible for the design of British aircraft should be hanged. Better yet, they should be forced to fly in their own creations!

Kupper eased back on the Mercedes to match their pace and carefully examined all the sky about him. Momentarily the sun was obscured by upper cloud so that even in that direction he could not be surprised. Nothing. Where is the fighter escort for these silly boxes limping back to their nest? We are not so naïve, Englishman. Come, now! If you hide much longer we will swallow your fat partridges. Come, now! Hurry. Your poor friends need you.

Kupper looked everywhere for Sopwith Pups, the one English fighter he respected. A Sopwith could turn inside an Albatros, and in knowing hands could be a nasty little beast of an airplane. If more than four appeared, he resolved to break away. Sellerman and Haube needed more experience. They were not ready for a real melee and once engaged there would be no hauling them out of the scrap. Even now, he knew, they saw themselves covered with glory. How sad, he thought. I can only see them covered with earth.

Again he searched the sky, sector by sector, making a complete circle so that he could not possibly miss a waiting escort. Still nothing.

He glanced back at Steilig and Zimmerman. Surely, if he had become blind they had not. They were looking down at him. He knew from the way they shook their heads that they were equally puzzled. Another circle. The slow F.E.'s would not get away although they were already trying. What had these poor crocks been up to? F.E.'s were now mainly used for reconnaissance. If these were on a genuine mission instead of serving as decoys, they had probably been photographing the results of the artillery preparation east of Ervillers.

Kupper decided to wait a minute longer. He had never had so much time to study an enemy airplane.

The F.E.'s were pusher biplanes held together by a multitude of flying wires. Between the wings a sort of bathtub contained the crew. The pilot was in the cockpit just forward of the engine. The observer was in the nose and had a Lewis gun to defend the craft.

The observers of both F.E.'s were standing up in their cockpits now, swinging their guns in the general direction of the Albatros formation. Their movements suggested great excitement—or were they just good decoy actors playing their roles to the very last curtain?

They had passed beyond the flak area now. In a few minutes they would be to the west of the German lines. These pigeons simply could not be allowed to escape. Where, where was their escort— *where?*

Kupper repeated his search of the sky, then chanced a look below. Perhaps there was some new kind of British airplane which could climb up from a lower altitude. No, not the English. They would send their men out in machines that should have been in a museum and the young men would not hesitate, first because they were British and second they had so little flight time they hardly knew the impossible from the possible. Those Englishmen who accumulated any respectable amount of combat experience before they were shot out of the sky were very few. So! Here again was the sickening sight of four young men waiting to be slaughtered. Brave young men. The observers were aiming their single peashooters as if they really expected a fair shot at an attacker. Somehow they had been convinced an attack might come from ahead. Jolly. Sporting. And ridiculous. Even Sellerman and Haube knew enough to take an unprotected F.E. in one pass. If they had listened to him only the day before when he had converted the Jasta mess into a makeshift classroom and again had gone over all the weaknesses of the enemy planes, they would know that a simple straight approach just slightly below the tail of an F.E. would be enough. The observer's gun was completely blind to that angle unless he chose to shoot his pilot in the face or saw off his own wing. If the companion F.E. maneuvered to cover the other's tail from above or below, simply slip to one side or the other, as required, and the gunsights of both airplanes would be hopelessly blocked.

Kupper made a final sweep of the sky and reached a decision. This was really a job for one Albatros, but since there were thirteen, let the engagement be shared. And who better than Sellerman and Haube deserved to score a victory on their first mission? When the matter was done with he would have to caution them against overconfidence; there would probably never be such a gift again.

Suddenly his resolve weakened. Stop. Why should four men die simply to provide a little seasoning for Sellerman and Haube? Perhaps in view of their hopeless position, the Englishmen would be reasonable. It was worth a try even if there was some slight risk. Perhaps.

Kupper raised his right hand, his gloved fingers spread wide. He slowly closed his fingers then brought his fist to the top of his helmet. "I will attack." Again he raised his hand, this time fingers together. He kept it steady for several seconds. "Hold your formation and speed."

He gave the Mercedes full power and dropped away swiftly until his altitude matched that of the F.E.'s. In a moment he had positioned himself so that only one F.E. could bring its gun to bear and if the observer fired he would almost certainly saw off his own wing. Even so Kupper maintained a distance outside the range of temptation.

He could clearly see the observer tracking him with his Lewis gun. The pilot, apparently frozen in either determination or terror, was flying the F.E. in almost a straight line. Poor chap.

Kupper fired a short burst from his Spandaus, then pointed upward at the hovering formation of Albatroses. Both the pilot and the observer looked up. There was no question that they could misunderstand his message. Come! Don't be utter fools! You're lucky —you have a choice of how your war will end. Be grateful. Take it!

Kupper described a slow arc with his arm and very definitely pointed his finger to the east—toward Germany. Then, as if shaming a naughty child to a corner, he moved his hand in a series of downward motions: turn east—start your descent immediately. As final authority to his gestures he fired another quick burst.

He saw the nearest observer lean back to confer with his pilot. They turned momentarily and gestured to their comrades in the far F.E.

Surrender, I beg you!

The nearest observer turned back very suddenly. Kupper saw him make a slight adjustment to his goggles, then his hands fell to the Lewis. Kupper watched the flashes at the end of the muzzle in horror. What kind of people were these? Even at this futile range, the child was firing.

Kupper peeled away and began a fast climbing turn to rejoin his squadron. In a moment he slipped into place at the head of the V.

He looked down at the F.E.'s. They were still holding a dive straight for their own lines. At least they knew the importance of

73

seconds or thought they did, because nothing except a twin miracle could save them now—not even the covey of planes Kupper spotted far on the western horizon. They were too far away for him to be sure of their type. They just might be the new British Camels, which intelligence reported were likely to be dangerous.

He made a quick estimate. They numbered fifteen, perhaps twenty. No matter. It was extremely doubtful that they had any association with these F.E.'s. And from such a distance they would never witness what was about to happen.

Kupper looked over his right shoulder at Sellerman and pointed his finger directly at his eyes. Then he moved his hand down in an arc and held it pointed at the right F.E. He repeated the signal to Haube on his left and pointed to the left F.E. Finally he raised his hand, made a fist, and brought it quickly down.

Out of the corners of his eyes he saw two Albatroses swoop down past him.

It was over in seconds. Sellerman and Haube had absorbed the lesson well, closing just as they should, holding their fire until the result was certain, and nicely covering each other when the job was done. Sellerman's F.E. proved to be a "stinker," smoke and flame pouring from it almost instantly. He must have hit the fuel tank with his first burst. The F.E. spun toward the earth trailing a long plume of smoke and flame and separated into several pieces long before it vanished through a delicate cloud. Kupper was certain the pilot and observer had been killed; they had made no apparent attempt to escape cremation.

Haube's F.E. proved a less spectacular victory. The pilot managed to throw it around fast enough for his observer at least to bend over his sights. But Haube slipped under his tail on the high opposite side and waited until his range was certain. Then he rolled into a shallow diving turn with both guns going and raked the F.E. from the pilot's cockpit to the tail. Well done, Kupper thought, but not difficult considering the tremendous advantage an Albatros had over an F.E. The tail came off and the F.E. snapped into a tight flat spin. It descended rather slowly, like a dead autumn leaf. Kupper was glad that the conquest seemed enough for Haube—he let the F.E. go without pressing the attack further. It was possible the Englishmen were still alive and with luck they might survive the crash.

They had not the time to wait and watch. Now Kupper saw more

74

than twenty airplanes in the approaching flight. They were coming in fast. He studied them a moment. A big flight of French Breguets, two-seaters, probably flown indifferently, but in such numbers they could hurt. Sellerman and Haube may have been blooded, but they were still far from ready for this sort of thing. Nor am I, Kupper thought.

As he swung around in a steep bank and descended at full throttle toward the east, he wondered if he would ever again be ready for true combat. Watching Sellerman and Haube make their kills had nauseated him. Now, he thought, when we are safely on earth again I must congratulate them. Well done, young executioners. Will I be able to hide my eyes?

Pilger stood beneath a barren elm tree watching the sky. He was alone by choice, for he had many things to consider. And they were not the sort of things he wished to share with Feldwebel Groos or any of the other men who had gathered according to custom and were awaiting return of the morning patrol. It was understood among all ground personnel, officers and noncoms alike, that no particular demands would be made of any soldier during this vague period which began spontaneously, endured for half an hour or so, and automatically terminated when the results of the patrol were known. It was not a period of thirsting for news or morbid fascination with those wounded, or a desire to learn the details involving those who failed to return. The gathering was more an instinctive display of respect and was thus attended by all except the mess cooks and servants who were preparing breakfast. It was a time for smoking and subdued conversation among all who stood along the border of the field. There was a great deal of looking up at the sky, of placing hands behind ears, of rocking back and forth on heels of boots, and the man who first heard or spied the Jasta's returning airplanes somehow became somewhat taller than his comrades.

Pilger was alone because he was heavy-headed with new troubles and he was also ashamed of himself. He found it easy to compare his remorse with his feeling on that strange afternoon during the second battle of the Masurian Lakes. He well remembered how he and a corporal of much better education had been detailed for a scouting patrol and had gone too far. To their dismay they suddenly found their retreat blocked by a Russian infantry regiment scattered along a low embankment. Pilger and his companion flopped into the bordering marsh and were forced to remain concealed among the reeds for three hours. They dared not move. The water was halfway up their bodies and very cold. Instead of marching on their way like reasonable troops, the Russians milled around on the embankment until they drew artillery fire. Then they ran away. But their departure had been too late for Pilger. The cold and the wet were too much. He had to ease himself.

"You look like you're pissing," the corporal whispered.

"No," Pilger lied. It made no difference that his pants were already under water. He was ashamed anyway.

Now he had done a thing that was much more shameful. He had read a letter, or the start of one, or perhaps it had been a report?

Pilger had come upon it when he cleaned Kupper's hut soon after the Jasta departed. All the letters Kupper had received were neatly stacked in a cigar box on his small writing table. This letter, or whatever it was, lay fully exposed upon the table. An ashtray made from a Mercedes piston held it in place, and Pilger had to move the ashtray in order to empty it. He was in the process of salvaging two cigar butts for future trading when the writing intrigued his eyes. He could not resist reading all that Kupper had written. Soon he was lost and his lips moved slightly as he absorbed the words.

Pilger could not recall having received more than two letters in his entire life—therefore they were holy things, wonderful, secret, silent communications between one human being and another. A man like Leutnant Kupper received many letters, as was his due. It was astonishing to discover that he also composed them—if it *was* a letter.

. . . I have been trying with everything in me to achieve hatred for the English and the French because I am convinced it is a very necessary element for my own survival. So far I haven't had any luck at all with the project. Maybe there is something deeply wrong with me. I hate nothing but sloth and stupidity . . .

. . . I actually admire the English. Their courage is incredible. They die magnificently. I neither like nor respect the French and consider them responsible for many of our national troubles, but I do not hate them. On the contrary, I mourn the twenty-odd French I have killed as much as the Englishmen I have slain and

76

wish there was some way I could give them life again—even if it meant the abandonment of my own. I will never forget a certain Frenchman over Verdun. His memory haunts me. . . .

Pilger had read the words several times and afterward searched without success for a beginning or an end. There was none. There were simply the two pieces of paper covered with Kupper's writing. How beautiful it was, Pilger had thought as he tried to shake off the feeling of guilt. Kupper's writing was perfectly even and finely turned, like that in an old book Pilger had once seen in Silesia. It was easy to read.

. . . I am torn, or rather being torn to pieces. There is my duty to the Jasta and of course to the Fatherland. Still, I do not believe we are entirely right in this war, but then I don't think we are entirely wrong either. I am only sure that we cannot win. We are hyenas. The world loathes us. America will come into the war and not on our side. There are already Americans flying with French and British squadrons. (I haven't encountered one as yet.)

Then Pilger had read the part which had impessed him so that he had left the hut in a state of profound shock. It persisted now as he stood alone looking up at the tree.

. . . I do not believe that I can bear to kill any more men regardless of their nationality. It cannot be my hand which squeezes the trigger—*this makes me a traitor!*
I have begged God for the truth. We are not here to enjoy the French countryside, or dress up in our uniforms bedangled with medals and salute each other, and command each other, and eat and drink and sing, and by our diligence and faith hope to build a future in this business. We are here as hired assassins, the sort of men with whom no decent person would conceivably associate if we were not in uniform. And certainly we are among the cheapest paid cutthroats in the world, although I hear the French work for even less. Where else can you hire a reasonably intelligent, highly trained, physically capable murderer for a mere fourteen hundred and sixty-eight marks a month? He will do exactly what you tell him to do as long as he doesn't stop long enough to realize that one killing in the air does not advance the front or even hold it—not one millimeter. Of course we also receive free room

and board, such as it is, and I have heard of some Jastas that are based in Châteaux. But we must pay for our wine in the mess and I may soon go into debt if this enormous idiocy continues.

I sometimes believe I know the truth, which then permits me to persuade myself with comfortable phrases. I tell myself that the decadent French deserve what they are receiving, or that the flower of Germany died because of English greed, or that the French have brought in black barbarians to mutilate our troops, and the only language our enemies will understand is written in iron. I tell myself these things over and over, and worse, I tell my men who are forced to listen and who may or may not believe me. The real truth is . . . my guts have melted with the snows.

Pilger massaged the stubble on his chin and delicately inserted one great finger in his nose. There was so much these days for a man to mull. New things grew like warts on a man's brain. It had not been so in the trenches at any time he could remember. There, a man's brain was almost fully occupied trying to avoid the next hunk of scrap iron.

This was all very bad. If men like Leutnant Kupper were sick of fighting then who was going to carry on with the war? Pilger sighed and after a moment farted. Ach! Things were in a stew. Bears were running from foxes. Perhaps it would be well to send men like Kupper to the trenches for a spell. They would not have so much time to think and feel sorry for themselves, and worse yet—feel sorry for the enemy. A man fought for air the moment he was dragged from between his mother's legs. And most men fought through all the rest of their days to keep strangers from pounding a shovel in their face. If Kupper's fancy education had not taught him that war was lice, bullets and blood, then he had been cheated. By now he should know that to be sweet to thine enemy was asking for a bayonet in the balls.

These things were necessary to a man—like onions to potatoes. Fornication and killing were equal urges, as Kupper ought to know. Pilger looked down at Louie the Alsatian, who rarely allowed his attention to be distracted from the sky until his master had returned. "Don't you agree, Louie?"

There were a great many other things a man like Kupper should know, then maybe he would stop writing silly things. Dangerous things such as Pilger had just seen scribbled right across the second sheet of paper—words hard to make out because they were not in the same script, as if they had been put down in a hurry. Or better yet, as if maybe he had just been drunk:

"I must find one thing to rescue me from total despair! I must know it still exists even among men at war . . . MERCY! Pray God that I will find it soon! Then perhaps I can relearn hope."

Pilger raised his leg and broke wind again. Watching the sky, he saw several planes approaching from the west. He heard a shout from the group of men who were gathered some distance from him. Louie began a frantic barking. It was said he would count up to thirteen airplanes and would not bark if one were missing.

The sound of Louie's barking was lost against the roar of engines. He could only jump up and down and bite at the fresh morning air as the Albatroses rose in a graceful *chandelle*. The signal of victory.

Very satisfying, Pilger thought. But something must be done about Leutnant Kupper.

Chapter Four

————————————— *At the front, the blood
of the wounded congealed—*

AFTER BABARIN discovered that the new hole punctured in the Nieuport's fuselage matched the size of his head, he exclaimed in wonder and told all who would listen how it had been made by a Boche 77-mm. ack-ack shell. Chamay, who had been sitting 145 millimeters from the forward edge of the hole, was not at all certain the fire had come from an enemy battery. All was confusion over the front now, with everyone much on edge in anticipation of the coming push, and the weather and visibility had been deteriorating steadily. Chamay believed the hole could easily have been made by his own ground artillery, since low cloud had forced him down to five hundred meters just before he was hit. He had shrugged his shoulders and tried to forget about it.

It was Babarin's duty to repair the hole, a project he had been able to postpone for two days because of the phenomenal weather. An April blizzard clawed at the canvas hangars and there was more snow than there had been all winter. When it did not snow it rained, and the temperatures stayed so consistently low the rain frequently turned to sleet.

Those few sorties flown by the 322nd Escadrille had been barren of results. Throughout the aerodrome, so comfortless in the damp cold, there was a vague scent of ultimate disaster. His Excellency had taken to wrapping a heavy muffler about his long neck and standing for hours on the small stoop which fronted his quarters. He would point his great nose at the leaden sky and hold it poised for minutes at a time, as if it could foretell some improvement in

81

the weather. Each day his hound face appeared to sag a little more until it seemed in imminent danger of total collapse. Officers and men obliged to pass His Excellency in pursuit of their duties saluted him, but avoided meeting his eyes, for they were altogether too melancholy and eloquent of majesty in deep private pain. Apparently it had taken a meteorological quirk in nature to seriously undermine Captain Jourdan's fundamental precepts. He was now, for the first time in his life, doubting the purpose of soldiering.

"No Boche will ever tag our Commander," Chamay had commented. "He is dying inside—before our eyes."

Babarin's problems were also complex and directly attributable to the foul weather. He had cut a linen patch somewhat larger than the hole in the fuselage and nicely pinked the edges. Normally he would simply glue the patch on and then shrink the linen by applying a pungent shellac-type mixture known to aircraftmen as "dope." But neither glue nor dope would flow at such temperatures and Babarin had ruined four similar patches trying to attain a firm adhesion. He built a small fire of twigs to heat the glue, but it failed in everything except the creation of smoke and stench. Sussote scrambled out of the hangar on his hands and knees and accused Babarin of trying to gas himself so he could be invalided home to Auvergne.

"Ça fait rien," Babarin answered haughtily. "The glue is not the true problem. We can sew on the patch if we must. What worries me is the dope—the consistency is important."

He wrinkled his brows in deep concentration and frowned at the hole. "We must be realistic. The twigs are too wet and so the fire is not hot enough. We must not be defeatists. We must also be logical. That is a very important quality for a mechanic—and don't you ever forget it."

At the time, Sussote had only a vague notion of what his superior had in mind, but when Babarin left him on a long search through the back of the hangar and returned bearing an acetylene lamp, he was filled with misgivings.

"Logic!" repeated Babarin. "Logic is the root and the spur of invention. For example—our duty is to place patch on hole. But the temperature is minus-five centigrade. The result? Dope has consistency of taffy. Eh, voila!—we must change consistency by creating warmer environment."

Babarin had removed the top of the acetylene lamp and stood

back to admire it while he caressed his mustache. According to Sussote's later testimony his eyes had taken on a faraway look which reminded him of his very own brother, André, just after he had fallen off the barn roof.

"*Alors!* The only wood available for heat is down by the little bridge. By the time we chop and drag it back here and dry it out, the war will be over. Also a man marching around in this weather looking for an axe will surely catch the grippe. If he dies there won't be so much as a medal for his family to take out and look at on Sunday afternoons. *Alors*—we must find other means of providing heat, and here it is all nicely done up in this little lamp."

Babarin's enthusiasm hastened his movements so that he began to move about the hangar workbench as a great chef exploits his kitchen. Sussote, watching as his gestures became more extravagant, was soon lost in the performance.

Babarin took up his tin-snips and fashioned a crude metal platform with which he tussled for some time before squeezing it into position on top of the lamp. Then he lit the lamp and placed it in the corner of the hangar. He found an empty four-liter can and carefully washed it out with benzine. The can had no top so he took up his tin-snips again and fashioned one from a discarded piece of engine cowling. "And while I am about it, I beg you to notice that I have left sufficient space around the rim so that the heated air will escape." During Sous-Lieutenant Miralle's subsequent inquiry it was concluded that this act of caution probably saved Babarin's life.

Finally, Babarin shoveled gobs of the gummy dope into the four-liter container, remarking throughout the process that Sussote should notice how it oozed instead of flowed, and that he would see how the reverse would soon be true—all thanks to logic.

When he set the can on the lamp and tenderly placed the top over the assembly, Sussote could no longer contain his doubts. "You know what that dope always smells like to me, Babarin? Like a hospital. Like that stuff they put people to sleep with when they cut them up."

"Ether," Babarin agreed brightly. He was viewing his rig with the utmost satisfaction, his arms folded across his chest, one hand poised so that his index finger could smooth the lower furrows of his mustache.

Sussote became increasingly uneasy. "I have a notion it is not wise to put fire near ether."

Babarin held up two fingers and pinched them together. "There is very little ether in dope. Perhaps a dram in that amount, perhaps even less. There is nothing to be concerned about, *mon vieux*. In a very few minutes we can commence work."

"Mais oui!" Sussote had started to say, just before the power of speech was denied him. Even as his lips pressed together the dim hangar was illuminated by a violent explosion.

Babarin was knocked flat on his back.

Sussote was hurled backward until he collided with the Nieuport's horizontal stabilizer, striking it with such force he sank to his knees.

When Sussote opened his eyes again he saw that the entire corner of the hangar had vanished, and where it had been he thought he saw a pleasant pastoral scene of snow-covered field, a small stream with a bridge, and some distant trees. It was also snowing, he later remembered. "It was like looking through the end of one of those glass balls you buy for children at Christmas—you turn the ball to make the snow fall and peek through the hole at the goings on inside."

Fortunately the water-soaked hangar did not catch fire although the torn fringes of the hole were smoking, and except for a slight cut on his right ear Sussote was unhurt. He went at once to Babarin, who was apparently dead.

Sussote was lamenting that his friend would be buried with such a badly singed mustache when the majority of the escadrille arrived on the run. Several men, under the impression that the Boche were trying a sneak attack, carried guns. Foulon, a corporal from Burgundy who had always been particularly excitable, actually went running around the hangar looking for Germans. Calmer men set about reviving Babarin, and Chamay arrived just as his dazed mechanic was being lifted to his feet.

Babarin shrugged his shoulders so expressively that Chamay knew instinctively who was responsible. He tried very hard to keep the acid out of his voice when he said that he was happy Babarin had apparently suffered no injury except to his mustache and dignity.

During the next half-hour the entire escadrille, including some visitors from the 14th Groupe de Chasse, came to view the vast hole in the hangar and comment on the triple miracle which had allowed the three Nieuports to escape with only superficial damage. After a brief preliminary inquiry Sous-Lieutenant Miralle, hinting darkly of sabotage, placed both Babarin and Sussote under arrest. Chamay's objections were coolly ignored.

Only His Excellency failed to appear in the hangar. Once he had learned of the slight actual damage he returned to his composition of a new plea for Spad airplanes. He was in haste to complete it before the arrival of his very special guest, a man whose presence in any escadrille was a distinct honor. The great Nungesser, ace of French aces, the equal of Guynemer and Fonck, had promised to come to *popotte* if the weather was bad enough to keep him on the ground, which it assuredly was. His Excellency planned to discuss his aircraft procurement problems with Nungesser and seek his advice. He had never met Nungesser, and some of the stories about him suggested he might not be overly attentive to serious discussion, yet Jourdan was determined to try. The right word to the right officer from such a celebrity might make all the difference.

As always, *popotte* would be at eleven o'clock, and several bottles of Volnay had been laid on for the occasion so the meal would last somewhat longer than usual. Jourdan intended to speak to him there, for it was doubtful if there would be any other opportunity. All of his pilots would certainly besiege Nungesser with questions, and who could blame them? He is, thought Jourdan with sadness, the very man I can never be.

Yet to envy Nungesser bordered on treason. Like Guynemer he was a symbol, an inspiration to all who flew for France. Of course he was not from St. Cyr and therefore could not be considered a professional officer, but in wartime, Jourdan reflected, one must take the broader view. Indeed, Nungesser's only military background was reported to have been a brief service with the 2nd Hussars, where he had acquitted himself well. Jourdan thought he might ask why Nungesser had transferred from such a distinguished regiment to the air. For the glamour? Nungesser was the personification of glamour. He would somehow manage to glitter if he were in the supply corps. Jourdan was well aware that seated at the same table he himself must, in contrast, appear very dull indeed. He had only four victories against Nungesser's thirty confirmed, which meant, by the law of averages, there must be another twenty unconfirmed. Jourdan raised his doleful eyes and watched the slow dripping of water through a leak in the roof. "God help me," he whispered, as if his yearning might be transferred upward through the melting snow. "Perhaps Nungesser will leave me a morsel of whatever it is he has on his plate."

Only one thing about the blizzard pleased Jourdan. With any better weather he knew his guest of honor would be aloft hunting Germans.

At precisely eleven o'clock Jourdan emerged from his quarters. He crossed the distance to the large canvas structure which served as the escadrille mess, adjusting his long stride so that he arrived at the entrance just as the second cook stopped banging on a 75-mm. shell case with his soup ladle. Today the clanging signal brought members of the escadrille on the run. Word of Nungesser's possible arrival had been enough to urge most of them into the polishing of boots and a certain sprucing of their persons and uniforms which His Excellency could never have inspired.

Hands in pockets, moving across the mud and snow in groups of two and three, they all came toward the mess. They inveighed against the cold although not one would consider a greatcoat to protect himself. They laughed and jostled one another with self-conscious hilarity, striving for ease they did not feel, pretending an indifference to this very special occasion. Their high spirits prevailed, although the tone became more subdued after they had stood in a shivering semicircle about their commander for a full ten minutes past their usual mess time. Yet they did not mind the waiting. If Nungesser scorned promptness then perhaps even His Excellency might, by example, depend less on the second hand of his watch.

Later, Chamay wondered if Nungesser had been waiting down the road for a suitable interval to elapse between his scheduled arrival and the time of his appearance.

At eleven twenty-six according to Jourdan's watch, they heard a roar of exhaust on the road beyond the bridge. Through the swirling snow they observed the open Hispano-Suiza roadster approaching at high speed. It skidded through a wild turn to make the bridge, bounced nearly clear off the surface as it passed over the hump, and spewed a wake of mud and snow as it turned down the line of hangars. It came toward them at full throttle; there was a moment when they were sure it would pass right on, then a squeal of brakes brought it to a sliding stop in front of the mess.

A stocky figure squirmed out of the roadster, reached back for a cane and limped toward Jourdan. His right hand rose to a salute so casual it was more like a wave.

"Forgive me for keeping you waiting."

His smile, thought Chamay, is unforgettable—more of a painful grimace which asked the observer to ignore the rows of gold teeth fencing his battered lips. He wore no kepi and the wet snow was matted on his heavy blond hair. He had been wounded and injured so many times his mere existence was the subject of debate. Chamay saw that his movements were curiously restricted. How many times, Chamay wondered, had he refused to die? There was a deep and angry scar which extended diagonally from Nungesser's lower lip and finished at the bottom of his chin. There was another, older gash just above his left eye. His uniform was black beneath the snow and there, worn as if his bone splinters had been hung together and pinned to his chest, were his medals; the Legion of Honor, the Médaille Militaire, a cluster of others which Chamay could not so quickly identify, and the Croix de Guerre with twenty-four palms. It was rumored that Nungesser wore his medals even in combat. Good enough, Chamay thought. He deserved to wear them in his sleep if he pleased.

"Welcome," Jourdan said, trying his best to smile. "We are honored," he added in a reckless attempt to abandon his stiffness. Then taking Nungesser's arm he led him inside.

Though Jourdan's troubles with armament and airplanes never left him entirely relaxed, a subtle change always transformed him once he had entered the mess. He invariably made pathetic efforts toward geniality, smiled frequently, and on occasions when wine and menu were pleasing, he had been known to laugh quietly. Such abandon seemed incongruous in Jourdan and secretly shocked those around him. Men further away remained undisturbed, since Jourdan's shy laughter was nearly as inaudible as his voice. Yet all shared his comparative elation. The cuisine in Jourdan's mess was the true first class element in the escadrille. The cook, one Stanislas Bouton, had been a talented restaurateur with his own establishment in Nice. He was a passionate man and it was said that in a moment of wine-soaked patriotism he had actually volunteered for service. Regardless of his initial urge, he had certainly given his all for France once enlisted. Now he was esteemed and protected by every man who ate his fare, and by silent agreement within the escadrille he was never allowed to venture beyond the confines of the aerodrome without a determined escort. Nothing must happen to Monsieur Bouton, no accident must befall him—particularly no kidnaping by another escadrille that might recognize such a valuable prize. All were concerned with his rather precarious health. "How are you feeling today, Monsieur Bouton? What a pity. Take care—are you seeing the doctor about it, Monsieur Bouton? How is your ague, your rheumatism, your gout, and above all, your liver?" The slightest rumor that something might be awry with Stanislas Bouton's physical chemistry caused as much worry and discussion as a minor Nieuport crash.

Jourdan's frequent defeats were somewhat eased by Monsieur Bouton's talents. Certainly on such a day his genius would remain true. They had discussed the menu when news had first come of Nungesser's possible visit, and had conferred seriously for an hour, revising the proposed menu according to the bothersome war restrictions and the appalling weather.

Bouton had waggled his pudgy fingers and said, "What grows better under water, *mon Captaine,* than watercress? So we will commence with a *potage au cresson.* Since we have eggs and cream, let us follow with a *quiche Lorraine*—puffy bacon, of course, and a chilled Pouilly de Mâcon. Unless you have an objection?"

Jourdan had no objection but reminded Bouton that bottles of Pouilly de Mâcon were simply not available.

After a moment of sulking Monsieur Bouton rallied. "Since I know where shallots are obtainable, we will forget the *quiche* and go directly to *filets de poisson pochés au vin blanc.* I will create a thin sauce which will give the illusion we have actually had the *quiche.*"

Jourdan had nodded his approval.

"Since it is April we must have *gigot de pré-salé rôti.* If it proves succulent and tender then we need only a Médoc to wash it down—and around the platter a fence of braised endives."

"We do not have Médoc," Jourdan had said.

"Not even from Bordeaux?"

"Not even a mediocre Bordeaux."

Bouton pulled hard at his thick eyebrows and tried to conceal his shock. Like the rest of the escadrille he was loyal to His Excellency and fully aware of his desperate need for encouragement.

"No matter," he said valiantly. "I can find mushrooms to enliven the platter. We will improvise and rely entirely on the Volnay, which is a permissible wine although one certainly could not call it well

88

bred. I have butter, olive oil, parsley to stuff the mushrooms, but no white vinegar. When I think of the lemons rotting in Provence . . ."

Monsieur Bouton clapped both hands over his eyes as if the spectacle of rotting lemons were actually before him. "But I have been saving a cheese, a Brie, which might rescue the situation. It will not be great, *mon Capitaine,* but again it will not be bad."

Now Jourdan could see that Nungesser was properly appreciative, particularly of the Volnay. During the course of the meal he had raised his glass toward each of his hosts so that by the time they reached the *fraises au sucre* and the marc, even the dour Delander was smiling. Those who because of their years and junior rank had deliberately seated themselves below the salt, were delighted at such comradely recognition. Chamay considered himself particularly fortunate since a third table had been brought in to form the end of a U. Thus all present could face the commander and his guest and the orderlies could serve from the open center. The Service Aeronautique was not given to fixed mess protocol, so the fact that Sergeant Chamay had found a seat closer to the guest of honor than Sous-Lieutenant Miralle or Folliet who was also a lieutenant, or Delander, or St. Hilaire, was not taken amiss by anyone. From his position Chamay could hear patches of conversation between Nungesser and His Excellency. He chewed his bread very quietly lest the crunching should obliterate what they had to say. He listened attentively while they discussed life in Paris, where Nungesser had been only the week before. Nungesser did a great deal of laughing yet Chamay was certain he detected a touch of bitterness in his voice. He told how rationing was a farce these days for those who had money; and it seemed that everybody except the refugees from Alsace and Belgium had plenty of it. Women were everywhere, Nungesser said, laughing. They delivered the mail, worked on the trams, collected tickets for everything, and in spite of their black overalls they still managed to look like women—and if you needed a woman on your next leave in Paris, as who did not, then bring her a bucket of coal and she would be yours! Nungesser had passed the window of the most elegant jewelry shop on the rue de Rivoli and there had seen a single lump of coal displayed on black velvet and surrounded by diamonds. They spoke of the Americans joining the war—what could one say? It was interesting, and heartening, and one must be careful not to count on it.

When the marc was served, His Excellency smacked his lips and apologized for the lack of fennel, which, had circumstances been otherwise, would certainly have graced the fish course. Nungesser replied that he was most content and his liver soothed by the rather special marc. Both men then fell into a solemn discussion of why it was that a decent meal could be found almost anywhere south of Lyon, whereas to the north this did not hold true. Nungesser objected. He claimed there was no finer food in all of France, which of course meant the world, than could be found in Normandy; *matelote de sole,* for example, or Vallee d'Auge chicken, or the oysters to be found in Courseulles, and the smelt of Cudebec, and of course Calvados—always Calvados.

Chamay wondered what had happened to the war. It was still there outside the windows, somewhere out in the blowing snow. Somewhere in the gloom and freezing mud only a few kilometers away men were dying. While other soldiers ate slop with their fingers, his commander and the hero of France discussed the Camemberts of Lisieux and Vimoutiers. Chamay reassured himself by studying Nungesser's array of medals and was greatly relieved when their conversation turned to a subject he considered more appropriate.

The Spad, Nungesser said, was an excellent airplane, although somewhat soft and lazy in a spin perhaps, and rather critical in airspeed before flare-out for landing. You cannot float it down but must keep some motor all the way to the ground. Otherwise it was a gem—a strong airplane in every respect. You could dive it without fear of losing your wings, and the landing gear was set far enough forward, Nungesser said, laughing, "so that even I can land one without disaster. And at last you will have a rudder big enough to do something except waggle at the passing birds."

All who could hear him knew Nungesser referred to the Nieuport's regrettable tendency to ground-loop.

"You will also like the Hisso engine now that summer has come," Nungesser said with a significant glance at the fringe of snow along the window sill. "We had some troubles with the water-cooling system during the cold weather." His sarcasm was followed by polite laughter in which even His Excellency joined. Then Jourdan asked when a deserving escadrille might expect to receive the new Spads.

Though Chamay tried his best to hear Nungesser's reply, he failed. Whatever Nungesser said to His Excellency was overwhelmed by a volley of laughter from the far end of the table, where Sous-Lieutenant Miralle had been vividly describing how after the explosion he had jokingly given the hapless Babarin the choice of a labor battalion or Verdun. And what had the man decided? Verdun! He even claimed that he had been wanting to serve there—which of course only proved that Babarin should be put away for congenital idiocy.

Chamay suddenly decided that he detested Sous-Lieutenant Miralle. He would not permit him to pack a member of his ground crew off to a labor battalion *or* to Verdun. Babarin's mistakes were sufferable. His loyalty inspired the drooping morale of others. Babarin, as much as Nungesser, was France. Transfer him? Over my dead body, Chamay thought.

He turned his attention back to Nungesser, who was talking about his earlier career flying Voisins in V.B. 106, an observation squadron. Loathing the duty, he had begged for a transfer to fighters without success. He had been shot down by ack-ack because, like a fool, he had innocently followed a Boche who had no intention of fighting. He had escaped with minor bruises and cuts, but the incident had made him so furious he had created a private insignia, painted it on his Voisin and resolved to fly it as much like a fighter as its limitations would permit. And one day, by the greatest chance, he had scored an actual capture of an Albatros two-seater. His superiors were impressed. *Voila!* A transfer! Escadrille 65 and Nieuports. To continue his luck he had immediately painted his personal insignia on a true fighter airplane. He had found it strangely satisfying. Now, seventeen wounds later, the skull and crossbones, candles and coffin, all painted upon a black heart, still identified his Spad.

Chamay could no longer resist the question which had flamed within him the moment Nungesser mentioned his insignia. He swallowed hard, leaned far across the table and asked, "Have you ever seen a Boche flying an Albatros with a target circle painted just forward of the tail?"

A sudden silence, which Chamay tried to believe was purely accidental, fell upon the room. Or perhaps it was the way Nungesser was looking at him, a half-smile playing about his battered lips, a strange inquiry in his eyes, as if he had been caught off balance.

"Yes," he said finally, and Chamay was aware that he was being scrutinized very carefully. "Do you have a special interest in that fellow?"

"I do."

Again the appraisal. Chamay was sure Nungesser was seeking something beyond the obvious badges of rank. His eyes were questioning, but he was not going to ask the reason for this special interest, thank God.

"Have you seen him lately?" Chamay said.

"No. They've had me in the hospital for four months."

Nungesser laughed and for a moment Chamay thought he intended to avoid further mention of the target. "I am the medics' favorite experiment. What I haven't broken through my own foolishness, they consider fair game—"

"So you have not seen the target for some time?"

Nungesser pinched at his eyebrows and studied his glass of marc for a moment. When he turned to Chamay his eyes seemed more friendly, anxious to share a mutual secret without revealing it to others. Chamay saw that Jourdan had been distracted by Lieutenant Diderot, who had a positive genius for saying the wrong thing at the right time. For once, Chamay was grateful to him.

"The last time was in October," Nungesser said. "It was our second meeting. I was after a balloon near Brimont and was sure I had them surprised. But our friend came out of nowhere with five others and I ran like a thief." Nungesser paused and kneaded his powerful hands. "But we had met before."

"Do you think he is still in business?"

"He is good—*very* good."

"Do you know anything more about him, his name, or his rank—anything would be important to me."

"I can tell you he is no beginner. We had a tangle last summer. I think it was in August. He was traveling alone then, but apparently he has given up the habit. I was also alone and we mixed for perhaps three minutes, then he dove away. If I'd had a Spad then I could have caught him, but with a Nieuport, he was soon gone." Nungesser shrugged and thoughtfully fingered the scar on his jaw. "If you should meet him may I suggest you be extremely careful."

"I have met him, Captain. He killed my friend."

For a moment Nungesser became absolutely motionless, his eyes locked on Chamay's. Again he passed his hand along his terrible scar. Then he said distantly, "You are young. And handsome. Many girls must have been in love with you and there will surely be many more. You have a lot of living to do. Do not be too brave—remember we all must lose friends."

At once he seemed to forget his words; there was his tortured smile again, the gold teeth showing. Turning to Jourdan, he tapped his watch, made apologies which were strangely formal for a man so hearty, and stood up. Immediately all the others rose, including Jourdan, who towered over him.

Chamay saw that his commander's hound-dog face was truly distressed at his guest's abrupt departure. Yet there he stood like an usher in a theater, his hand held toward the door as if indicating the most convenient exit. As all the others pressed their farewells and thanks for Nungesser's company, Chamay hung back. Then, just as he reached the door, Nungesser turned deliberately and beckoned to him.

"I have seen something in your eyes which disturbs me. Hate the Boche all you please, but you are hating a single man—and that is dangerous. And if you meet one day? He will not know you and so he will not be angry, and so he will shoot ever so much better than you."

Nungesser clapped Chamay playfully on the arm. "Good aim and anger are not compatible. Why make your enemy such a gift?"

Nungesser turned to Jourdan and they conversed briefly in low tones. Later when all had gathered about Nungesser's car to wave him away, Chamay was certain they had spoken of him. For as soon as the Hispano-Suiza disappeared in a swirl of snow, Jourdan beckoned to him. "Come walk a few steps with me."

They strolled in silence, brushing the wet snowflakes from their faces. Finally Jourdan spoke and his voice held a wistfulness Chamay had never heard before. He suddenly decided that His Excellency was a very lonely man.

"You remind me of my younger brother," Jourdan began. He was such a professional soldier that Chamay found it incongruous that Jourdan actually had a family like an ordinary French citizen. Somehow it seemed improbable that he should ever have been a child or have loved or lived in a house or had any roots whatever except in his unit. As a soldier, Chamay thought, His Excellency has always been in perfect command of himself; now he is ill at ease, as if the effort to transform himself into a human being is almost too much for him.

93

"Like you, my brother was a bit of a hothead. I remember when we were children we had some petty argument, and he chased me through our orchard with an axe. In some ways you even look like him—"

Jourdan hesitated so, that Chamay was certain he was trying to communicate something deeply personal.

"My brother was a Dragoon officer, the Thirty-first Regiment. To show his contempt for the Boche he led a charge waving his sword and wearing white gloves. He was killed before he could run five paces. The official file states he was killed by machine-gun fire. I believe differently. I knew he had really been killed by his own gallantry."

Chamay was at a loss for an appropriate reply.

"Do you think my brother accomplished anything for France, or discouraged her enemies? I do not. In one heroic gesture he threw away his expensive training and subtracted from the power of his unit. He left his men leaderless. The majority were killed and the charge failed."

Jourdan paused and toyed with his swagger stick. "That was during the first month of the war. Perhaps if my brother had known how long it was going to last he would have acted differently, but I doubt it. He had the same *élan* you have—the same be-damned-to-consequences way of fighting."

They had come to Jourdan's quarters and for a moment Chamay thought he would be invited inside. But he saw that Jourdan was engaged in some monumental inner struggle—it was almost as if the power of speech had been temporarily denied him. His fingers rubbed nervously along the smooth surface of the swagger stick. "Nungesser assures me we will have Spads very soon, any day. I would like you to go for the first one—"

He paused and again the contest between what he wanted to say and what he would permit himself to say seemed to reach a climax. Chamay sensed that if he spoke even a few words about appreciating the honor, Jourdan would make a full retreat behind the wall of his rank.

Finally Jourdan said, "I am aware of your special hatred for the Boche, Chamay. I hope you will manage to control it." As he stepped up on the wooden platform which served as a stoop to his quarters and looked down at Chamay, the perpetual weariness which hung like a clock from his shoulders seemed heavier than ever.

"I hope you have not misunderstood me," he said to the air above Chamay's snow-covered kepi. "I loved my brother very deeply. It is not easy to think he was awarded the Medaille Militaire—when he should have been court-martialed."

Chapter Five

April *1917*

IN SPITE of the first decent weather in weeks, Easter Sunday proved a dark day for the flying personnel of Jasta 76. The bombardment of the German line had been going on for three weeks, a prolonged and nerve-wracking proclamation of the forthcoming grand attack. Kupper was more than aware that their physical endurance had been pressed to the limit during the preceding days of flying in weather so cold that every patrol became an agony. There had been no choice but to take off again and again, and chase the poor enemy artillery spotter airplanes obliged to fly in the same weather. There had been surprisingly little fighter protection for the clumsy observation planes, so although the hunting had been uncomfortable, Jasta 76 had placed among the high-scoring units. Kupper had four additional victories confirmed for the week preceding Easter Sunday and one classed as a probable. His total stood at twenty-five and he had been assured by Geschwader Kommandeur Deitrich that a *Pour le mérite* would soon be dangling around his neck. Steilig had scored twice early in the week and then once more on his twentieth birthday, for an impressive total of thirteen. Hochstetter had knocked down a wandering English Camel, which must certainly have been lost to have been so far south, and the kill had brought his total to six. Keim had a Nieuport confirmed and one not yet official because it had crashed far behind the French lines. And Zimmerman had sent one Caudron splashing into an enormous shell crater near Paissy.

Since their initiation, neither Haube nor Sellerman had scored, although Kupper was quick to praise them for several "assists" given their comrades. Without such teamwork, he insisted, it was very likely that some of them might not have returned. Boelcke had been right: The only way to survive in the sky these days was to fight as a team. It was the German way, and one had only to spend a few days over the front to realize it was the right way. During four days in April the British had lost seventy-five airplanes!

"We fight hand in hand," Kupper had told his pilots as they gathered around the big brass samovar one freezing morning. "You must *never* leave formation and go off alone no matter how tempted. You have two eyes—one for the enemy and one for your comrades. Even if you are lined up for a sure and easy kill, if you chance to see a comrade in trouble, break off instantly. Go full throttle to your friend who needs you. If he fails to return, you won't be able to say to him, "I'm sorry—I was busy just before he sawed off your tail. Apologies, old fellow, but when I looked around again you had disappeared."

Kupper pounded home the policy in every way he could devise, sometimes in deadly earnest, other times in banter, and often as a stern command. He had killed enough men. Now his mounting desire was to save as many of his own as he possibly could. And the results of his campaign had been remarkable. The cost of all the recent victories had been nothing more than a spattering of holes in three of the Albatroses. The only damage to his men had been frostbite and a peculiar combination of tenseness and great weariness. Combat drained a man's morale and nerves, and his tolerance depended largely on his powers of recuperation. On a few occasions Kupper had had enough presence of mind to glance at his watch before and after engaging an enemy aircraft. He had been astonished to discover how an action which seemed to take twenty or thirty minutes had actually taken three or four. The longest melee in which he had ever been involved occurred when he had served with Boelcke's original Jasta 2. They had dropped down on a formation of English Nieuports over the Somme and there had been so many clouds at actual contact level that the fight became mostly a game of hide and seek. Even so, the whole affair was finished in approximately twenty minutes. Kupper had reached the conclusion that long chases around the sky were to be avoided if at all possible. The aftereffects were insidious and the behavior of your prey so unpredictable. Even if you had the advantage and were sitting on the enemy's tail waiting for a decent shot, you never knew what his terror might make him do. A rat race took all your concentration and the minutes consumed became increasingly precious. Kupper recited his laws until he hoped his pilots knew them by heart. Never forget that your enemy may be a scoundrel and all of his comrades may hate him, but they would rather see you die than him. They will come swooping down upon you if you are not quickly in and quickly out. Ten seconds, twenty seconds perhaps, thirty at the most—shoot, run, and live.

Kupper had at last concluded that it was not the effects of combat but the continual flying in bad weather which had caused the alarming physical decline in his pilots. They looked like ghosts and walked as if in an exhausted trance. It is always touchy when the enemy is flushed, but when a man must also worry about hitting trees and hills on his way to and from the fighting, a grinding fatigue begins to possess him. His alertness becomes ever more difficult to spark. He makes dangerous mistakes.

Kupper was convinced that young Haube would not have killed himself on a routine circling of the airport if his physical reactions had been normal. Easter Sunday had been clear, so Haube's sudden loss of his flying senses could not be attributed to vertigo or visual confusion brought on by a gray horizon spinning beneath gray clouds. Haube had been flying next to last in the formation. Kupper had seen him roll into a steep bank, which was not remarkable if the boy was feeling frisky on such a beautiful day. Yet then, instead of slipping down or flattening into a final glide, he seemed to hang in the air for a moment. Kupper distinctly remembered warning Haube about the Albatros' tendency to spin quickly and easily. But it would recover easily, too, if you simply did the right thing. Haube *might* have had barely enough altitude—*if* he had been quick enough.

Suddenly he was on his back and dropping straight down. Whatever he did, if he did anything, had been wrong. The Albatros hit the mud tail-first and crushed the weary young Haube almost beyond recognition.

Kupper thought that the effect of the crash on the Jasta had been out of all proportion to Haube's actual performance. By great good fortune he had achieved one victory. He had not flown more than twenty sorties altogether and there had been nothing extraordinary about his character except a rather charming smile. It was understandable for Sellerman, who had been his close companion, to be so inconsolable—the two had trained together at *Jastaschule* and had almost lived in each other's boots since their first flying lessons at Schleissheim. Yet even the implacable Pilger expressed his regrets. If Haube had been killed in a regular engagement the sense of loss would certainly have been of much shorter duration. Aviators were expected to die—out of sight. But Haube had chanced to kill himself directly in front of everyone and it was embarrassing.

Kupper had dutifully written Haube's mother in Breslau. Her son had to be a hero so pride might ease her desolation. His letter told in detail how bravely her son had fought against a host of the enemy and how when the battle was done her boy had managed to return to the aerodrome and there his wounds had overcome him.

It was the best Kupper could do. Why should Haube's mother know it had been a dry patrol and that not a shot had been fired? When he reread his stilted lies Kupper hoped his writing had not become illegible. His hand was trembling more than ever—a trembling that was becoming a shaking and which, for hours after Haube crashed, refused control. Now he was not only conscious of it when he shaved but often when he ate, and unless it could be stopped, then soon it would be shaking when he pressed his gun triggers.

Haube! Just another young German with a smile! Like the flaming Frenchman over Verdun, his hair on fire, his screams echoing down through the soul! "Oh, Haube!" Kupper groaned. "Your clumsy mistake has brought him back to haunt me!"

Just at dusk of Easter Sunday he gave the letter to Pilger for mailing and then went for a long walk in the nearby woods. The patches of snow on the ground muffled his steps and gave the twilight a soothing quality. Kupper hoped the physical exertion would permit him to forget both Haube and the Frenchman.

Once his commander had gone Pilger took out his knife and slit the envelope. He pulled thoughtfully at his lower lip as he read the letter. He grunted with particular approval at the part which recommended that Frau Haube might take some solace in the fact her son had joined with legions of other young men who had died in honor for the Fatherland.

When he had finished he smoothed the letter several times with his enormous palm, accompanying his gestures with small, barely audible, noises of satisfaction. Finally he resealed the letter with mucilage he had stolen from Baumgarten, the records clerk, and mailed it.

Leutnant Buchman's observation post was located in the charred ruins of a church tower overlooking the valley of the Aisne. On clear days Buchman claimed he could see Reims from his perch, but Soissons, which he thought might be more interesting, was concealed by a series of gently rolling hills.

Buchman scoffed at all suggestions he might live through his twenty-sixth year if he would wear a helmet while on the job. He hated helmets. They pinched his temples and gave him a headache and their weight gave him a backache. He reminded his critics that his tower was far enough away from the nearest French line to discourage sniping. Far more dangerous, Buchman insisted, was the possibility of the entire tower collapsing, or if he missed a step between the sagging boards which had formerly served as the bell platform, he would fall thirty meters to what was left of the stone altar. A helmet, Buchman said, not only made him top-heavy, it also made him feel like a turtle. So he exposed his taffy blond head to the remote chance of French snipers as the lesser of two evils. His courier, Stein, took the opposite view. He never exposed himself to the enemy and would not have climbed up to the belfry even if its precarious strength could have supported two men. And he always wore his helmet. Buchman thought him the kind of fearful nitwit who would protect himself in every way and inevitably kill himself on his motorcycle.

Buchman was fully aware of the importance attached to his job in *Flugmeldedienst*—flight-reporting service—which was why an officer had been assigned to it; yet even more than the military trust he liked the sense of functioning alone while encircled by millions of men who had no choice but to function together. Stein was not really a part of the job except to serve as messenger if the vital telephone lines to the *Flugmeldestation* should be damaged.

Buchman and a long line of fellow officers stretching from the North Sea to Switzerland had been trained as observers of military hardware and the movements of troops, so each in his sector might analyze developing situations and pass their intelligence to the rear. Sometimes in a matter of seconds they had to differentiate between enemy artillery and their own, and they were expected to detect enemy activity no matter how cleverly camouflaged. During Buchman's daytime tours of duty very little that happened within a radius of twenty kilometers escaped his keen eyes. He was particularly valued by those *Jagdgeschwader* now based at the new aerodromes within reach of this telephone. He not only served as a possible confirmation for their victories, but could also summon help when a patrol was obviously in trouble, or he could report when and approximately where a German plane might fall. His most routine job was the immediate announcement of invading enemy aircraft formations—type, course, approximate altitude and number. Such vital information enabled the Jastas to act quickly and often meet the enemy with the advantage of altitude or sun.

Buchman's spectacular head of hair was well and fondly known to members of Sebastian Kupper's Jasta 76. He had become sort of a landmark on the desolate shell-ravaged plateau and the pilots thought him wonderfully bold and doubtless quite crazy to occupy so forward and exposed a position alone.

As a consequence of his job Buchman was far better informed on the course of the war than the ordinary infantry officer. His business involved actual material and human beings moving about, rather than mere figures, symbols and lines on paper. Thus his sense of the war's true flow was better than that of many staff officers who depended on his reports.

Buchman normally arrived at the church just before dawn and once he had ascertained that the telephone lines were in order and the pattern of the enemy's day established, he would send Stein off on his motorcycle with orders to return in two hours with his sidecar filled. Stein might be an old lady who would wear his helmet in bed, yet Buchman appreciated his talents as an accomplished thief. He pillaged every mess within his one-hour cruising radius, and while the supply depots of the surrounding 19th Reserve Division offered very little worth stealing, the presence of three Jasta messes only twelve kilometers to the rear could not have been more providential. There was also a 77-mm. antiaircraft battery on the fringe of Vauclerc which must have been blessed by the God of War himself. While digging gun emplacements, they had chanced upon a buried treasure of wines which had been hastily cached during the late summer of '14. Now the soldiers from whom it had originally been hidden were doing their utmost to conceal it from other soldiers.

Fortunately the battery's complement was only forty men including the two officers, all of them grimly determined to enjoy their find and not give it away. A twenty-four-hour guard was posted at the limestone cave which held their prize and orders were to shoot and *then* apologize to any overly curious stranger if he wore a German uniform, and not to bother with the apology if he was a civilian. The two officers were mere Lieutenants who lived in daily terror of inspection by a superior from Staff, who might wonder at the aura of well-being which pervaded the entire personnel of the battery.

Stein passed the unit every day, often enough so that in time his thief's nose assured him that something was not as it should be. He discovered the secret when he gave a drunken batteryman a ride in his sidecar. After allowing a suitable time to pass lest his informant be shot, Stein approached the supply corporal and extracted a bounty of two bottles a day for keeping his mouth shut.

Thus did Stein and his officer make banquets of their midday meals.

Leutnant Buchman, like every other German soldier, had long known that the spring must bring an Allied offensive. Preparations had been in progress all along the front and in Buchman's general area between Craonne and Reims the plains were now studded with blockhouses. The whole of the German armies had drawn in like a muscle tensed for protection. They waited behind a line known as *Siegfried-Stellung*—later called the Hindenburg Line. Already, Hindenburg and Ludendorff had conferred at Kreuznach and concluded that their house was in order and able to withstand the inevitable storm. Since it was Ludendorff's birthday they drank an extra toast to the success of the new policy of inviting the British and French to blood themselves against their stoutly entrenched German armies. If all went as planned the enemy would never recover its lost strength.

No one needed to inform Buchman that preparations for the French offensive had begun. He was hoarse from yelling at the telephone during several days of almost continuous barrage. Miraculously the tower had been hit only once, and Buchman thought it might have been an accident, since no following shells burst in the immediate vicinity. Yet he now occupied his belfry with increasing misgivings as he sipped at an ice-chilled bottle of still champagne and munched on the last of his sausage. During the morning he had considered lowering his heavy tripod binoculars to the ground because a gale force wind caused the tower to tremble and sway until pieces of the plaster wall actually broke away from the wood and clattered down to the altar. One huge chunk struck Stein's helmet, knocking him flat and giving him the fright of his life. But now, as afternoon approached, there were signs of the wind's easing and there were even occasional patches of blue sky—the first Buchman had seen since Easter Sunday.

The atrocious weather had arrived four days previously and Buchman knew he would always remember the first morning with its squalls of snow and sleet and the motorcycle ride back to the tower in the gloomy dawn, which had proved as hazardous a journey as he ever cared to make. Buchman deliberately held to his belief that a man could become used to anything—and certainly he was as easy under shellfire as any man—but wild rides on a motorcycle in the slithering clay of Champagne with the likes of Stein at the helm were more than he cared to repeat. Yet he had been obliged to endure them for four days, clutching the sidecar with his frozen fingers as it careened across the neoarctic landscape. He was determined not to display the slightest unease in front of the one man he directly commanded, because it was obvious Stein had taken fiendish glee in this daily embarrassment of his officer. Buchman had observed him grinning almost continuously as mud and snow flew in all directions, his silly helmet bouncing down over his eyes until he must have been temporarily blinded, and his grubby hands always too busy to wipe at his nose drivel. It had been a minor contest, thought Buchman—the kind of thing that keeps all combat soldiers everywhere from falling down on their knees, beating their heads against the ground and bawling their hearts out. Or just turning tail and running home to mother. Stein had been trying to frighten his officer so that for once he could be on top looking down, and Buchman knew he was stuck with the tradition that a German line officer was a brave man.

It had taken only a day for news to travel down from Arras, where the British had already attacked. And it was not good news likely to be given out by the Wolff Büro, which published war communiques every Saturday and Sunday for release to the German public. The Bavarian regiments had given way and the 1st Guards

Regiment, which finally halted the advance, had had *every* officer killed.

More snow had fallen than Buchman had seen all winter and during the four-day tempest he had spent most of his daylight hours yelling into his telephone, not with vital information as he would have preferred, but with frustrating explanations to 19th Division staff and to his regular Flugmeldestation that as a consequence of snow squalls he could not see a goddamned thing.

There had been brief intervals during which Buchman had seen much more than he desired. He had tried to persuade himself that it had been a trick of the afternoon light that had revealed to his powerful binoculars more black faces than white among the assembling enemy troops. If Intelligence knew what they were talking about—and thanks to a freak incident they were remarkably well informed for a change—then the black faces he had seen would be Senegalese of the French 10th Colonial Division.

Over a week ago, Buchman knew, there had occurred a violent skirmish with some units of the French Fifth Army around Sapigneul. From his tower he had been able to watch the German artillery preparation for that minor attack and he had wondered how any creature in the shape of a man could remain alive. Yet apparently a great many Frenchmen *had* survived, because the attack became a "counterattack," which was Staff's bland-faced way of saying the original attack had been a failure. Still the fortunes of war were not all on the side of the French and one extremely valuable prize resulted from the confusion. The company commander of the French 3rd Zouaves had entrusted a sergeant with the plan of attack and ordered him to take it to the rear. Why this had been thought so necessary at a time when the unit was under heavy fire, no one could understand. The sergeant became lost, went the wrong way and was captured. His plan, which gave general indications of the forthcoming offensive by the whole French Fifth Army, had been carefully analyzed and there had been more than enough time to make suitable defense changes, particularly around Fort Brimont.

The French, thought Buchman, were going to walk into an iron-solid hell, and he could well understand the confidence prevailing among those junior staff officers with whom he played cards almost every night. Theirs was still a paper war and things looked good on paper, or could be made to look so even if they didn't.

Buchman was of another mind about his own slice of the front. The presence of so many blacks disturbed him. There was a rumor that the Senegalese were immune to gas, which Buchman knew was ridiculous, but the stories of their predilection for mutilation before killing, or for mutilation alone, just for the sheer joy of it, were supported by photos of unfortunate German soldiers which he had seen during his training. And, Buchman thought ruefully, he had heard quite enough jokes from fellow officers as to how he might sound as a soprano. He certainly would not tell Stein what he had seen, lest the scoundrel take off and leave him without emergency transport when most needed. As for himself, Buchman had resolved that when the very first French helmet appeared above the brow of hills forming a natural barrier two kilometers south of him, then, with or without permission from his *Luftschutzoffizier,* he was abandoning the tower.

Now Buchman studied the greasy-gray horizon and tried to imagine what it must be like in the sodden gullies and ravines where the French were trying to deploy troops in weather which must have been manufactured in Germany. He decided that if he were an Allied general he would demand battleships for transport of his troops across the sea of mud and snow which existed between his own lines. The entire front was said to be a quagmire all the way to the North Sea. It was madness to launch a major attack just because it was April and supposed to be spring. The French, of course, had let the silly English become mired in the mud first; and now they seemed determined to commit the same idiocy. It would be amusing, Buchman thought, if so many men were not going to die.

The sense of depression which the glowering weather had brought left him as soon as he saw the afternoon sun pouring down cold golden shafts of light between new gashes in the cloud. Within half an hour everything to be seen from his tower sparkled with a wet sheen which gave an illusion of life even to inanimate objects. He glanced down at Stein's helmet so far below him and watched it become a jellyfish floating in the depths. The barbed wire entanglements crosshatching the churned landscape in all directions took on the clear sharp lines of a fishnet. On the nearby horizon Buchman could see a part of a twisting curve made by the Aisne and he had often thought how fine a place it might be to fish in, if times were different. Now the narrow stripe of water caught the sun, and the shimmering vision filled Buchman with joy. The splinter of light was such a contrast to the bleak and monstrous scene below, a detail so sprightly and brilliant that he fancied it hurt his eyes. "God!" he said to the wind, "it is fine to be alive!"

He was still enchanted with the light on the river when just above it he saw four aircraft. Since they were bound toward him he immediately went to his binoculars. Four—no five. There had been so little enemy aerial activity during the past three days that it was almost a pleasure to reach for the telephone. After a moment he returned the telephone to its leather case. Those were German airplanes—triplanes. Only the German Air Force flew the stubby little Fokkers and there was no mistaking them. In his binoculars Buchman could see the three wings of each airplane set one above the other. They were coming home then from a raid. The poor pilots, he thought, must be like frozen herrings. With the most intense light behind them it was impossible to see their color, but if they were from a neighboring Jasta then Buchman was reasonably sure they would at least waggle their wings as they passed. "Welcome home," he murmured.

He stood back from his binoculars and saw the triplanes had changed course just enough to miss his tower by one or two kilometers. He was vaguely disappointed. He admired aviators, and in his mind's eye he saw himself as one of them. These fellows had certainly not been cringing in their hangars because of the rotten weather. If he ever met them he would praise their courage and chide them for snubbing his tower.

Buchman could hear their engines as they slid between the cloud base and the stark gray ridge to the west. With the snow beneath them, Buchman decided, they looked exactly like ducks bound south in late autumn.

The triplanes were closer now. He bent again to his binoculars hoping to catch the leader's identification markings if nothing more. Was it the light? Sometimes in shadow the color red could appear as black, particularly in the late afternoon, but—

They *were* black! Some new Jasta must be moving down from the north, but if so, why had they made a sweep so far into enemy territory? When a Jasta transferred from one aerodrome to another the pilots usually loaded their airplanes with as many personal effects as they could carry and sometimes even lashed odd gear on the wings. So they were rarely in the mood or condition for an encounter with the enemy.

There *was* something different. *Ja!* It *was!* On the fuselage of two airplanes Buchman had seen the unmistakable English roundel! Instinctively his hand had again gone to the telephone and then hesitated. How clever someone was being—so clever that an experienced observer had been almost deceived! Here, where the French predominated, English airplanes were rare birds, yet Buchman knew them well from the dumpy, BE-2's to the saucy little Sopwith Pups. In his spare moments he had even troubled to memorize their performance figures. No! This rather obvious deception had really not been so clever! If they needed a disguise, then why choose the *only* German airplane so distinct in design that no Allied airplane could possibly be confused with it?

Buchman thought it strange that Flugmeldedienst had not warned him of a surprise. If they had been as careless in informing the flak batteries, then these returning heroes might be in for a hot reception.

The triplanes were just disappearing over the end of the ridge when Buchman turned his back on them and reached for the telephone. He spoke to the same Luftschutzoffizier who had always been his liaison, and after remarking on his lack of honesty at cards the previous night, he said it was not surprising such an unscrupulous fellow would fail to tell the truth about a certain patrol. Card cheats would inevitably receive their just deserts Buchman added with a smile, as would those other geniuses at staff who thought he didn't know a triplane from any other type.

There was such a long silence at the other end of the line that Buchman wondered if the connection had been broken. Finally his friend's voice was on the phone again. There had been no special patrol. A quick check with intelligence had revealed no German Jasta on the Western Front known to have chosen black as their unit color.

Chapter Six

April 13, 1917
With intruders from the north—

FOUR DAYS AFTER EASTER a large battered package arrived for Leutnant Kupper. He had been walking with his Alsatian before the final patrol of the day and the motorcyclist who delivered the package found him only a few paces from the officers' mess. He saluted and was gone before Kupper thought to ask his unit. He saw a letter pasted on the package addressed in Maria's unmistakable rolling hand. He tore off the letter at once and standing heedless of the falling snow quickly glanced at the pages in what he called a "first reading." Later in the privacy of his hut he would read the letter again and again, trying to envision what lay behind each word and sentence so that he might better sense her mood and all that went on about her. Brushing the wet snowflakes away from the paper, he hoped this time she would be less concerned with Pilger.

. . . Major Kurt Degelow, a friend of my brother's and a true dear, is returning to his regiment today. When he came to call at the house last night I asked him if he could deliver a package for me even if I had no idea exactly where you were. He agreed *before* he saw the size of the package! He said that as long as I could give him your Jasta number he doubtless could find you sooner or later. I hope it's not too much later, because what is in the package is a ham from Kempinsky's! It is your Easter present —and may God help Major Degelow to find you!

Kupper frowned at the snow which threatened to blot the letter, then decided to finish it later. He sniffed at it, closed his eyes and smiled. Then he refolded it reverently and placed it inside the flap of his tunic. God bless Major Degelow indeed! And he was a dear! Furthermore, he must certainly be a combat officer, since he had kept his word and not eaten the ham himself. It would have been so very easy to say he had never been able to find Oberleutnant Sebastian Kupper, or that some accident had befallen the package on the way. The major would certainly receive his heartfelt thanks through Maria.

Kupper hefted the package and for a moment was tempted himself. Such a ham, which must have cost Maria a fortune, would last weeks in this weather if kept in his own quarters. He glanced up at the English Lewis gun which the trophy-minded Steilig had taken from one of his conquests and remembered the day he had hung it above the door of the mess. It was a prize of a very rough engagement with the famous British 56th Squadron. There was not a man in the fight that afternoon who at one moment or another had not thought he had only seconds to live. "This is for all," Steilig had said when he placed the gun over the door, "and for those who will come after us."

At once the idea of keeping the ham to himself sickened Kupper. God in heaven! What is happening to me? There is a place for hyenas and it is not at the front!

He kicked open the door, held the package at arm's length before him and shouted at the top of his lungs, "Hola! You poor spoiled clowns! Prepare your miserable bellies for a feast!"

They left their magazines and cards and letter-writing to gather around him. Steilig came first, his perpetual look of wariness suddenly ceased, Sellerman smiled for the first time since Haube's death, Hochstetter advanced, his eyes more mischievous than ever, and Keim viewed the package as if it contained a land mine. Zimmerman approached it as lightly as a dancer finding his partner, and all the others found some way to express their curiosity.

"A ham from Kempinsky's!" Kupper shouted. He saw at once how they pretended to disbelieve so their anticipation could be prolonged. They said it must be some sort of a trick—for who in these times could manage such a delicacy even in Berlin, let alone at the front? A few officers forced themselves to look away. It was childish to become so excited even if the parcel really did contain a ham.

Kupper tore at the package and a mess orderly came running with a knife. In a moment Kupper held the ham before him. They stood about in a semicircle and regarded it as if it were a jewel of equal size.

"Dear God," Hochstetter breathed in awe.

"It is a mirage," said Keim.

"It couldn't have been sent here by mistake instead of to the Kaiser's mess?" Zimmerman asked. They all laughed, for everyone knew the Kaiser had no appetite and the officers obliged to eat with him were always complaining of starvation.

"Who is it from?" Steilig asked, wetting his lips.

"My fiancée, Maria."

"May God bless her forever!"

They escorted the ham to the mess table, moving chairs lest Kupper collide with them and drop his precious cargo. When it had been set in place Hochstetter slipped his hands inside the cuffs of his tunic and bowed solemnly three times. "Kempinsky's!" he intoned, "in my former life I practically lived there, and in my next life I plan to do the same."

"Do you mind?" Steilig asked as he bent to sniff at the ham. After a moment he straightened, clicked his heels smartly and saluted. "It is sublime!" he said.

Even Sellerman's brooding eyes became alive again. As the others debated when and how the ham should be consumed so that it would be rendered full justice, Sellerman jumped on a chair and begged for attention. "We have more champagne than we can drink!" he cried, "enough to bathe in if we wish—but our beloved commander is willing to share the only Kempinsky smoked ham on the Western Front! Let us send to a jeweler and have him create a special medal for pilots of Jasta 76. The order of Kempinsky's to be awarded after contributing five victories to the Jasta record!"

"The first will be awarded our noble commander!" Zimmerman yelled.

"With diamonds rampant on crossed pig's feet!"

"No!—start a campaign to promote him to captain!"

"No! *Major!*"

"An insult! He should be at least colonel-general!"

There was much laughter, and Kupper was overjoyed to see at last that the spell of gloom was broken. I may have them back again full of spirit, he thought, and if Maria can help me accomplish that with her ham then it is even more priceless than she ever supposed. He decided to commence now while the mood of his little band was so ready.

Kupper glanced at the telephone standing in its leather case on the small organ which the now long-dead Von Esser had rescued from a burning French church. The telephone had not made a sound all day. Von Esser, the only true nobleman to serve with Jasta 76, had been a gay soul and certainly would have said, "Now, while you *can!*"

The others stood looking at Kupper so hopefully he was reminded of little boys before the window of a candy store. They were still in their flying boots and their faces were filthy with the grease they smeared on against the cold. They are so thin, Kupper thought. Except for Keim they seemed dangerously frail. Standing so in the fading light, they appeared like a band of ragamuffins, for they were as usual wearing every manner of clothing to keep warm and only their breeches and leather puttees struck the military note. My miserable-looking children, Kupper thought, how red your noses are, how tangled your hair, how eager your eyes!

He glanced at the telephone again and beyond it to the window. He saw that the sun had broken through the cloud deck and had shot a bar of cold bronze straight across the aerodrome. But it was a pale sun, certainly the last few minutes of it this day, and when the clouds again slipped over it darkness must quickly follow.

Kupper set his mouth in a grim line and while the others watched hopefully he sauntered over to the frog which almost every Jasta kept in a glass jar. There was a small ladder in the jar and if the *Laubfrosch* climbed it the weather would be good. If the frog remained on the bottom the weather would be bad. Jasta 76's frog had been christened Madame Bizot because of a remarkable resemblance to the village mayor's wife.

"I am consulting Madame Bizot," Kupper said, looking down into the jar. "She is sitting flat on her bottom. Obviously there will be no fit flying weather the rest of the afternoon." He nodded at the telephone, "And this instrument has not rung all day. Obviously the wire must be broken somewhere between here and Flugmeldedienst. It certainly cannot be repaired until tomorrow."

He strolled to the window and pretended to study the clouds packed against the ridge. The sun conveniently faded and he shook his head forlornly. "Under the circumstances, gentlemen, I am afraid we shall have to cancel our evening patrol."

Deliberately keeping his face to the window, Kupper heard a murmur of approval behind him. The sound helped to convince him that he was doing the right thing. What would the evening patrol bring in weather like this except benumbed spirits and possible frostbite and a further tensing of their nerves? This rare chance to relax must not be lost. The Geschwader Kommandeur would of course want to know why the patrol had been canceled, since in fact the weather was flyable. I will decree it nonflyable, Kupper thought, and be damned to the consequences.

He turned to the others and smiled. "Pilger!" he called to the doorway which led back to the kitchen. There was a heavy thumping of boots and Pilger appeared so quickly Kupper knew he had overheard everything. He must have been standing just behind the door. His head was slightly bent as if resting on his jowls, and having assumed a posture which merely suggested attention he allowed his great hands to hang loosely at his sides. Kupper also thought he saw accusation in those pale eyes, then put it down to his own guilty imagination. But there are times, he thought, when Pilger goes much too far.

"Fetch buckets of snow—chill twenty bottles of champagne immediately. Tell cook we want vegetables to go with this ham and the best of his cheese. We want a clean tablecloth tonight, and napkins, and three bottles of brandy. All of this in thirty minutes."

Pilger showed no sign of having heard his instructions. He simply turned on his heel and disappeared into the gloom of the narrow passageway. In an instant the thump of his boots was gone.

"Now, gentlemen." Kupper smiled at them. "May I suggest we retire to our quarters for a wash and return here promptly for a celebration." Kupper raised his eyes to the Kaiser's portrait, which was surrounded by a wreath of artificial leaves. What a pity we cannot have a more inspiring symbol, he thought. Then to the others he said, "In full uniform, if you please."

Laughing, they made a rush for the door. Kupper followed and watched them trot past the mechanics and armorers who were standing in the snow waiting half-frozen for the evening patrol. They too would be more than delighted to hear it was canceled.

From the officers' mess to the line of Albatroses it was some one

114

hundred meters and from there across the hedgerow to the line of officers' huts another hundred meters. Kupper was pleased to see them making a race of it. It was good for their lungs. He could hear their panting laughter and they were strung out across the snow like children let out of school, their arms flaying the wind, their flight jackets flapping and scarves streaming. Louie the Alsatian was beside himself with excitement. He barked continuously, chased a little way after the runners and then hurried back to his master for approval. Kupper was surprised to see even the dour Keim caught up in the fun. There he was, actually jogging along like a fat puppet.

Feldwebel Groos left the line of Albatroses and came to Kupper, his eyes questioning. What was this? Had the crazy pilots gone crazier? As always when addressing a superior, Groos stood at rigid attention. He is the most mechanical of all my tin soldiers, Kupper thought. When the war is over and he is returned to his box will someone take him out and wind him up again?

Kupper smiled and was on the point of telling Groos he could dismiss his men for the day when he saw a look of astonishment cross his face. Almost simultaneously he heard the rattle of machine-gun fire and the snarl of engines.

He saw Groos reach out for his neck. The next instant Kupper had been thrown to the hard ground, his chin pushed in the snow with Groos sprawled across him. He heard a sharp pounding sound and watched a line of eruptions kick up the snowy earth a few yards beyond his face. He squirmed around just in time to see five black triplanes pulling out of a dive and zooming for the purple sky.

"*Die Engländer sind gekommen!*" Groos shouted.

Kupper pushed him away. He had seen the rondels clearly enough. The English had come! In *triplanes?*

The black triplanes had started a circle of the aerodrome in preparation for another pass. Kupper looked toward the stubble field and saw the men who had been rollicking only a few moments before rising cautiously from the snow. Except for one. It was Keim. He lay on his back. One leg was bent and moving slightly.

As the others started for him Kupper called out, and his voice was harsher than he ever believed it could be: "Hurry! Let him be! Hurry!" He waved them toward the line of Albatroses and broke into a run for his own.

The mechanics and armorers were still within a few feet of their

115

posts and had taken what shelter they could beneath the Albatroses' engines. At Kupper's shouted commands and Feldwebel Groos's furious urging, they quickly returned to their senses and stood ready to spin the propellers.

Kupper was the first to reach his Albatros. The propeller was being spun even before he was fully down in the cockpit. As he yanked his seat belt tight and felt the Mercedes shudder with power he was grateful for two things. The engines were hot and easy to start because the mechanics had all in readiness for the usual evening patrol. And the place chosen for parking the Albatroses had proven its worth in a way he had never really foreseen. The area was a small depression between three wooded hummocks which formed a pocket. The bitter weather had forced Kupper to find a place where his mechanics and armorers could work efficiently. Here, because the pocket was fringed with tall elms, they were protected from all but eastern winds. It offered a dividend in concealment and position.

The low-flying English must not have been the Albatroses until it was too late. They had shot up the five empty storage hangars and the next best target had been a splotch of men running across the open field. Now the English must come in from the east or climb and make a steep dive if they would bring their guns to bear on the pocket.

On the opposite side of the field Kupper saw that the triplanes had chosen to climb and dive in for the kill. He understood. The sun had flashed out again, just touching the treetops orange. If the English came in low from the east that blessed sun would be directly in their eyes. Their climb would give the Jasta precious seconds.

Kupper glanced down the line and saw Steilig already in his Albatros. His propeller was spinning. Kupper thought he looked rather strange sitting in the cockpit without goggles, flying jacket or helmet. We will all freeze, he thought.

Beyond him Hochstetter was also ready and most of the others nearly so. Zimmerman was just climbing into his cockpit, and young Sellerman was still running for his Albatros, which was the last in line.

As Kupper raised his fist and the chocks were yanked from in front of his wheels, he was vaguely conscious of Louie's wild barking. Then he shoved full throttle to the Mercedes.

116

He emerged from the wood pocket tail-up and dragging a veil of snow. He bounced the Albatros in the air just before he might have struck Keim's prone body. Glancing down he saw a splotch of red on the snow beside Keim, but he was also sure he saw him wave.

Kupper banked steeply to the right. The English could do no harm where they were. He would be waiting for them when they came down. *Triplanes?* They looked like Fokkers and yet they were not.

He flicked his head around long enough to assess his own strength. The wonderful Steilig was climbing to join him. There were three other Albatroses in between and climbing off to the north—probably Hinkmann, Just, and Schröder.

Zimmerman was just passing over a clump of men formed around Keim's body. Sellerman—? Trapped in the pocket if he didn't get out in thirty seconds.

These impudent English had flushed their quarry. Now with surprise and altitude to their credit they were certain to destroy any airplane left on the ground. Kupper counted four still in the pocket as he saw the triplanes peeling off into a dive. If they had done the same thing on their first pass there would not have been an Albatros left to Jasta 76.

Sellerman! Hurry!

There was no way to stop the triplanes in a dive. Kupper saw pilots and men running away from the doomed Albatroses. Only one airplane was creeping away from the pocket.

Sellerman! *Gott Verbot!* Jump out and run or fly! You have five more seconds!

He was starting to move at last! He was rolling fast now and off the snow! Kupper held his breath. He choked on his own spittle as he yelled at the violent evening sky. "Spare Sellerman! He is only a child! *Bitteschön!*"

But no sound came from his lips.

He wiped at the water flooding his eyes from the wind, and saw what he knew would happen. The first triplane swooped down toward the mauve earth like an avenging hawk. He was almost straight above Sellerman, who had yet to climb above fifty meters. A quick rattle of the Englishman's guns and Sellerman's Albatros appeared to quiver in agony. It fell away drunkenly on one wing and exploded against the snow. Black bits flew in all directions and the largest remaining part skidded tail-first across the middle of the aerodrome. When it stopped, Kupper closed his eyes for only a second. When he opened them again the pieces of Sellerman's Albatros had burst into flames.

But the English had blundered. They had *all* come down to work over the aerodrome. Having driven away the Albatroses they seemed to think they would stay away while they shot up the tents, which were of no consequence, and the line of officers' shacks, which were of even less, and the Jasta mess.

The spectacle of the English shooting at mere structures gave Kupper hope. They were wasting priceless minutes. He continued his climb toward the west.

There was a low deck of cloud at one thousand meters. It was broken and torn with the freezing evening wind. Kupper saw how the indigo, green and violet vapor forms illuminated by the last of the sun, matched the lozenge camouflage design on the Albatros wings in a marvelous way.

Once he achieved the base of the clouds he eased back on his power until the others could close in.

He signaled for a line abreast and with himself as pivot called for a right turn back to the east. He could see their anxious faces, Steilig, Hochstetter, and Zimmerman. All bare-headed, bare-handed, yet still too charged by fear and anger to feel the cold. It could not last. They had been caught pitifully unprepared and any chase after the English was out of the question. They must do what they could in a few minutes—before they froze rigid in their cockpits.

Now the aerodrome was in shadow. Only the surrounding hilltops were sharply outlined and all the garish colors became softer in the lavender of evening. The black English triplanes became suddenly more difficult to follow.

Now, Kupper decided. We must dive on them immediately while we still have wits and trigger fingers. Or we must run away. He raised his right hand to blow on his fingers and discovered his whole arm was trembling.

There were only three triplanes visible. Where were the other two? In these few minutes little had changed. Keim's body was a minute black fragment still in the same place. The blaze about Sellerman's crumpled Albatros had subsided and a trail of heavy black smoke blew almost horizontally away from it. No life on the ground. Where were the other two Englishmen?

There. Low over the forest, their black wings melting into the stark trees. The English must have missed their original target and stumbled on Jasta 76. They were not coordinated. It was difficult to believe the English would risk five new type airplanes on such a deep strike.

They were joining up, swarming directly over the aerodrome. They were taking their time. Looking for us, Kupper thought.

Quickly! He pulled up and entered the cloud. He saw the others follow. They could hold this concealment for a minute before vertigo set in. He was not as yet satisfied with their position. Stretch it a minute more. He wanted an almost straight-down line of descent on the English. If he tried a long-angled power dive out of the sun then their speed would build so much the Albatroses might start shedding wings. And without speed they would never jump the English unless they could approach unseen. So he thought to cut his throttle and drop straight down on them, guns going. It was a rare opportunity with the cloud at just the right level and the position of the enemy fixed.

In spite of the slip stream's roar and the steady noise of the Mercedes, Kupper had the weird sensation he was flying on tiptoe. For the moment it lasted he was able to forget the cold.

He glanced at the others. Steilig was only a few meters away and plain enough in spite of the cloud. Hochstetter just beyond him was merely a fuzzy shadow in an airplane. Zimmerman the farthest away was only a blob of color. Beyond them, invisible in the murk, would be Hinkmann, Just, and Schröder. Each would be flying on the wing tip of the other, and as they had practiced so many times, Kupper's signals and maneuvers would be repeated down the line.

Like a diver about to attempt a hazardous plunge, Kupper took a deep breath. Dear God, it's cold! Yet inside of him a fire flamed so intensely that only his skin suffered. He had known this terrible heat many times and knew he would never become accustomed to it. It sent blood pounding at his temples and drove it racing and throbbing through his limbs until they became wonderfully taut and quick as powerful springs. The fire cleared his eyes and gave to his most simple movements a resolution and certainty he had never quite believed. Here was death, there was life.

He was about to fight for his life.

He raised his hand, made a fist, and saw Steilig repeat the gesture. Then he cut back his throttle until the Mercedes began to backfire. He shoved forward on his control stick and seconds later emerged from the cloud in a near vertical dive.

Steilig? Yes. Behind and to his left. Hochstetter? Yes. Zimmerman? Yes. He wanted his veterans close at hand.

As the thrumming of the Albatros' flying wires changed to a wild screech, a series of sharp visions rushed upward toward Kupper. There was Keim's tiny form still sprawled in its place. There was Sellerman's funeral pyre. There were the English triplanes circling for altitude.

Kupper kicked hard right rudder, eased back on his stick and brought the nose of his Albatros around until it was locked on the lead triplane. When its wingspan filled the ring sight between his Spandaus he would fire.

In seconds Kupper knew he was certain to make a kill. He saw colored streamers flowing back from the triplane's wing tips. The flight leader. He saw the red, white and blue rondels rising toward him. He saw a helmeted, bundled figure in the cockpit. A face looking up.

Even as his fingers were ready to close the triggers Kupper knew he had made a mistake. Like the German Fokker triplane this English variety was apparently capable of standing on its tail long enough for a good burst of fire. And this Englishman had not been asleep. His guns were flashing. His white tracers were smoking straight at Kupper's face.

A series of holes appeared diagonally outward from the Albatros' right wing root. And the same on the left! The Englishman had sufficient control and the nerve to kick rudder while he was firing! In a near vertical climb!

Kupper broke away to the left. He had not fired a shot.

He hauled back on the stick and jammed full power to the Mercedes. He rolled into a vertical bank, hoping to swing around to the triplane's tail. He tightened the turn until his cheeks sagged. But where was the triplane? The sky was suddenly full of black triplanes and multicolored Albatroses. Where was the Englishman with the streamers?

Suddenly suspicious, Kupper glanced behind him and knew. There!

120

Directly in line with his own rudder sitting right on his tail. Too far away to shoot—yet.

This was no ordinary Englishman. It had been a long time since anyone had been on Sebastian Kupper's tail. When the Englishman had forced him to break away from the dive he must have anticipated his recovery and thrown his triplane around instantly.

Now he was sitting back there—waiting.

Kupper thought to tighten his circle even more, then changed his mind. A triplane could always fly inside a biplane. If the pilot was skillful he could normally outmaneuver anything in the sky. And this Englishman was no beginner.

I am playing his game, which is all wrong, Kupper thought. All triplanes are slow. I'll make a straight run for it. The sun is gone. Use the forest, put myself against the dark trees, make a poor target so he won't risk a long-range burst. I am in trouble. Serious trouble. Quick! Now!

Kupper suddenly rolled out of the circle and dove straight for the forest. Instinctively he brought his shoulders together trying to make himself as small as possible. "God help me," he whispered. "God keep the wings on my ship and make me small!"

If the burst didn't come within the next few seconds he knew he would be safe. He waited forever. He was skimming the treetops before he forced himself to look back.

The bronze sky was clear. There was no triplane on his tail.

Kupper wiped at his eyes and, still at full power, began a wide turn. Caution! He searched the sky. Nothing? Yes, there to the south of the aerodrome were two Albatroses. Where were the others? And the English? Convinced he was alone, he began a climbing turn for altitude. He sighed mightily.

There were the English—low on the horizon—black specks already. All five of them westbound for home! The men in the triplanes were not clumsy amateurs like so many of the English pilots. Kupper could think of only one reason why they might retreat. They were strangers to the area. They must have flown a long away, perhaps from as far as the Arras sector. Night was coming on fast and they must be short of fuel.

As Kupper started his descent for the aerodrome the cold seized him and caused him to shudder so he could hardly manage the controls.

In his final glide he saw one Albatros had landed in the southeast corner of the aerodrome. It bore Schröder's chessboard device behind the cockpit. Kupper wondered if he still believed aerial combat was like a game of chess, since his position on the aerodrome so far from the mechanics was a certain indication his landing had been forced. He was still seated in his cockpit and several men were running the length of the aerodrome toward him.

Kupper saw two more Albatroses approaching from the south. They were low down and barely visible in the dusk so he found it impossible to be sure Steilig's flaming sword decorated the fuselage of the lead airplane. The second Albatros did not appear to have any decoration. It must be Hinkmann.

Hochstetter was just turning into his final glide. There was his monkey plainly outlined.

As he dropped over the fringe of trees on his own approach, Kupper saw several men gathered about Keim's body. Flashing past just above them, he thought he recognized Pilger hovering over those kneeling in the snow. Then his wheels brushed the earth and he passed through a ribbon of smoke from Sellerman's wreckage.

Taxiing slowly toward the wood pocket, he glanced at his watch. He remembered that his decision to cancel the evening patrol had been made about 1830 hours. It was now 1845.

It had been a disastrous fifteen minutes for Jasta 76. English time was an hour earlier than German. The victors would be home for tea.

As his mechanic and armorer came running to catch his wing tips, Kupper realized that his feet and hands had gone numb. He waited until he was sure he could control his shuddering before he laboriously lifted himself from the cockpit.

The losses on the ground were obviously serious and his own display over the aerodrome had been anything but inspiring. His men had certainly been watching. Somehow he must regain their respect. Somehow. The pilots would know they had done their best, but how to convince the ground personnel? By chance they had witnessed their first aerial combat at close range. How could they understand that a mere five English machines could rub the Jasta's nose in the dirt? They had seen their champions gored and would need reassurance. Very well. Officer behavior was designed for just such calamities. Some military wizard had long ago discovered that

German soldiers were quick to sense defeat and these must not be allowed to believe it was fear that made him tremble so.

Pilger held the short wooden ladder while he descended from the cockpit. When his feet reached the ground he paused and leaned against the ladder. God he was tired! But here was Pilger, huge as ever, staring at him. He dared not slump as he longed to do.

"Keim?"

"He will be all right after some mending."

"Sellerman?" Why did he bother to ask. There was something else in Pilger's eyes, a furtiveness he had never seen before.

"What else? What are you going to tell me?"

Suddenly Kupper knew. He had been so benumbed with cold it only now came to him that some familiar element was lacking in his return.

"Where is Louie?"

Pilger squinted. A strange metallic tone came to his voice when he said, "Louie is dead. He was afraid and found the wrong place to hide—in number three hangar tent."

Kupper shook his head and all the stiff control he had so carefully guarded left him. He did not give a damn what Pilger thought. Or anyone else in the Jasta. His beloved Louie was gone and he wanted to weep.

The sudden softness in Pilger's voice surprised him. He said, "He was my friend too."

Then they came to him, ground officers and men, with reports on the wounds which were deep and many in the body of Jasta 76.

Corporal Mannerich slightly wounded, Private Jung seriously. Two slugs through the chest. Both men had taken shelter underneath the five Albatroses which had never left the ground.

One tent hangar had been destroyed and bullets had penetrated over a hundred barrels of fuel which should have exploded but did not.

The Jasta mess had been punctured a hundred-odd times along one wall and the stove had been holed eight times. Fortunately there had not been a man in either structure.

These were little things which were told to Kupper first, as if it would be indiscreet to relate the more serious damage until the inconsequentials were out of the way.

Leutnant Keim would be all right. He had been hit by two slugs which had broken his hip and caused a great loss of blood. He had been given a shot of morphine and a tourniquet was now holding back the blood.

Schröder's Albatros had been badly shot up and he had been hit in the thigh and the arm. His arm was broken. An ambulance was on the way for both men.

Sellerman was dead, of course—from the looks of the wreckage he had gone instantly. What was left of him was unpleasant if the Herr Kommandant would care to look.

Zimmerman had just telephoned from a supply depot near Sissonne. One of the triplanes had put ten bullets through his engine crankcase. His immediate landing had been in the only clear space available, a stone quarry. The Albatros was badly damaged but Zimmerman was unhurt. A supply officer was bringing him back to Jasta 76.

As he listened to one report after another Kupper became aware that Pilger had been carefully watching him. Louie, he thought. Pilger knows I cannot concentrate now. Pilger! Stop pressing me!

Yet now, as if he must add his quota of gloom to the moment, Pilger directed Kupper's attention to the fuselage of his own Albatros. It seemed to give him sensual pleasure to stick his great forefinger in a line of holes which passed directly through the painted target device. One hole cut the bull's-eye. Kupper instinctively hunched his shoulders.

"Date them," he said to his mechanic.

Steilig came to him, his face and eyes red with the cold wind and his mouth set in an angry line. "I could not take my man, Sebastian. I could not get to him. He was always inside of me." Kupper saw that he was breathing heavily as if he had wrestled the English triplane with his arms. His voice was hoarse and ashamed. The cold dauntless Steilig with eleven victories was shaken at last.

Hochstetter came and tried to smile. "I can wait awhile for the next surprise party."

Hinkmann came and said someone in Flugmeldedienst should be shot.

The four officers stood in stunned silence until Steilig offered his open cigarette case. The others accepted. Pilger stepped close to them immediately holding a lighted match. He saw their trembling hands and lips and concealed them from the soldiers by deliberate use of his great shoulders. When they quieted he stepped away.

They drew deeply on their cigarettes, their eyes meeting again and again, questioning, and then focusing on the ground in silent thought. They realized they must force themselves to join Kessler, Mueller, Meyer and Just who had never been able to leave the ground and were now down by the smoking wreckage with what was left of Sellerman. They could not walk away in the opposite direction and simply leave him there for a cleanup detail. He had died within a hundred meters of Haube's grave, in sight of the officers' mess.

Kupper dreaded what they might see, but he said gently, "Let's go down there."

When they had reached the wreckage Kupper became aware Pilger had followed them. He was annoyed. This was an affair for flying officers only and it struck him there was something ghoulish about the way Pilger was staring at the smoke. He seemed to be deliberately inhaling the stench.

Just, Meyer, Kessler and Mueller were waiting near what was left of the Albatros' tail. They raised their eyes to Kupper but no one spoke.

Kupper tried to pretend Sellerman was not in the black and smoking pile of junk before him. He wanted to run away. Perhaps the infantry could take war served raw, he thought. They had no choice. But airmen were usually spared the ultimate details. Steilig and Hochstetter, in spite of their numerous kills, had never seen a man die except at a great distance.

A slight change in the wind blew the smoke directly at them. As they moved in a body to escape it Kupper wondered if he dared chance a vision which might never be erased from any of their minds?

Yet they were being watched. All the men in the Jasta—the armorers, mechanics, the cooks, Feldwebel Groos and his corporals—were standing silently in the dusk waiting to see what these defeated and exhausted officers would do about their fallen comrade.

Only Pilger has the gall to be with us, Kupper thought. Or is he our self-appointed shepherd?

Kupper tried to swallow. He found his throat too dry. He braced his shoulders and, keeping his eyes on the snow, walked around to the side of the wreckage. He sensed the others were following, yet he dared not glance behind him. He stopped and turned reluctantly toward the wreckage. He had no idea what was proper now. He supposed they should salute, but every pilot's fear of the vision at close range of what could so easily happen to him was upon them all. And he could not salute the snow at his feet.

It drained nearly all his physical strength to raise his eyes. There it was. Leutnant Basil Sellerman, age twenty, formerly student of law at Tübingen. Killed in action at approximately 1830 hours, April 13, 1917.

There it was. So pitifully small. A charred doll, complete except for one leg which had been jerked off, leaving a red-raw stump which was cooking slowly. The thing was Pilot-Officer Sellerman after completing approximately sixty hours flying time, of which less than half had been combat. A poor investment for His Imperial Majesty's government. There had been the cost of his training, his salary of fifteen hundred marks a year including benefits, and the total destruction of his expensive airplane. No—more likely the accounts were just about even. The thing had scored one victory on his first patrol and presumably it had cost the English government a like amount to share the contest.

Suddenly Kupper dropped to one knee and bowed his head. This thing deserved a prayer for itself. The salute could come later and would be for the exclusive benefit and encouragement of the many spectators gathered without invitation at young Basil Sellerman's last rites. This would not be like the customary funeral—arranged at leisure when the pilot had fallen on the enemy side. There was no band to play "Jesus My Refuge," and certainly no one felt like a chorus of "Song of the Good Comrade."

When the others had kneeled Kupper began the Lord's Prayer in a monotone. He continued even through Hochstetter's siege of retching.

When he had finished he silently asked the thing's forgiveness for repeating the only prayer he knew. Then he stood up and looked directly at the nightmare that he knew would join the flaming Frenchman. Now the show, for the men.

He saluted the thing and walked away.

In a moment Kupper sensed he was being closely followed. He

turned to make certain although he knew instinctively it must be Pilger.

"Do you want to see Louie? He's still in the tent."

"No. I want to remember him the way he was." He also wanted to tell Pilger to go away! To leave him *alone!* To take his hulking body out of his sight forever! He did not want to see anything ever again which might even vaguely suggest war.

When he was certain he would keep his voice reasonably even, he said to Pilger, "Take care of him. See that he is buried—as a friend."

Pilger veered off toward the number three hangar tent and Kupper was certain he heard him grumbling his dissatisfaction. What does he want me to do? Give my dog a full military funeral to mock my dead Sellerman?

When he neared the flight line he beckoned to Feldwebel Groos.

At first he thought it appropriate to choose a place near the wind sock, where pilots of Jasta 76 would be reminded of one Leutnant Sellerman every time they circled the aerodrome. Perhaps long after I am gone? No! It was a morbid idea and would certainly do nothing to boost morale.

"Put him down at the far west corner of the aerodrome. Beside Haube. See to it there are flowers. Do it at once."

He must force Sellerman into his grave. There was no time for any further sentiment. There were reports to make out covering the total loss of two aircraft and extensive damage to five. Requisitions must be sent for replacements, which hopefully might be the latest model Albatros D-V. There was considerable work to be assigned on the damaged aircraft—Eiserbeck, the technical officer, had already esimated it would be a week before Jasta 76 could become fully operational.

Two new pilots must also be demanded from Fourth Army Flugpark, and this time Kupper was going to insist that they be more experienced than either Haube or Sellerman. He would tell them that eagerness was not a shield against bullets and he was tired of burying children who should be flying kites instead of lethal weapons.

They must have another truck convoy of fuel sent in if the Jasta was going to have any safe reserve. Fortunately the English had missed a considerable bank of drums which had been covered with

127

camouflage netting. Kupper was not certain, but he thought there might be enough fuel left for a week's normal operations. When the enemy really started their offensive, then they might use a week's supply in two days.

At least one task would give him sour satisfaction. When Staff jumped on him for being caught by surprise, as they certainly would, he would challenge them with some pointed questions as to how it was that no less than *five* English airplanes, operating out of a field that was God only knew how far distant, could have crossed the lines unobserved and attacked an aerodrome more than twenty kilometers behind the lines.

"Groos? Did we receive any warning call after we were in the air?"

"No, Herr Leutnant. I spoke to Corporal Maletsky at message center. There had been no signal of any kind. Usually they call us if a fly jumps off a Frenchman's butt."

Was it possible, Kupper wondered, that Flugmeldedienst did not *know* of the penetration, or even of the attack? He would put his call through before he did anything else. Perhaps this whole defeat might cost him his rank. Certainly it would not speed his promotion to captain. He no longer cared. As commander he was willing to accept all just blame but he would not withhold his low opinion of Staff's intelligence unit. Let them think of reprisals. They could not send him to any more dangerous duty than he already enjoyed. He would also broaden their obviously limited knowledge of the new English triplanes. Not only would they outperform an Albatros, they were flown by the most skillful pilots Kupper had encountered since his last brush with the French Storks. In truth, Jasta 76 had been lucky. If the English had not deliberately broken off the engagement it might have been a total loss.

He turned to look at Groos's pitted face. It was immobile and his thoughts were apparently unaffected by what he had seen. And why not? Here was a man who had been at Verdun.

"Where did they take Keim and Schröder?"

"The ambulance came from the *Feldlazarett*. I suppose they will be there still."

"Make certain. I want to know all you can find out about their wounds and where they will be sent. Send Zimmerman to me as soon as he arrives."

128

They paused before a half-round structure of corrugated iron. On specific orders from Staff it had been sandbagged around its perimeter and served as the Jasta message center. The only safe place in the Jasta, Kupper thought wryly. Staff protected themselves even vicariously.

Full night had descended upon the aerodrome and patches of stars were visible through the low, broken clouds. The cold wind swept circular trails of snow across the low doorway to the message center. Instinctively Kupper reached to button his tunic. He felt Maria's letter and wondered how many hours it would be before he could read it. Ah, Maria . . .

"See that Leutnant Zimmerman reports to me when he arrives. And tell Pilger to bring me some hot tea."

"Would Herr Leutnant care for some biscuits?"

"No."

Groos saluted and started away. Kupper's voice halted him. He had suddenly remembered something which shocked him anew. The ham from Kempinsky's! He never wanted to see it again, for it looked exactly like the stump of Sellerman's leg.

"There is a ham in the officers' mess. Take it away. You may share it with your men."

Kupper shuddered, glanced up at the stars, opened the low door and ducked inside the message center.

Chapter Seven

——————— *With a package from*
Kempinsky's—

EN ROUTE to the officers' mess Feldwebel Groos counted the many matters which must be dealt with before he could consider his day's work finished. He must plan to delegate things so that he himself would actually do nothing at all except threaten the most vile punishment if they were not done.

The Jasta had suffered a terrible kick in the belly. What a kick! Actually he gave not a damn about the Jasta's reputation as long as it did not smell *too* badly, but it should be borne in mind that at any time it might be sliced up by *Jagdgruppe* and the personnel distributed all over the Western Front. This might be bad for Feldwebel Groos.

So just in case an axe should be lowered on Kupper's neck after today's miserable performance, a man should consider the various ways of protecting himself. He must be sure all his men understood that if anything went wrong Feldwebel Groos would emerge blameless. The culprit would be clearly identified whether he had anything to do with the bungle or not. It was a technique Groos had developed over his long years in the army and it was the principal reason why he had held the rank of Feldwebel for so long. He was well aware of his uncanny ability to foresee what was going to be right, and take the credit for it. Thus even the most abused private was convinced sooner or later that Groos was an excellent noncom.

He had already been at pains to claim it as his idea to keep the Albatroses secluded in the pocket of wood. Therefore he had personally saved the Jasta. When the attack was over, everyone within

131

range of his abrasive voice had been invited to wonder what their status might now be if the English had spotted the Albatroses on their first pass over the aerodrome. Groos had shaken his finger portentously in the general direction of the front and explained their doom in terms he was certain would be understood.

"Those thuds you hear over the hill are not just some senile *Landwehr* bandsman playing with his drums. It is the French—coming this way. If it were not for me most of you would be on *your* way to stop them this very night. And if you think life here is a pain in the ass, and I am not the best friend you ever had since you last gnawed on your mother's tits, then wait until you meet a Feldwebel who has been in the trenches too long! Ha!"

In the military life, according to Feldwebel Groos, there were three types of hanging. For an officer's balls they employed a silken ribbon. Noncoms rated a comfortable leather thong. But when a private was hung up by his balls regulations specified barbed wire and they had better not forget it.

There were many things stored in Feldwebel Groos's military mind. He could still recite oddments he had been forced to learn as a recruit—the history of the Prussian Royal Family, the history of the last war in 1870, the peacetime stations of all the army corps, the garrisons, divisions and brigades of his own corps with the names of the generals commanding, and he could still take a carbine to pieces and put it back together again while blindfolded. All very useful information, he had often thought.

Feldwebel Groos considered that he was, and since 1914 had been, in a double war. One must first survive against the enemy, which had been a great deal more difficult at Verdun than here, in spite of today's rude visitors. Long before the English started down on their second pass Feldwebel Groos had made himself cozy behind two spare Mercedes engines. It was always comforting to have steel between you and steel. And he had taken careful notice of the fact that he had arrived in the shelter of the engines a bare second before that hard-skulled Pilger threw himself down in the same place. Fortunately there had been ample room for both of them, but if there had not been, Private Pilger would have found himself out in the cold. Or would he have? There was something about Pilger—he occasionally displayed signs of being too clever for his own good. He was part of the double war, which was to survive

132

among your own troops after you survived the enemy. Thus far, Feldwebel Groos considered he had been more than ordinarily victorious in this secondary war, but now, he thought gloomily, men like Pilger were not making it any easier.

He quickened his pace toward the officers' mess.

He must first get Pilger cracking on some tea for the commander. What a strange one that Kupper was! A fighter, *ja.* There were his victories to prove it. And perhaps he was a good aviator. Who knew? They all bounced their landings and they all killed themselves sooner or later. But as an officer he lacked many qualifications. For one thing, Gross remembered, he looked *at* a soldier instead of *through* him. In the peacetime army he would never have made Oberleutnant.

After he had Pilger out of the way, he would take up the matter of the ham, which regrettably he would have to share with thirty men. He saw no way of preventing Kupper from asking any one of them how he had liked the ham. He often spoke to privates. Could Kupper be a Communist? And if the man said he had never heard of the ham, then where would Feldwebel Groos be, even if Kupper *was* a Communist? Hung up with a leather thong, that's where! And foreseeing such possibilities was how one survived in the secondary war. Rule one: Do not leap at something which looks good. If it's alive you may frighten it away. If it is dead it may be poisoned. If it is a material object it may be set to explode on contact.

A ham! To share such a great delicacy with a mob of ignoramuses was a sacrilege. Groos thought he would as soon defecate in his own boots.

The officers' mess was deserted. There was a single oil lamp burning near the piano and Groos saw the glow of fire through the new bullet holes in the stove. He would set some men to repairing the stove in the morning. Spoiling officers was imperative. It kept them off your neck. He glanced at the magazines spread out on the reading table, *Die Deutschen,* the *Leipzig Illustrierte Zeitung, Der Krieg,* and *Kladderadatsch* with a photo of a generous-mouthed girl on the cover. Groos could not remember ever having been alone in the officers' mess so he reached for the copy of *Kladderadatsch* and stuffed it under his tunic. The secondary war. He knew what he would do with the girl when he finally crawled into his bunk this night.

133

Now where was Pilger? And the ham?

He was about to leave the mess and search for Pilger when some long-polished instinct told him to remain still. Had he heard someone beyond the door leading to the kitchen, or had he not? If so, all was silent now. Groos held his breath. There was a slight tinkling from the stove, nothing more. Yet he was not satisfied. He took three ponderous steps to the entrance door of the mess, allowing his boots to crunch down full force on the wooden floor planking. He opened the door and after a moment deliberately slammed it shut again. Then he waited, motionless, listening.

He was both disappointed and puzzled at the continued silence. He turned to open the outside door again with the intention of actually leaving. Suddenly he heard a snuffling sound from beyond the kitchen door, a panting like a beast rooting in the earth, Groos decided.

He tiptoed toward the kitchen door, pausing now and then to listen and readjust his weight when his boots pressed too heavily upon the floor planking. At last he was able to reach out and seize the handle. He yanked open the door.

A single candle outlined the giant Pilger crouched over the wash counter on which there was something Groos could not see. Pilger spun around in angry surprise and as he did so Groos saw the ham.

"*Achtung!*" Groos said hoarsely.

There was a strange look in Pilger's eyes Groos found unnerving. Perhaps it was a trick of the candlelight. God knew he had seen rough soldiers in his time, but suddenly Pilger had dropped out of the human race. His whole face was smeared with grease so that it became a polished hide; bits of ham fat clung to his lips and cheeks and his half-opened mouth seemed to shelter fangs instead of teeth. And his great lumps of hands were slimy with grease.

As Pilger came slowly to a loose attitude of attention Groos wondered what he would do if this animal suddenly attacked him. Though he was a strong man and he knew how to kill, this beast was making his bowels churn.

"Ah—" said Groos, simply to make a sound. The spectacle of Pilger folding himself back into his soldier's shell was somehow obscene. For a moment Groos wondered if he could accomplish the feat.

"My friend, you are in trouble. That ham belongs to Kupper."

"I know that."

"What kind of a nerve do you have?"

"Kupper is not going to eat it. Neither will the other officers."

"Who informed you of this?"

"No one has to tell me. I know officers. They saw Sellerman. Their stomachs are not like yours and mine."

"Thank you for including me. It may interest you to know that Kupper has just given the ham to me. It was my idea to share it with the men. You have already had more than your portion. Now you will wash your filthy face and hands and make some very hot tea at once and take it to Kupper, who is in the message center. While you are doing those things I will try my best to think of some punishment so that the next time you decide to have a private banquet you will not so easily forget your Feldwebel."

Pilger nodded and obediently moved a water pot to the center of the stove. Then he bent over the wash sink. He pumped water into a tin basin and rinsed his hands. Finally he sloshed water around his face as if he enjoyed it.

Groos was amazed. Only a few moments before he had been face to face with a monster and now here was a big country boy who behaved as though he had just been caught with his fingers in the jam pot. Even his movements were humble. It could not be that he actually feared being accused of a serious crime. As Kupper's batman he had more reason to be in the officers' mess than I have, Groos thought. And apparently he had not helped himself to anything but the ham. It would take a bit of thinking to hang something on the kind of lunatic who would return from leave two days early, but of course there was always the future.

"Well now, Pilger, maybe I won't be too hard on you. Remember we are old front hogs, real veterans—both of us. But how would you like to be back on iron rations, potato-rind bread and chestnut-leaf tobacco again? How would you like the dear lice for bedfellows again, with a few hundred rats to keep you from getting lonesome? How would you like a ninety-eight rifle in your paws just for old times' sake and a nice barrage of green-cross shells laid down just for you so some officer could yell "Forward"? Think of those things, Pilger. You know what that life is like. And I advise you to remember that this is a long war and I will be very annoyed the

135

next time something interesting develops and you fail to inform me first."

Pilger nodded again and held his silence. He dumped a spoonful of tea into a tin pot and took down one of the heavy cups hanging on the wall. Watching him pour the boiling water into the pot, Groos decided he moved exactly like a polar bear he had once seen in the Berlin Zoo.

Suddenly both men froze in position and listened. After a moment they relaxed. The big guns on the line were at it again. Beyond the cracked window the heavy carrumping had begun and they both knew it would last all night. And maybe forever, Groos thought.

"How would you like to be back in the infantry, Pilger, let us say with my old outfit the Nineteenth Division?"

"How would you?"

"Just imagine—all of my old friends right up there on the ridge tonight, those who are still alive, that is. I suppose you know we had a seventy-nine per cent loss at Verdun? Now there they are still at it like stout fellows, taking their medicine without caring for themselves. Winning the war is all the nineteenth cares about—and I would not be surprised to find some old comrade of mine up there, a Feldwebel say, who could use an experienced man. They need your sort up on the ridge. Yes, indeed. A small recruit could do your job here, some youngster who might keep me better informed."

"Kupper needs me—more than you think."

Groos's vast experience enabled him to receive the message, decipher it, and know he might hear something useful if he proceeded cautiously. Anything Pilger might confide would, of course, have its price. "On the other hand, I would not *personally* favor sending a man with your combat service back for more."

"Why not?"

"For one thing I value your cooperation. When the younger men see a veteran like yourself snap to, it makes things easier for me."

They listened to the guns for a moment. Then Groos said, "About Kupper? Why do you think he needs you so?"

"He wants to stop fighting."

"Ha! Who doesn't?"

"If men like him stop, then soon enough every man in Germany will quit. Then where will we be?"

Groos eyed the ham. He had shown his strength long enough.

Now he would relax. Grasping a chunk between his thumb and forefinger he tore it away and popped it in his mouth. He chewed at it thoughtfully. "When peace comes," he said, "on Sundays we can wear our medals and go to the park and listen to a band play 'Heil dir in Siegerkranz' and maybe I can find some old whore to stab once in a while."

"What about Germany? What about the Fatherland?"

Groos stared at him in wonder. The pitted folds of his cheeks slid down to drape the corners of his mouth. Had he been wasting his bargaining skill for this sort of thing? This hypocritical bastard in the shape of a man! Trying to sell the Fatherland to another front hog who knew what it was to be shelled as well as he did, to his own Feldwebel, as if he was a raw recruit—page-boy!

"Don't give me that hero manure, Pilger! The Kaiser has to shovel it to keep his job, but it always ruins my appetite. Now you get out of here, you and your goddamned bugle blowing. Take your teapot and get out of my range before I have you sent to Russia! *Raus!*"

Pilger obeyed without the slightest show of resentment. But as he carried the pot and cup toward the door he suggested that Groos regard the last button of his tunic which looked so peculiar with the corner of a magazine peeping out behind it.

Let him go, Groos thought. The smart bastard will hang himself sooner or later and I will have the pleasure of pulling the trap.

He turned to the ham. That overgrown gorilla had consumed more than a quarter of it and had obviously not even used a knife. Since there was so little to share among so many, hardly more than a nibble for each man in the Jasta, Groos calculated, it was best he chop off his own portion here and now.

He took a great knife down from the rack above the stove and using his fat finger as a measuring unit, set the knife blade near it. Then he remembered that Lance Corporal Blum and Private Lehmann would not want any ham because they were Jews. He brought up two more fingers and moved the knife that much farther into the ham. Ha! The Hebrews had a damned fine religion! He sliced down through the ham with purpose and great satisfaction.

Groos leaned back against the wash counter alternately chewing and sighing with appreciation. He longed for a suitable liquid to wash down the ham and after a cursory search of the kitchen spied a half-liter of wine standing in the cool of the potato bin. His first instinct was to reach for the bottle and remove the cork at once —then his secondary war habits took charge and queried the action. Someone had obviously reserved this bottle and intended to finish it. Now, if it was one of the cooks or his orderlies, then ownership was meaningless. In their safe and cozy jobs they were expected to take the welfare of their Feldwebel very much to heart. On the other hand, if the wine belonged to an officer who had asked that it be set aside in such and such a way until he could finish it, then there could be the very devil to pay if it vanished. And back on the one hand—was there a label on the bottle of any kind?

Groos listened to the thundering guns for a moment and he thought of the difference a few kilometers could make in a war. The ridge called Chemin des Dames: they were taking a pounding up there tonight. It was hard to believe that just beyond a few hills men were crawling around like maggots until they connected with a piece of hot iron. Then if they were able to, they twisted in the mud and screamed for a while.

This had turned into a fine war for men who knew what it was like up there and were now faced with such a weighty decision as to whether a half-liter of wine should be stolen.

Groos seized the bottle, pulled the cork with his teeth, arched his neck for maximum range and spit the cork in the general direction of the front. As if in reply to his challenge the noise of the barrage suddenly increased.

Hauptmann Siemelkamp, Commandant of the 28th Supply Depot, Fourth Army, was also acutely aware of intensified thundering in the west. Because he needed at least some acquaintance with the Luftstreitkräfte if he were to impress people during his next leave in Bohemia, Siemelkamp had personally delivered young Zimmerman back to his Jasta. These aviators were now the glamour chaps and Siemelkamp knew it would be much more interesting to say he had served with them even briefly, rather than to have been in a supply depot so far behind the lines. Therefore Hauptmann Siemelkamp had dismissed his chauffeur and had personally returned Zimmerman to Jasta 76. He wanted no witnesses to his journey, no truths to belie later descriptions of his adventures at the Western Front. Like the majority of his personnel he only heard the sound of enemy guns when the wind and all other conditions were favorable and then they made only the faintest mutterings. But here! Hauptmann Siemelkamp was genuinely grateful to his wife when he thought what it must be like at the real front. While Bohemia might be far removed from Berlin, his wife's family had been influential enough at court to secure a captaincy for him, and necessary orders were arranged so that Hauptmann Siemelkamp commanded a depot well out of harm's way. Actually both his direct commissioning from civilian life and his posting made rare military sense. Siemelkamp had managed one of Prague's largest stores prior to the war, and had developed a knowledge of inventory and warehousing far beyond the competence of the average supply officer. Since donning a uniform he had also acquired a military manner any professional Prussian officer might envy.

As a result of his crash Zimmerman was covered with clay-mud and asked to be dropped at his quarters before reporting to his Jasta commander. Siemelkamp had been shocked to see the primitive huts these glamorous aviators occupied. How disappointing! He was in the act of bidding Zimmerman a patronizing farewell when the distant barrage commenced. Only Zimmerman's repeated assurance that the guns were nearly twenty kilometers away and that there was not the slightest chance of a shell falling near them kept Hauptmann Siemelkamp from crawling under his Opel and waiting until the dreadful sound ceased. Zimmerman explained that it might continue for hours. If a roof over the Hauptmann's head would make him feel more at ease, he might try the officers' mess.

Siemelkamp was in such a hurry to reach its shelter he had no time to brood upon Zimmerman's ingratitude for the lift or his clumsy sarcasm. When he first rushed into the mess itself and stumbled into the magazine table, his fear of the barrage and his contempt for officers who would not even leave a light in their private refuge combined in a howl of rage. Looking frantically for assistance and sympathy, he saw a crack of light and found his way to the kitchen door. He threw it open to discover a mere sergeant drinking wine and gnawing on a ham such as Siemelkamp had never seen in his own supply depot.

For a moment the sight of such a large and beautiful ham canceled his fear of the barrage. So this was how the Luftstreitkräfte truly lived! At least the sergeant had the discipline to put down his wine bottle and click to attention when he saw an officer.

"What are you doing here, Feldwebel?"

"Having a snack, Herr Hauptmann."

"So I see." The man was obviously a thief—and a bold one at that.

Siemelkamp's uneasy eyes searched the shadows beyond the candle. They returned to the ham, then again swung upon Groos and concentrated upon his Iron Cross first class. He saw his shoulder straps were edged with the infantry's white and for a moment had the uneasy notion that he might have discovered a deserter. "Where is the kitchen staff?"

"Asleep, Herr Hauptmann. We have had a bad day."

"Is that why you don't turn up some lights? Or are you being as inconspicuous as possible while you help yourself to officers' food?"

"The French bombers like bright lights, Herr Hauptmann."

Siemelkamp caught his breath. He had not considered bombers in his fears. He yearned to bolt for the front door, jump in the Opel and make full speed for the depot. Yet there was that luscious ham. "Do the bombers come here?" he asked.

"Not yet, Herr Hauptmann. But if we make a lighthouse for them they certainly will."

"Then put out that candle! At once!"

"Oh, this is nothing to worry about. It cannot be seen from above and it is low enough so it cannot reflect on the snow."

"Are you sure?"

"Quite sure, Herr Hauptmann. If it were otherwise we would all long be dead."

Siemelkamp shuddered. "Are you the Battalion Sergeant-Major?"

"No, Herr Hauptmann. We do not have a battalion. We are part of a Jagdgruppe. I am only the Jasta Feldwebel."

"How informal," Siemelkamp said. He was not at all clear on the army tables of organization. "And your commanding officer is only a Leutnant?"

"*Ober*leutnant—"

"If he learned you were stealing his food he would probably have you shot."

"Leutnant Kupper gave me permission."

Siemelkamp again reminded himself that his victim wore the Iron Cross first class and therefore the usual bluster of telling a man he was a disgrace to his uniform and rank would hardly do. He must somehow get rid of this scoundrel.

"Permission for what? To steal his food?"

"I am not—"

"You *are* a dunce to try to convince *me* that an officer would say to you, 'Look here, my fine fellow, you're looking a bit thin about the middle. Run down to the mess and have a go at my ham.'"

"That is the way it was, and—"

"Preposterous! Fetch your Leutnant immediately. I will enjoy watching his face while you repeat your story."

"The Leutnant is very busy at the message—"

"*Raus!*"

As Groos marched to the door Siemelkamp looked at his retreating back and thought how beautifully they had understood each other. One did not become a Feldwebel with Iron Cross first class and transfer from the infantry to the flying service without knowing that a direct order from an officer must be instantly obeyed. And the scoundrel would take all night finding his Leutnant because he knew very well his mission was a sham anyway. The Feldwebel was an experienced soldier. He did not expect to be punished for his crime, because he would simply be unable to find his Leutnant. Likewise he would not expect to find the ham waiting if he chanced to return. He would understand that a supply officer naturally developed the habit of acquisition.

Siemelkamp turned to the ham and rewrapped it with the same skill and precision which had marked his early clerking in a department store. When he had finished he blew out the candle and made his way toward the front door of the mess. It was a short and distressing journey. He stumbled over the magazine table again and nearly dropped the ham. And as he left the open door and ran the few steps to his Opel, he swore the barrage was becoming louder.

Some three minutes later Siemelkamp sat back in the seat and eased the Opel's speed. He was free of the aerodrome and with two hundred and fifty-one divisions in the German Army it was exceedingly unlikely that any liaison would again be established between his depot and Jasta 76. And if by chance he should ever be questioned about what happened to a certain delicacy which was still in its unmistakable Kempinsky wrapping, then he would deny any knowledge of same. And since he was an officer that would be the end of it—except possibly for that too clever Feldwebel.

Yet all was not as it should be. No matter how many times Siemelkamp tried to convince himself that his imagination had taken charge of his reason, he now knew the barrage *was* getting louder. And he began to see less and less activity along the road and much more barbed wire stretching out from it and disappearing into the rumpled mud and snow. The few soldiers he saw carried rifles strapped on their shoulders, full battle kit, and wore helmets. Everything was unfamiliar.

He slid to a stop before a road barricade and was told by the guards that the thin cross of light from his headlamps was too bright. He must extinguish them entirely if he wished to proceed further. Siemelkamp experienced the greatest difficulty in conversing with the soldiers. All four were from Hanover in Prussia and in Siemelkamp's opinion looked and spoke like Teutonic savages. They told him he was very near the front and he wanted to weep. None of the soldiers had ever heard of the 28th Supply Depot, much less knew the way to it.

Siemelkamp demanded they send for an officer and one man tramped off through the snow—most casually, Siemelkamp thought. After a seemingly endless wait during which he several times felt the earth tremble so violently he was convinced he would soon be killed, the soldier returned with a Leutnant Buchman.

The Leutnant had obviously been asleep and for an instant Siemelkamp thought to apologize for awakening him. As he was about to do so a series of heavy explosions occurred somewhere in the darkness behind Siemelkamp and it was all he could do to stutter through his demand for immediate guidance out of the area. He was unfortunately lost, he explained, and must deliver the most important dispatches to the rear—namely to the 28th Supply Depot, if the Leutnant knew its location.

Siemelkamp became inwardly furious when he saw the blond young Leutnant yawn even as a series of concussions shook the night. The insolent nerve of the man! Yawning in the face of his superior officer, and not seeming to care about the explosions or whether he lived or died.

"I only know what the French are up to, Herr Hauptmann. I

leave the disposition of the German Army to others more qualified."

An isolent fellow, Siemelkamp thought. But this was no time for a lecture. The young ass was yawning again. He must not go to sleep standing up—he must get me out of here.

"I am sorry you are so weary, Leutnant, but then aren't all of us who fight for Germany? Now if you can telephone perhaps, and inquire the route to the 28th Depot—"

"I'll put Corporal Stein with you. He knows every cowpath on the Western Front." Buchman yawned mightily. "And Herr Hauptmann, when you are safely back in your cozy depot would you send us what we really need up here?"

Hauptmann Siemelkamp feigned a solicitousness he did not feel. Every explosion, even the most distant, seemed to squeeze his bladder. "Of course! Anything at all I can do. It is only a matter of making requisition forms—"

"Just send us about two thousand cartons of sleep."

It took another ten minutes to produce Corporal Stein, whom Siemelkamp detested on sight. He thought he had a most unsoldierly bearing, he looked like a Jew and his helmet was much too large for him.

Leutnant Buchman recommended that he follow Stein's motorcycle, but Siemelkamp would have none of the arrangement. He knew the wildness of German dispatch riders and was not going to risk losing him en route. He ordered Stein into the seat beside him. He could find some sort of transportation back when they reached the main road.

After a complicated series of turns Siemelkamp was obliged to admit that Corporal Stein knew his way. What little sense of direction Siemelkamp had managed to retain had long been lost and to bolster his spirit he decided that Stein was something of a genius. Thus he was entirely amenable when Stein recommended they stop while he ascertained if the next road, which ran along the side of a plateau, was open. He slipped away into the blackness after cautioning Siemelkamp about displaying any kind of light.

It was a terrifying place to wait, for in the distance Siemelkamp could actually see the flashing of guns. He became so frightened he was suddenly compelled to stand up in the Opel and open his pants. There was no time to dismount so he simply stood trembling in the light of the flashing barrage, urinating over the Opel's side.

He was even more relieved when he saw Stein was running toward him from a ruined church tower. Bless the man! He was at least doing his best, and yes—the road was open.

They had not traveled far when they came to a barrier across the road which Siemelkamp thought looked strangely like the first. There were also four soldiers here, although he had no time to examine their faces. Apparently they recognized Stein, for they waved the Opel through.

A few meters beyond the barrier Stein recommended that they stop. He quickly dismounted and assured Siemelkamp he would have no trouble finding his way. He must simply carry straight on to the railway crossing, after which he should turn right and follow that road directly to the 28th Depot. As for himself, Stein said he had many friends in the area and would find a billet among them.

Siemelkamp was pleased to notice Corporal Stein's otherwise offensive appearance was at least accompanied by a smart salute. He returned it, muttered his thanks and drove off as fast as he dared. It was not until several minutes later that he began to wonder about Corporal Stein walking to a billet. Peculiar. Was it possible the last barricade had been the same place he had first seen Corporal Stein? Yet as the cannonade began to fade, Siemelkamp's suspicions were replaced by rich pleasures of self-congratulation. It had, after all, not been a bad day. And he had at last been in combat and would have much to tell.

He was beginning to formulate suitable episodes for his adventure when he chanced to look down at the opposite seat and saw that the ham from Kempinsky's was gone.

BOOK TWO

Chapter Eight

April 16, 1917
Confusion in Champagne

THIS WAS THE MORNING.

In his mind General Nivelle could envision the whole of the Craonne Plateau with, as he had imagined it so many times before this morning, his armies swarming up the slopes and capturing hundreds of thousands of Germans, the great proportion of their cannon, and mountains of war material.

This was the dawn Nivelle had waited for and prayed for and fought for against those critics both military and civilian who insisted the Germans were too strongly fortified against direct assault; those cowards and pessimists who had insisted that some other way must be found to emasculate the forty German divisions amassed behind the Hindenburg Line.

"There is no other way," he had told them all. "Action is the basis of war!"

In Paris, when he had first outlined his plan, Nivelle held his audience spellbound. He was a cool and organized speaker although the words he chose resounded with patriotic ardor. His physical appearance, so carefully groomed, was alone sufficient to command extraordinary attention and respect—a firm, sturdy jaw exactly molded to inspire confidence, a heavy though sensitive mouth surrounded by a gray bristling mustachio and a token goatee which he occasionally touched if he wished to emphasize a point—all well displayed upon the pedestal of his high uniform collar. And for color there were his three long rows of ribbons. Yet it was Nivelle's eyes which customarily entranced his listeners—large, strangely soft

148

eyes which utterly redeemed his stiff military poise. With such eyes he could expound as he had at Verdun, and be believed. "Let our moral greatness be equal to the task confided to us; the safety of our country depends on it." The eyes of a dreamer; eyes fulfilled when he advised young recruits, "Throw away your hearts before the assault—throw them into the enemy's trench!"

And no soldier, recruit or veteran, ever questioned Nivelle's personal *sang-froid*. He had been compared to Napoleon.

Here along the Craonne Plateau, amid the wooded ravines and rolling hills which rippled away from both banks of the river Aisne, Nivelle was convinced he might avenge Sedan. In one gigantic attack he would liberate all of northern France. His sincerity and devotion had even persuaded Haig to subject the British armies to his command for the duration of the battle.

Thus, from the Forest of St. Gobain in the west to the Moronvilliers Massif in the east, all along the River Aisne from Missy to Mount Sapigneul and thence south and east in ragged line from Berméricourt, Brimont, and Courcy—all the way to Auberive on the Suippe, the greasy click of breechblocks and the clanging of ejected shell casings became grace notes in the mighty pandemonium of dawn.

"*L'heure est venue!*" Nivelle proclaimed. "*Confiance! Courage!*"

The Craonne Plateau expands into several high plains separated by ravines which project to the south like claws and serve as admirable cover for machine-gun emplacements. The northern side is more like an ancient massive rampart with the Aisne serving as a moat. A road known as the Chemin des Dames transverses the crest of the plateau from the Laon–Soissons road to the village of Craonne. Here the Germans waited with particular confidence.

Fog choked the valley of the Aisne. Black smoke spouting from thousands of petty conflagrations combined into one gigantic, evil-smelling union which merged with the fog and made it ever thicker and more ominous. There were the "departures" of the French artillery, each of which had long left the muzzle of its gun before the poilus' ears were further tormented by the sound of ripping canvas. There were the "arrivals" coming from the German artillery, which announced their imminent intrusion with a terrifying whistle if they were big shells, and coupled announcement with explosion if they were small.

The 340-millimeter guns shook the earth and the very atmosphere itself, the 200-millimeter mortars pounded the scrofulous hills forming the bulwark below the Chemin des Dames and rechurned the hideous ooze of blood, flesh, bones and sopping clay which had been originally mixed days before. The 150- and 105-millimeter guns and howitzers spewed up smaller chunks of the soggy terrain, and the whip-sharp explosions of the 75's were everywhere.

It was the morning of April 16, 1917.

After their dreadful exertions in Artois against the German line, the British were resting. Now it was the turn of the French. Nivelle had planned it so, although he spoke not of sacrifice but of glory and certain victory.

The objectives were neatly prescribed to the hour and minute. The French Tenth Army would capture all the heights between the Aisne and Juvincourt by zero plus three and one-half hours. The final objective for the night, upon which it was assumed the triumphant troops might rest, was extended to Amifontaine, a mere seven kilometers.

The First Army would scale the heights and command the Chemin des Dames by zero plus four hours and thirty minutes. One hour and a half later they would be as far east as Anizy le Château, where they would be allowed to pause lest they outrun their supplies.

Moving toward Laffaux was the I Colonial Corps. They had recently taken to naming their bayonets "Rosalie" or "Josephine," and in a sudden spasm of name-giving, the Battalion d'Afrique, which was a penal unit, became known as *"Les Joyeux."* They had accepted service in trench mortars with enthusiasm—and why not? French military discipline had made their present life so miserable the suicide club could not be much worse.

To the east, General Mangin, the hero of Douaumont, commanded the French Sixth Army. His poilus had buttoned their coattails back over their bayonet scabbards so they could run faster and catch more of the retreating Germans. Their hoarse voices were lost in the overall thunder and their cold morning curses evaporated in their steamy breath.

There were many battalions of black troops in Mangin's array. All of them carried special scimitar-style knives and many of them murmured *"Coupe-coupe"* softly to themselves while they stamped their huge feet against the slippery clay in a hopeless attempt to

150

keep warm. They did not appear in the least afraid of the impending combat, but their heritage had equipped them poorly for such penetrating cold. Waiting like patient animals for the attack to begin, they brushed at the mud on their gigantic pantaloons in an effort to warm their freezing hands. The continuous explosions which caused many other troops involuntarily to pray left the Senegalese apathetic. They would stare dully at the ejaculations of earth and debris and beg only for warmth.

From his belfry on the plateau, Leutnant Buchman occasionally observed scattered groups of General Duchêne's Tenth Army through rifts in the smoke and fog. They were squeezed into a gap between Heurtebise and Craonne and their apparent inactivity puzzled him. He knew very well how military confusion often created stagnation, but he had not expected the French to be so orthodox.

Farther to the east Mazel commanded the French Fifth Army, and yet farther west stood Pétain with the Fourth. He was instructed to restrain his troops until the next day.

All of these half-million human beings were obliged to obey the commands of a single Frenchman in far-off Compiègne. Nivelle was their life or death.

The grand attack commenced through fog which often blinded the French artillery yet was rarely thick enough to conceal the troops from German machine guns. By ten o'clock, when it began to rain along some parts of the front and snow along others, the slaughter was proceeding according to German expectations. By ten o'clock the I Colonial Corps found their heroic attack upon the plateau of Laffaux and Vauxaillon had gained them very little. The German VIII Corps from the Rhineland, and particularly the tough 16th Division, saw the French appear through the fog suddenly and die suddenly. Those who did not die vanished into shell holes. Because of the fog few officers knew the exact whereabouts of their own men, much less the progress of other units. They were only certain that the artillery barrage which was supposed to ease the way for them had been badly placed. They were also now certain of their need for reinforcements if they were to hold even the few meters of earth they had achieved. They were certain their supply of ammunition had been reduced to an alarming degree, and the final certainty was of German counterattacks.

151

All else was chaos.

They managed to take Laffaux and Nanteuil-la-Fosse which were far short of their assigned objectives.

By noon the VII Corps had captured Courcy, Loivre, and Berméricourt, and the XXXII Corps wriggled through the secondary German positions which had been established between the Aisne and a graceful little stream marked "Miette" on the officers' maps. No man looking upon it could hear the stream, although he must know it was making a rippling sound. No man dared drink of it.

By noon the lowering clouds lifted just enough to allow the debut of a few airplanes. According to the locale, there were Albatroses to be seen, an occasional trio of Fokkers, more L.V.G.'s, a very occasional Caudron, which was almost immediately shot down, and even rarer braces of Nieuports or Spads, which appeared scudding along beneath the low overcast. Resentment at the absence of French airplanes festered among those foot soldiers who were not too stunned to be capable of any reaction except fear. And so the airplanes were not cheered. Often both Frenchmen and Germans screamed maledictions at the leaden sky and refused to understand that airmen must see to fight.

In front of Loivre and Brimont, the French 23rd Regiment of Infantry, which was called *"Les Braves,"* and the 133rd Regiment, known as *"Les Lions,"* clawed at German concrete with their puny weapons and died. The Russian Brigade fought with much less enthusiasm and also died. Just to the north of Loivre the 14th Division, composed of the 44th, the 60th, the 35th, and the 442nd Regiments, crept and ran and plunged and pressed themselves against the stinking muck, and died. As did the 9th and the 10th Divisions, who died in front of Craonne.

At two-thirty, when the flowing of blood temporarily eased, the Germans counterattacked and recaptured Berméricourt. Terrified and exhausted troops of the I Colonial Corps were thrown back into their assault trench. Those who could recognize anything at all discovered themselves mired in the same mud they had left at dawn.

At dusk the confusion was compounded. In the sector where the I Colonial Corps had fought so desperately, the French artillery believed that the lines had fallen back far enough so they could open up with their 75's. They did not know the target area was still occupied by their own Senegalese. Thus the awful losses among the blacks were multiplied; and beset by German machine guns as well as their own shelling, 6,300 were killed of the original 10,000 engaged. Occasional survivors rallied around the few officers left alive and attempted to frighten machine guns with grenades and scimitars, but the majority streamed to the rear and demanded immediate transport to Paris by any possible means. As a bewildering tide, they invaded stations and clambered into trucks and overwhelmed the field hospitals. Once away from the lines no one knew what to do with these grinning incomprehensible blacks. And so they let them freeze.

And up and down the lines mud-caked lips found words. Voices, hoarse with fear and bitterness, said, *"On est tombé sur un bec."*

The Gros Legumes, of whom Nivelle was the grandest, had made shocking miscalculations.

By midnight it was said the French had lost fifty thousand men. And at midnight a gale wind brought sleet and snow.

At midnight Paul Chamay lay in his bunk listening to the wind and begging it to cease. He had not left the ground all day.

At midnight Captain Jourdan telephoned a fellow graduate of St. Cyr from his new base near Ferme d'Alger. He apologized for the 322nd Escadrille in a voice wretched with humiliation. They had not given proper protection to the few artillery spotters who had so courageously taken to the air. Not once during the day had there been visibility enough to see the limits of their own aerodrome.

Sebastian Kupper washed his hands at midnight for the third time since dusk ended his patrols. The weather had been discouraging, yet what remained of Jasta 76 struggled into the turbulent air and slipping between cloud, snow squalls and terrain, managed reasonable success along the Chemin des Dames, and during the afternoon they had ranged as far as Auberive. Another victory for Steilig, another for Hochstetter, both of them old French Voisins trying to spot the artillery. It was easy enough except for the weather. Zimmerman had bagged a Caudron over Berry au Bac.

Kupper had shot up some ground troops concentrated in a hollow which had appeared safe from shelling. He had no idea how many had fallen to his bullets, but he remembered the way so many had looked up and opened their mouths in surprise. He could not actually see their eyes, yet the impression of them persisted. So between midnight and dawn he was obliged to leave his bunk twice. He opened the door of his hut and leaned out far enough to vomit. When the dry retching subsided he washed and rewashed his hands. Killing men on the ground was like shooting pigs in a sty. He kept seeing blue bundles tumbling over one another and then lying still.

On the morning of the seventeenth a May bug was seen by certain men of Pétain's Fourth Army. Some of them claimed it was the biggest insect they had ever observed, so huge they doubted a normal bird could lift it, and therefore in spite of all other negative signs the traditional harbinger of spring had certainly arrived to relieve the crisis. Even though they held out the hard-shelled insect to all who would look, they were soon discredited.

For on the morning of the seventeenth it snowed.

Jourdan set the monotonous pattern for the men of the 322nd Escadrille. He would step out of his quarters and tilt his great beak upward as if there was any real sky to regard. Then he would examine the limitless nothing as if he could see. After a time, when his eyes became streaming with tears from the wind, he would wipe at them and sigh. Then he would lower his head and disappear into his quarters, a man overwhelmed by ill fortune. Watching him, Babarin discovered that he repeated the performance at regular intervals. He said to Sussote, "He's a fifteen-minute cuckoo—he lost his clock in the snowstorm."

All morning the brief ceremony was imitated by the personnel of the escadrille. There could be no flying until Jourdan gave the order, but each man preferred to make his own estimate as to when that might be. Thus for a few minutes there would be thirty men standing about profaning the weather and the next few minutes the same group would be in the shelter of their hangars, then another group of ten might stand outside jumping up and down with their hands jammed in their pockets and turning in every direction for some slight sign of improvement and finding none. The constant thudding of the guns beyond the impenetrable curtain of cloud and snow did nothing to ease their impatience. "Everything is ready," Babarin said, staring at the Nieuports clustered in the hangar tents. "Everything except God."

154

It seemed to be true. While a few other French escadrilles managed to make at least a token appearance over the front, the 322nd could not make a sortie until the second afternoon of the offensive. Then Jourdan led his flock to the west of Reims, where he found the weather improved enough to climb above a hundred meters. The formation was only seven Nieuports, the maximum operational at the time.

Just as they saw the artillery flashing along the active front, Chamay became uneasy about his Le Rhone engine. A new and quite foreign vibration seemed to possess it from the moment the short climb began. The Nieuport trembled in a way he had never sensed before; his hands, feet and rump told him the whirling Le Rhone was ailing, and the pungent smell of burning castor oil became stronger than ever.

Chamay pulled slightly away from the formation and pressed his ignition button several times, allowing the Le Rhone to slow and almost stop, then releasing the button in time for it to surge with power again. He hoped the blipping might ease the vibration, yet it seemed to have the opposite effect.

Suddenly the vibration increased, the Nieuport shook so violently Chamay thought it would shake itself to pieces, then a moment later he knew his sortie was finished. He saw the propeller stop dead in a diagonal position and beyond it the rest of the formation pulled swiftly away. As he shoved the nose down to hold flying speed and began a turn toward Reims, he could plainly hear the guns at the front. For a moment he was more absorbed with the remarkable echo they made against the low ceiling than with his inevitable return to earth. If he had learned anything at Pau, then the fast approaching fields should present no great hazard as emergency aerodromes. Yet now he saw that the only field he could possibly make appeared much smaller than those they had used for training. The light was flat and weak; it was not at all like those gay sunlit afternoons when he had practiced with Raymonde.

And this field was covered with snow.

The ground was rising at an alarming speed. Yet he must keep speed or the little Nieuport would fall off into a spin and the ground would come up forever.

There were stone fences and hedgerows. The field became rumpled instead of flat as it had appeared from a greater height. He pulled back on the control stick. The sighing of the Nieuport's flying wires diminished as he realized he had been holding much too steep a glide.

Directly below his glide path he saw a long supply convoy partially concealed behind an embankment. He swooped over it and saw the face of a long clay ridge rushing at him. He held his breath and cleared the rim. Now the earth sloped gently toward his chosen field. He must lose altitude soon or overshoot.

He dipped the Nieuport's left wing, shoved the nose down, and pushed hard right rudder. The Nieuport slipped gracefully down in a steep descent, flying wires wailing. He straightened the ship just before the ground and saw he had made a poor choice.

The thin blanket of snow on the ground had appeared to merge with an enormous camouflage netting and the flat light made the illusion nearly perfect. Now he saw that the netting concealed a full battery of heavy guns.

He banked as steeply as his few meters of height would permit to avoid the first long guy wire supporting the netting. Suddenly there was the choice of a second wire or smashing into a wall of sand bags. He chose the wire and saw it bite into his left wing. The wing caught the ground, broke away from its roots, and as Chamay watched in dismay the Nieuport spun around, slid backward a short distance and came to a violent halt.

He pushed up his goggles and saw that he was being surrounded by artillerymen.

"Are you hurt?"

"No." He raised himself in the cockpit and stood for a moment looking at the damage. Jourdan would be aggrieved and Babarin shocked. How could his pilot have made such a clumsy landing?

"We don't see any holes. Did the Boche shoot you down?"

"We didn't see the fight." The artillerymen were of the VII Corps, and Chamay instantly recognized the hint of Basque in their accent. Many were from Bayonne, big fellows in the main, although they were a mixture of obvious recruits and older men. They reached to assist as he swung his legs out of the cockpit. When his feet touched the ground he thanked God and then his hosts.

"You were lucky we weren't firing. We're just preparing to move up."

156

"Were you flying alone against the Boche? We never see one of our own flying machines."

"Where do you aviators hide all the time?"

"We try not to hide. Now let me see if I can examine the motor."

Chamay saw the Le Rhone had smeared everything in its vicinity with black oil. He bent down to look underneath it, as if he knew what he was actually looking for, and thought of Babarin. Had he made a mistake in continuing to trust such a man with the life of his engine which, in a sense, was his own life?

A huge artilleryman with a full black beard, a great snout of a nose and protruding eyes leaned down so that his head was level with Chamay's. He spoke in the patronizing tone of a man who considers himself an expert on many things. "You will never fix that motor, *mon vieux,* even if you could repair the wing."

"You seem to be right." The artilleryman had taken the obvious and made it a personally discovered fact. Chamay resented his proprietary air, nor did he like the way this Goliath turned his head and regarded him so suspiciously. The artilleryman lowered his voice still further and nodded his head like an understanding conspirator. "I am not surprised that these things can be arranged," he said. "Perhaps if I was an aviator I would do the same, since I am also a sensible man. It is becoming a common thing and no wonder since a truly sensible man is not anxious to die."

"I don't like your insinuation," Chamay said evenly. He straightened and saw the artilleryman follow him. Somehow he appeared even bigger than Chamay had supposed. White teeth appeared in a hole encircled by the artilleryman's beard and his eyes became amused.

"Ah—don't take offense, *mon vieux.* Only this morning we had other guests drop in from the sky. They are across the road now in the schoolhouse, or what is left of it. They contrived to make such a bad landing, their flying machine could not possibly take them back to a dry bed and a comfortable mess. They claimed to have been hit by ack-ack which was very clever of them, true or not. Now their government will give them some kind of medal which they can wear in their old age when less sensible men are long dead."

"*Their* government?" Chamay asked without really caring. He

157

wanted to find an officer and try to arrange for some kind of transport to Reims. From there he thought he could make his own way back to the escadrille. "Are they English?"

"No, Boche. A prize pair of villains who caged themselves, you might say. We are keeping them in the schoolhouse pending the arrival of all those thousands of prisoners we are going to capture up on the line. From the looks of things I believe the schoolhouse will be more than big enough to hold the complete bag and our two fellows will die of loneliness."

"You have German airmen *here?*"

"Two of the most heroic turds you could imagine and obviously the only sensible men in the German Army."

"Can I talk to them?"

"If you can speak their hideous tongue—why not?"

The white teeth gleamed in the beard again, and then the artilleryman closed the aperture and spat in the direction of the road. Chamay saw that his irascible manner concealed his true thoughts. He was a master of *blague,* the subtle way of saying one thing and meaning quite another, the deliberate burying of sincerity lest one be considered naïve.

"Would you be good enough to lead the way," Chamay asked, in a tone he hoped was sufficiently careless to match the artilleryman's cynicism.

Chamay was not disappointed in his first close-range sight of the enemy. Both Germans were like the Teutonic images which had so long marched through his mind. They were younger than he had envisioned but quite as heavy and down-looking as he could have wished. When he asked the bearded artilleryman why no guard stood over the prisoners he was assured it was unnecessary. "They wouldn't run away if you poked a bayonet up their butts. They are afraid they might meet a Senegalese."

They were standing shoulder to shoulder in the crumbled corner of brick and plaster which comprised the remains of the schoolhouse wall. Both Germans were bareheaded and their hair was cropped so short Chamay at first thought they were bald.

As he stepped away from his escort of curious artillerymen, Chamay saw the Germans whisper to each other, then stiffen. He stood before them a moment in silence while they examined every detail of his clothing. They seemed puzzled until Chamay brought

158

his hands from behind his back. His left hand still clutched his helmet and goggles. The Germans relaxed slightly.

Chamay's German was entirely academic, but he knew they were relieved to see an airman. He recognized the black and white ribbon on the Iron Cross in the button line of the shorter German's tunic. And he saw that his pants leg was dark brown with blood.

"You speak German?" he asked Chamay hopefully.

"A little."

The short German nodded to the crowd of artillerymen behind Chamay.

"Then inform these stupid men we demand our rights under the Geneva Convention. We are both acting officers. I am Rummer and this is my pilot, Linsingen."

Both men gave quick little jerks of their heads and Chamay wanted to laugh. They were behaving so like Germans. "We demand safe transport to an officer-prisoner camp," said the youth who had identified himself as Rummer.

"You are not in a position to demand anything." Chamay nodded at Rummer's bloodstained pants. "Are you badly hurt?"

"No. I demand treatment. We cannot stay here all day."

"Do either of you speak French?"

"No."

"Too bad." Chamay turned so half of his face was hidden from the Germans and winked at the bearded artilleryman. "Sergeant!" he said knowing he had promoted the beard at least one rank. "These prisoners are a nuisance. Tonight they will become more so. Take them down the road to the Senegalese."

Chamay spoke with deliberate lethargy, as if he was a field commander and the full weight of the offensive had fallen upon his shoulders. Rather a good imitation of Jourdan, he thought. He started to walk away and at once heard quick murmurings of excited German behind him.

"*Kapitan!*"

Chamay paused. His suspicions were confirmed. One or both of the Boche understood French. He clasped his hands behind his back and returned to the Germans. "*Ja?*"

"We demand—we *ask* you keep us here."

"Why are we so honored?"

"You are an airman. You understand us."

159

"And the Senegalese would not. You are quite right. Then unless you want to be their guests you will answer a few questions."

"According to the Geneva Convention—"

"I am making the rules here. What kind of an airplane were you flying?"

"An L.V.G.," Linsingen said softly. Perhaps it was concern for his comrade's wound, Chamay thought. He seemed less defiant than Rummer. Chamay knew that in the German Air Force the observer was in command of a two-seater reconnaissance airplane. The pilot merely acted as his chauffeur. It could be that Rummer's determined silence was his idea of retaining command.

"So? One of your new ones? A Spandau gun forward and a Parabellum machine gun in the rear cockpit. A Benz motor. Handy to fly for its size, but not too fast. Right?" It was all Chamay had been told about the new type L.V.G. which had only recently arrived at the front. He hoped his quick recital of its major virtues would give the impression he knew much more. For an instant he wondered what the penalty would be if a real interrogation officer came along and found a mere Air Service sergeant, and one who had just crashed his machine at that, questioning valuable prisoners. But official interrogators were not going to find out what he wanted to know.

"How many flying hours do you have?"

"Sixty-seven—"

"Where did you learn to fly?"

"At Kempten."

"And you?" Chamay looked steadily into Rummer's cold blue eyes. He saw the defiance mounting in him.

"I am not a pilot." Chamay could not decide if his sneer was an expression of contempt for all pilots, or if it was intended as a personal insult.

"You must have gone to school to become an observer. Where?"

"Juterborg."

Chamay had no idea whether the men were lying or not. He did not really care. Let them think him an absolute fool for asking such fruitless questions if in the process he could learn what he really wanted to know.

"Were you spotting for artillery when you were shot down?"

"No."

160

"What then? Not just out for a joy ride?"

"Reconnaissance," Linsingen said forlornly.

"Alone? One slow two-seater *alone?* I must say your escorts can't be very interested in what happens to you people."

Rummer spoke. He was obviously not pleased with Linsingen's behavior. "There was a mix-up and the fighters never joined us. The visibility was very bad."

"I know." Chamay allowed a sympathetic note to creep into his manner. Now he must play all-airmen-together. He smiled and regarded Linsingen as he might a newly discovered comrade. "Have you ever flown an Albatros?"

"No."

"What a shame. They must be a wonderful machine. Personally I would give anything to fly one. They are far superior to anything we have." He waited a moment. "Don't you agree?"

Linsingen hesitated, then said, "Of course."

"Now I suppose you could also have been a great ace if you had been given an Albatros instead of an L.V.G.?"

From his personal experience Chamay was convinced every reconnaissance pilot in the war secretly considered himself cheated. Given a fighter plane he would certainly have been an ace.

"I am curious about one of your Albatros pilots. He has painted a target circle on the fuselage of his Albatros. Do you know him?"

Both Germans were silent. They appeared not to have heard his question.

Chamay waited. His eyes met Rummer's and he saw only cold arrogance. It must have been just such a man, he thought, who had murdered Raymonde. Suddenly he felt his heart quicken. A rage he had never known before gripped him with such force he could hardly breathe.

"*Answer* me!" he shouted. He heard a voice sounding like his own and yet like that of a stranger.

Silence. There was something about Rummer's manner, a Teutonic insolence which triggered Chamay's fury. He raised his right arm deliberately until it was level with Rummer's face. Then with a quick rotation of his shoulders he swung the back of his hand to Rummer's face and sent him sprawling to the floor.

Chamay moved to stand over him as he struggled to his knees. "Answer me!"

161

Rummer wiped at his bleeding mouth but held his silence. Chamay swung around to Linsingen. *"Answer* me!" he shouted.

Linsingen started to speak, then firmly closed his lips. Chamay stepped in front of him. "One of you is going to tell me what I want to know—*now."*

The Germans remained motionless. One of the artillerymen coughed. Then there was silence again.

Suddenly Chamay's leg shot out and his heavy shoe struck Linsingen in the groin. He grabbed at himself and sank to the floor with an agonized gasp.

"Sergeant! Take it *easy!"* the bearded artilleryman called. But Chamay barely heard his voice. He moved quickly to Rummer, hauled him to his feet, and slammed him against the wall. He glanced over his shoulder at Linsingen who lay with his knees doubled up against his body. He was moaning softly.

Chamay said, "The Senegalese are not so gentle. Now will you find your tongue?"

"What is it you want?" Rummer's voice was barely audible.

"Do you know of an Albatros pilot with a painted target circle?"

"No."

Chamay slapped Rummer hard with the palm and the back of his hand. He continued to hit him until his head wobbled. "You're lying! He must be an ace—what you call a *Kanone!"*

Still Rummer remained silent. Pressing him hard against the wall, Chamay deliberately raised his knee. "This is your last chance. What is his name?"

"Kupper."

"His rank?"

"Oberleutnant."

"Given name?"

"Sebastian."

"How old is he?"

"I don't know."

Chamay believed him. "Is he about your age?"

"No. Much older. I have only seen a photo in *Der Krieg."*

"How many victories does he have?"

"More than twenty."

"What Jasta is he with?"

"He commands his own."

162

"What is its number?"

A hesitation. Chamay drew back his hand and closed his fist. "I think it is Jasta Seventy-six."

"Where is it based?"

Suddenly Chamay knew he would learn no more for Rummer's face had turned to stone. His eyes were still proud, but they were frightened and Chamay's anger left him. He was actually relieved when the bearded artilleryman placed a hand on his shoulder and said, "Let him be. He's lost a lot of blood and will faint on you."

Chamay released Rummer and looked down at Linsingen. He had pushed himself to a sitting position. Instinctively Chamay reached to help him to his feet, then changed his mind. Be damned to this Boche—and all of them.

He turned away quickly and strode out of the schoolhouse. In a moment the bearded artilleryman joined him. "You are a rough man, *mon vieux*. Are all airmen so—inhospitable?"

"I see no reason why we should welcome them to our country."

"But they were helpless." The artilleryman shrugged his shoulders. "Oh well. It is not for me to deliver a lecture. Getting you back where you came from presents a thorny enough problem."

"If I can reach Reims I'll find transport to my aerodrome."

"You're bound to risk some shelling on the road to Reims, but there's more risk in the traffic which is all coming this way—toward the war. If you start hiking all alone to the rear, some overeager officer may take you for a deserter and things could become very sticky."

The artilleryman leaned close to Chamay and his voice became confidential. His breath was pungent with wine and for the first time Chamay realized he was a little drunk.

"It so happens," the artilleryman said, "a certain sergeant-major has made many unkind remarks to me. A month ago when we were moving up from Épernay he stole a bicycle. It is a very good vehicle and he is so proud of it that it occupies the place on the *camion* where formerly I found a dry place to sleep. I have become unreasonably fond of you in spite of your rude manners. Now who ever heard of a deserter riding a bicycle to the rear?"

"You can tell the sergeant-major I traded him an airplane for it." Chamay smiled. "After I'm gone."

Chamay alternately pedaled and walked the bicycle for three

hours. At last a snow squall moved away and revealed the ruins of Reims on the horizon. The journey had become a nightmare. All along the way he had repeated Kupper's name. Sebastian Kupper!

The realization that his long search might soon be ended and the constant repetition of the name helped to calm his growing sense of uneasiness. For the continuous parade of men and the machines of war often seemed about to engulf him.

The bearded artilleryman had been wrong—traffic was moving in *both* directions, to and from the front, and the stream which Chamay followed soon became a horrible river of dazed and blood-soaked Frenchmen.

All the way he saw only one group of German prisoners. They were hardly more than a dozen sitting quietly enough on the embankment which bordered the road. There was no guard, and though the passing troops stared at them curiously they were otherwise ignored. For a long way there was only the clicking and clanking of equipment; a strange and sullen silence gripped the apprehensive troops slogging from reserve up to the line. It was not only the dank and dispiriting weather. Something Chamay could not understand had gone very wrong with the big push; he became increasingly certain that the angry, bitter, frightened faces he encountered by the thousands, the growing despair he thought he saw in every man's eyes, must foretell a catastrophe.

There were times when the press of wagons and trucks filled with wounded made it absolutely impossible for him to proceed faster than a walk. He received a special shock when he passed a company of Tirailleurs from a Moroccan division. One sharpshooter recognized him as an airman. He called out an insult to Chamay which was caught by the wounded in the truck just ahead. A chain reaction soon swept the columns on both sides of the road.

"Shoot the *costaud!*" The cry went up and down the lines. Some unseen soldier picked up a handful of mud and heaved it accurately to splatter against Chamay's cheek. "Running for home, of course!"

"That's where they keep the aviators! On bicycles!"

"We should have the Boche! We know they are not afraid to fly!"

"Where oh where have our flying men been?—lying in bed to deep a dry skin!"

Laughter. Howls of glee. Another plash of mud bouncing off his shoulder. Troops marching in the file nearest the center of the road often unslung their rifles and made prodding gestures toward Chamay with their bayonets. Some were grinning, others were not.

"Shoot the *costaud!*" The chant passed from column to column until even those men far ahead who could not possibly see Chamay joined in. "Shoot the *costaud!* All the airmen have gone home to mother!"

"The last is on his way!"

"Shoot the *costaud!*"

At first Chamay tried to smile. He quickly learned to keep his head and eyes down for many tried to spit in his face.

It helped to think of Kupper. He was one man—a battle, not a war. And for the first time since he had joined the service Chamay was uncertain of final victory. He had thought he understood the peculiar morale of the French poilu which so often found its greatest strength in hardship. But here along this road he feared for France. There was not the slightest sign of *élan* among the dejected troops, and the snatches of conversation he heard before all attention turned upon himself became a continual echoing of disasters:

". . . a hundred thousand men lost already and only a few meters gained."

". . . Nivelle is a fool like all Gros Legumes, and the French in particular."

". . . forty-eight tanks caught, an easy target when a bridge for crossing the trenches was not completed; their petrol tanks were set afire by machine-gun bullets and the crews roasted alive."

". . . counterattacks—the Boche were lobbing gas shells at random, there was gas everywhere and a man did not know if he dared breathe from one moment to the next."

". . . of the Two twenty-seventh Regiment of the line, all very experienced men, five hundred out of thirteen hundred were killed or missing."

". . . out of a battery of thirty-six seventy-fives supposed to lay down the barrage, sixteen were blown up by the Boche."

". . . our trench mortar shells were landing on concrete and the Boche were laughing—a hundred and twenty thousand men lost—a hundred and fifty thousand. Yes, a French airplane was seen. It was flying backwards."

The leaden sky brought an early night and with it a violently gusting wind carrying the perpetual burden of rain and snow. Cha-

165

may had been unable to find transport in Reims so he continued on the bicycle, alternately riding and walking as the weather and road permitted. He was grateful for the darkness when it finally cloaked the roads. No one spat at him.

He had not eaten since late morning. In an attempt to forget his ravenous hunger he concentrated on a note he intended to drop on the first German aerodrome he could find. He would address it to Oberleutnant Sebastian Kupper, Jasta 76—bold lettering in German. *"You murdered my friend over Verdun, 15th December 1916, 1000 hours. I will find you."*

Between Reims and the 322nd Escadrille's aerodrome he became lost four times in a maze of minor roads, so that it was nearly one in the morning before he arrived home. There was still a light burning in Jourdan's hut. Chamay went directly to it. His Excellency would be worried.

"Chamay!" The exclamation of surprise seemed to struggle upward through the folds of Jourdan's long neck. There was unashamed delight in his eyes and for the first time since he had joined the escadrille, Chamay saw his commander's face wrinkle in a full smile. He had been perched on a box engaged in his endless battle with the military telephone system. He slammed down the telephone immediately and extended his long arms to Chamay. For an instant Chamay thought he was going to be embraced, but His Excellency halted a meter away. "Welcome," he said fervently. "Welcome home!"

"Thank you."

"I was worried. I did not see you break away or go down."

Hesitantly Chamay described how his Le Rhone had failed. "I confess to the worst landing ever made. The Nieuport will never fly again."

"But you were not injured?"

"Not so much as a scratch."

"Then it was a very good landing." Again Jourdan attempted a laugh, a croaking unpracticed sound of a man who has not found cause to laugh for a long time.

Chamay had expected at least some doleful regrets for the loss of a valuable flying machine. Escadrille 322 was now an even poorer relation than before. There was not a spare airplane left, since the cripples had been robbed piece by piece to keep a mere seven flying.

166

"I presume I will be grounded for a time," Chamay said, in what he hoped was a properly remorseful tone. His Excellency's ever mournful mood had a way of reflecting itself in his men when they actually stood face to face with him. An interview with Jourdan called for the *masque tragique*.

Yet now, still smiling and emitting little clucks which presumably were signals of laughter, Jourdan was even bouncing as he paced. Chamay watched in amazement as his commander abandoned all reserve and executed a sort of dance.

"No, my dear Chamay! You will certainly *not* be grounded!" Jourdan clapped his hands together three times as if summoning a genie from the oil lamp on his desk. "That is," he continued, "you will not be grounded for more than two days, which should be the maximum time you will need to clean yourself up and make your way first to Paris and thence—" He paused, and for a moment his hound dog look disappeared.

"You will prepare yourself for earliest departure to Le Bourget, where you will pick up the escadrille's first Spad! Eight have been reserved for us. Serial numbers four sixty-five through four seventy-two. When we have our full quota this will be a quite different war."

Chapter Nine

———————— *April 1917*
Paris

CHAMAY RODE a fuel truck as far as Épernay, where he waited seven hours until he found a train bound all the way through to Paris. It was a composite train with a few freight cars, but the majority of the cars were loaded with wounded brought in from field stations all along the front. Many had been given only the most cursory treatment. On every hand Chamay heard the same woes he had heard on his journey of the night before. Things were going from bad to worse. The offensive was a disaster, there were far from enough medics and the advanced field stations were overwhelmed with thousands of wounded when they had only planned for hundreds. "If you can still move, *mon vieux,* get away from the field stations. If you can't move beg someone to move you if they have to strap you on a donkey and light a flare on its tail. Move, keep moving, get out of the way, *mon vieux,* before there's a full retreat or a mutiny or both. Always keep moving your head or your hands or wiggle your ears or something, or the tired medics will dump you in with the dead."

Chamay had found a place near the door of a freight car and established himself on an empty ammunition box which he surrendered almost at once to a poilu who said he had been thrown thirty meters by a shell blast. Although no wounds were visible he had suffered a terrible concussion. "Of the whole body, monsieur. I suppose every bone is broken." Chamay could not decide whether the man was really hurt or simply wanted to sit on the box.

The first two-thirds of the train was made up of passenger cars converted into mobile field stations to shelter the seriously wounded. The walking cases and an odd assortment of individual soldiers were jammed into the freight wagons. No one had bothered to examine Chamay's papers when he boarded the train and he soon began to wonder if his companions had been treated with the same casual indifference. They were apparently from every sort of duty and regiment. They seemed to have drifted in from all sectors of the front, assembled by a sort of miserable magnetism for one another, and somehow found this train bound for Paris. Most of their uniforms were spattered with blood in at least one area and the majority were bandaged in some way. Many wore dirty paper tags on their chests on which had been scribbled the details of their injuries and what had been done about them.

The majority of the men seemed stunned into silence. Yet there was another category of wounded in Chamay's car which aroused his suspicions more than his sympathies. Certainly they had managed a remarkable recovery or had never been much hurt in the first place. One artilleryman displayed a third finger which had been smashed by a breechblock. He bemoaned his fate, for in the future which of his remaining fingers should he use to excite the girls? No one in the wagon seemed to resent his being released from battle simply because of a smashed finger. Perhaps he just walked away. Who cared? Now, monsieur, it is *me* who matters! We are going away from the front and we are bound for Paris. That is quite enough.

The train made many stops all through the night and each time Chamay noticed that a few more passengers were acquired. There was a cook who had been scalded and even a few who made no pretense of having been wounded. If asked, they would cough and say they had been gassed. But they bore no tags on their chests and they often forgot to cough. Before the night had passed Chamay became convinced they were deserters.

The train reached the outskirts of Paris during the early morning and halted alongside a column of ambulances. The seriously wounded were taken from the passenger cars by sweating litter bearers and placed in the ambulances. The process was difficult because of a water-filled ditch between the train and the road which was of insignificant width if a man was unburdened, but much too wide for a single step by a man carrying the weight of a stretcher. Each wounded man had to be set down while the bearers straddled

170

the ditch, then picked up again so the bearers could swing him across the ditch, then set down a second time on the opposite side so the bearers could resume their normal positions. No one, including the officers in charge of the transfer, seemed in the least concerned about the clumsy and time-consuming arrangement.

If it were not so hard on the wounded, Chamay thought, the scene might at least merit some bitter laughter. There was no mind which could come unraveled quite like the military mind, he thought, and Mars himself could not solve its dark tangles, but what genius had conceived this ridiculous operation? As the agonizing procedure continued and the bearers wore regular paths between the train and their ambulances, the places they crossed the ditch became muddied and slippery on each side. Soon the bearers were obliged to approach the ditch with the utmost care and Chamay saw several slip to their knees in a desperate effort to avoid dumping their charges. Word spread up and down the line of men waiting by the train that the bearers were all foreigners—Serbs, Greeks, Russians, and even some Austrian prisoners. So, Chamay thought, the military jewel who had planned this rendezvous between train and ambulances must also have been a foreigner. "There—at kilometer nineteen— the distance between track and road is shortest. Incline to track bed is a small degree." Splendid! Except that the ditch was not big enough to be marked on a map and if anyone had bothered to make a preview of the site it must have been dry at the time.

Chamay paced unhappily back and forth along the track trying to allay his increasing frustration. The biggest push of the war was on and where was he? Waiting. Waiting while precious hours flew, waiting practically in sight of Paris, all in one piece, a healthy and angry soldier-pilot not only grounded but earthbound at a location where he could do absolutely nothing at all. He should be at Le Bourget this very afternoon learning all he could about the Spad. By tomorrow afternoon he should be swooping down on the escadrille and the next day perhaps in combat.

He increased the speed of his pacing, and to further divert his mind from the apparently endless chain of litters, tried to remember how differently he had viewed many things only two years previously. There was the day he had returned from the Congo with his father and gone directly to the recruiting office of the Service Aeronautique, which was in the Invalides. A service order then to Dijon and the *vestiaire* at the depot. A uniform, two pairs of shoes, socks, underwear, overcoat, tin cup, bowl and spoon. How silly. None of the items were used after the first week and the one franc a day pay of a soldier second class hardly paid for the tailor-made uniform which at least came near a fit. Then the departure for Pau as an *élève pilote*. Pau and Raymonde—a miracle having Raymonde for an instructor. Then the second miracle—meeting Denise on a sunlit afternoon. Pau, where the repair shops were as important as the low gray hangars, and Annamite labor troops were continuously employed picking up the pieces of crashed airplanes and junking them or hauling them away to the repair shops so another student could humiliate himself. Pau, where a man learned how *perte de vitesse* led to a *vrille*. Pau, where Raymonde made life a lark in spite of the severe routine, and his *equipe* of twelve was considered the most rambunctious and yet the most promising. Thanks to Raymonde, the swift progress from *La Mare de Grenouille,* so called because the usual student landings most closely resembled the escape of a frightened frog. Ah, it was a hell of a fine life then!

Suddenly he remembered the two Germans in the schoolhouse. Where had they been during that glorious summer? And exactly where and when had Paul Chamay been transformed into the kind of a man who would torment two such helpless men? God almighty, he thought, I am no better than a Boche! We are all lost.

He stopped to watch the transfer of the wounded. Less than a third of the ambulances had departed with their loads. Unless something drastic was done the parade was obviously going to take all day. He passed a group of infantrymen and heard them say the more seriously wounded were dying while they waited. Perhaps it was true. Chamay had noticed that several of the lumps transported from the cars to the side of the road now lay utterly still. It was starting to rain and no one troubled to move those litters though others were carried right past them.

Chamay resumed his pacing, but he could not avoid the spectacle between the track and the ditch. The endless stream of wounded oozed from the train like slow dripping blood from a great reptile.

He had seen enough. He was wearing his best uniform, dark blue tunic, Croix de Guerre with two palms now, his almost new kepi, and belt. He had been the focus of endless interest among his fellow occupants of the freight car—so few of them had ever seen an aviator, much less talked to one. Very well. Perhaps the same interest could now be used to some advantage.

He walked forward to the locomotive and after discussing the delay with the train crew asked to borrow their coal rake and a pry bar if they had one. After answering a barrage of questions about how high and fast an airplane flew and how many Boche he had killed, he doubled the number of his victories and the tools were handed down.

He walked back to his freight wagon dragging the rake and pry bar behind him. So far, he decided, a pretty uniform could be very useful. He devoutly hoped it would work as well among his fellow passengers for what he wanted now was muscle and a great deal of it.

He returned to his own freight car, halted for a moment, and stared thoughtfully at the wooden door which could be moved along heavy steel tracks. He inserted the rake handle underneath the track and tried to pry it away from the body of the car. In spite of his most strenuous efforts and a great show of grunting he only succeeded in slightly bending the rake handle. But many of his traveling companions had collected around him.

"What in the name of God are you trying to do, monsieur?"

"The sergeant is gone out of his wits."

"No. It is only *cafard*."

"You are shoving your way into trouble, Sergeant!"

"If you want to close the door just push it."

Chamay persisted until he had attracted more than a score of men. Some came drifting into the crowd all the way from the end of the train. Finally he turned to them. Did they want to wait all day with Paris just over the horizon? And what about the poor fellows who were waiting to be carted off the train? Who, even if he could only use one arm, would refuse to help those miserable bastards who were leaking so badly they must be nearly dry of blood?

He turned to attack the door again. Between efforts he would pause and outline his scheme, panting out the words in bunches. It was important that his audience be governed by emotion rather than sober consideration for they were men just escaped from great unpleasantness and the last thing they wanted to do on this gray, soggy morning was commit some military folly, petty or otherwise, which might adversely affect their immediate futures. There were just enough officers about to make a man cautious.

173

Chamay could not budge the door. "Lend me a hand for one moment," he asked a slight infantryman who had only a moment before asked if Chamay was suffering from shell shock. The man scratched at his beard in surprise and then halfheartedly pushed on the pry bar. He began to push harder when he heard a few favorable comments from the crowd. Soon another man joined on the bar and then two more picked up the coal rake and tried to insert it along the bottom edge of the door. More joined in until the full lengths of both the pry bar and coal rake were solidly covered with straining hands. Yet they could not move the track or the door a millimeter away from the body of the wagon.

Now more men pushed their way into the contest, until for lack of any better space they were pulling on the track and the door itself with their bare hands. They grunted and cursed the door and shouted encouragement to one another and exclaimed how much more force they could exert if they had two good hands and arms, or a better right leg, or a left leg without a chunk out of it, or if their wrist or their collarbone or their Achilles' tendon was not broken—how they would tear the door from its moorings!

Soon there were more than a hundred men gathered around the door and when one group of shovers and pullers fell away exhausted another group would immediately take their places. Every man on the train who could lift a little finger wanted a chance at the door although the new arrivals were far from sure why.

The door screeched and splintered where the pry bar and rake pressed against it, but it remained wedded to the wagon. Chamay was discouraged. An officer was coming along the track. He did not appear to be the type to join in an attack on the door. Someone said he was in command of the train.

At last a blacksmith from Picardy laid his great paw on Chamay's shoulder. There was only a bloody bandage where the tip of his nose had been and he was breathing noisily through his mouth. Put men inside the wagon he advised, as many as possible. Close the door. Command the men inside to push, which must spring the door sufficiently to insert both pry bar and rake on opposite sides. Then all heave suddenly and together. *Voila!*

A few moments after Chamay accepted his suggestion there was a great rending of wood and screeching of metal as the door exploded from the side of the wagon. Those men who had been pressing from inside fell after it in a heap. There was much laughing, the first triumphant laughter Chamay had heard in weeks. Now he did not care if his companions were deserters, genuine wounded or just malingerers.

Far more hands reached for the door than could find a place. Though only twenty men managed to squeeze themselves into the positions of honor so they might actually carry the door down to the ditch, Chamay estimated their escort at more than two hundred. Everyone was talking about the business of the doors and each man, it seemed, had further ideas.

The stretcher bearers were delighted with such a firm bridge and soon there were four bridges across the ditch torn from as many freight cars. The transfer of the wounded proceeded with ease and speed so that by noon the train was empty of litters and the last ambulance gone.

As the whistle warned of impending departure the train commander came to Chamay. He was an elderly, bland-faced captain. Chamay saluted although he had almost forgotten how.

The captain spoke solemnly. "I suppose you are aware the destruction of government property in time of war carries the most severe penalties?"

"I am."

"If the doors are left where they are then proof of their destruction would be most difficult, if not impossible."

The officer turned away, his bland face unchanged.

All the way to Paris the men who remained on the train were strangely thoughtful. It was as if they suddenly realized that all Gros Legumes were so far removed from details they could no longer recognize reality. It was as if a miraculous shell had burst gently among them, filling the stinking car with a fragrant smoke and peppering their minds with shrapnel clarities, so that for the first time since they marched off to war they knew it was only the little man on the spot who brought triumph or despair to any situation. And in the explosion of realities, at last they esteemed themselves as little men. Already in their minds the doors had taken on a golden hue, and they knew they would remember them forever. The doors—because of a few scraps of splintered wood they had been able to stare directly into the face of reason. Which was a great deal more than the Gros Legumes dared do.

The train snorted into the Gare de l'Est an hour later. Chamay found the station suffocated with troops and civilians. How we all smell, he thought. A wet uniform with a secretly frightened man inside of it exuded a special odor not to be duplicated by any other garment.

He made his way through the press of bodies, carts and enormous ramparts of sandbags in search of a train which would take him back in exactly the same direction he had come—to Le Bourget.

He moved unhurriedly, not minding when the crowd became so thick he could not move at all. The troops were of no interest to him now, but the civilians seemed like people from another planet and he was fascinated with their scraps of conversation.

"In the past fortnight I have been given a bottle of whiskey, two vegetable marrows, half a kilo of sugar and six logs of wood . . ."

"The price of wool is outrageous!"

"Twenty francs for a partridge and I had to wait an hour for a table . . ."

"*C'est la guerre!*"

"A tiny cauliflower cost me two francs!"

"I was going to make his muffler with a Tunisian stitch, then I thought it would be easier using the daisy . . ."

"*C'est la guerre. . . .*"

For a moment Chamay was completely surrounded by the family of an officer whose leave had been canceled. His three small children wore puttees like their father's and their hat bands had apparently been chosen to honor those places he had already fought—Verdun, Marne, Ypres. The children were weeping soundlessly.

The gate leading to the Le Bourget train proved to be the least crowded in the station. A woman had replaced the usual male functionary. She told Chamay there would not be a train for three hours.

"You are positive, madame? I dare not miss it."

"Nothing is positive these days, m'sieu. Only last week we had a train from Brest which was two *days* late."

The woman glanced at the stars and wings on Chamay's collar and his Croix de Guerre. "If you will be here not later than thirty minutes past four I promise the train will not go without you."

Three hours! Say less ten minutes for reserve!

Chamay forgot his weariness and charged through the milling crowds until he came out into the boulevard de Strasbourg. He was

176

so preoccupied with subtracting minutes from hours and how he would ration his time he was nearly run down by a taxi and almost immediately afterward by a horse-drawn dray with a driver who obviously thought he was in the artillery. The traffic and noise, the multitudes of men and women in civilian clothing, staggered him. It seemed incredible that only a few hours before he had watched the unloading of so many Frenchmen who would never again contribute their bit to traffic. And only yesterday he had been flying for his life. Yet here all was big-city confusion and the main reminder of war's presence was the generous sprinkling of uniforms on a civilian field of apparently universal black.

Or almost so. Chamay was immediately challenged by a pair of tarts who obviously mourned for no one. They were frowsy and reeked of brandy, so he was not tempted to change his sudden resolve. He would try to see Denise's sister, Hélène. She must have some later news. Denise's last letter had been strangely noncommittal about everything.

Hélène's address was engraved on his mind. Number eleven, rue de Rennes. There he had addressed his letters to Denise.

. . . because this has been our first decent day, Babarin has been grinning all over the place and clucking around my Nieuport like the mother hen he is. Even His Excellency tried to smile . . .

. . . I got one Boche today. He crashed in a wood near the old château at Fère-en-Tardenois. Most unusual—they don't come so far over to our side these days . . .

He started walking briskly along the boulevard de Strasbourg. The rain was light and it amused him to see how carefully the civilians protected themselves with umbrellas. After several collisions he decided it was safer to walk in the street. If he must be killed by traffic that was one thing, or shot down by a Boche quite another, but if Jourdan learned one of his pilots had been blinded out of the war by a civilian umbrella he might very well borrow a bayonet and fall on it.

In spite of the air of prosperity there appeared to be an undertone of gravity, a general sense of near explosion marking the faces of most civilians. He wondered if word of Nivelle's failure had already leaked through the official communiqués. Perhaps that was why the more seriously wounded had been unloaded outside Paris.

He passed a cinema. People were waiting in line to enter. A long line. He passed a tea room and a large restaurant. Both were overflowing with people. At the same time he noticed piles of rubbish along the street gutters. Thousands of people could amuse themselves in every way, but there were apparently not enough hands to clean up the streets. He passed another cinema queue and then, at the intersection with the rue de Turbigo, saw a crowd gathered around a speaker. Whatever the point of his argument, it seemed inextricably mixed up with accusations against President Wilson of the United States and the new restrictions on restaurant menus. Chamay paused long enough to hear the speaker say something about the government's threat to close the confectionery shops, then he switched immediately to a description of how the Germans were solving their glycerine shortage by boiling down fat from corpses of their own dead soldiers. Didn't the fool know the word *Kadaver* in German applied only to animals, or didn't he want to know?

He walked on, now quickening his pace.

What can I do, precious Denise, to deserve your affection? I have been taught to kill and that is really all I know except some education in the classics (of no use whatever) and a passable smattering of five languages including Arabic, which is also of no use whatsoever unless I can find work guiding tourists to the pyramids.

He came upon a stone parapet which was plastered with a huge advertisement for a revue at the Fémina. He stopped to study the provocative display. If a man had time!

Why hadn't Denise written? It had been more than three weeks. More! Nearly a month had passed since he had sent off pages and pages.

. . . what do we have? The usual sordid affair between a married woman and a man who is free? I hope not. I believe not. Why should romance wilt the instant there is an exchange of vows? Are we so hypocritical that we can believe forever afterward a healthy man or a healthy woman will *never* stray (which can be accomplished almost as vividly in the mind as in the flesh, but that sort of straying is permitted). Forgive my naïveté. If I should have very bad luck and be killed I will have plenty of time to repent and say, "What a sinner I was to have so enjoyed that lovely body." And if I live to be ninety I will have still more time . . .

All mail to the troops in Champagne had been held up for two weeks now without explanation. Yet before, when the mail was still coming through regularly, there should have been at least one or two letters from Denise.

He walked on, quickening his pace, looking back often for an unoccupied taxi.

Brave, fine Paris! Who would want to return from the front and find Paris wallowing in defeat and gloom?

Heedless of those who stared at him he increased his pace until he was half running.

Hélène was so much like Denise—the same full laugh, an expression of all the joys of living. It was too much to hope Denise might be staying with her. One chance in a thousand—but then this was not exactly a luckless day. What good chance being sent for the escadrille's first Spad and then having three loose hours in Paris!

He walked and half ran all the way to the place de Chatelet before a taxi pulled up beside him. It was already occupied by an elderly couple, who explained they had sent three sons to the front and if a soldier walked in the street instead of strolling along the sidewalk then he must be in a great press to get somewhere and it would be their pleasure to see that he did.

"But I am going all the way to the boulevard Raspail where it meets with the rue de Rennes!"

"Come—we live in Montparnasse. So much the better!"

Chamay eased himself onto the small flap seat which faced his hosts. They were Parisians. The man had been in the Colonial Office and immediately recognized Chamay's name. He said he had once enjoyed a luncheon with Chamay's father in Djibouti.

"That was another world," the man said, shading his eyes as if the memory of Somaliland brought sun to the dark afternoon. "France was an empire and the tricolor was regarded with envy and admiration and fear from Senegal to the Cameroons, to Rabat, to Mangareva, Caledonia, Cayenne. I've been in them all and I will never see them again because we are going to require a much smaller colonial department when this present adventure is done."

179

Chamay was troubled to hear the war labeled an adventure by so intelligent a man. But he kept his silence, as he believed his father would have recommended.

When they passed over the Pont au Change his host pointed his cane at the line of fishermen and adviser-assistants. "See there, Sergeant, the voluntary mobilization of our national energies. I suppose there are twenty-five to thirty men along this bridge—idling while France bleeds to death. Interesting, is it not? And disgusting. Wait until you go to the cafés and see Paris in all her glorious gluttony."

The woman placed her gloved hand on her husband's. She looked at Chamay sympathetically. "Forgive us. It is difficult not to be bitter. We are so alone now. Our three sons are never coming home."

Chamay's host also seemed anxious to change the atmosphere he had created. He managed to chuckle. "But you, Sergeant, are bound on an extraordinary mission. I can be sure of it simply by looking into your eyes. It is not a military mission."

Chamay smiled. "Thanks to you, I now have more than two hours."

They dropped him by the kiosk where the rue de Rennes sliced across the boulevard Raspail. They wished him every success.

How many times had he written this address on envelopes!

What is there to do in Dijon that is so distracting, or did the postman break his leg, or did you break your arm? Have you collected the volumes waiting for you at Hélène's? Babarin asked if I was writing a book. I told him yes—*The History of Love-Making from the Cro-Magnon Times until Now* . . .

The concierge proved to be a dark woman with a mustache which Chamay judged the feminine equivalent of Babarin's.

"But Ma'moiselle Hélène has moved to a more elegant place. She and her sister are so kind—"

"The mail? Did you forward it to them?"

"Of course, monsieur. Always. I know how important mail is. You need not tell me. I lost my husband in nineteen fifteen and never knew the old goat was dead until a month later. One cannot rely on the post these days, monsieur. It is like everything else in poor France."

Precious minutes passed while Chamay became the target of a monologue. The concierge had some very firm ideas about what

180

should be done with the Boche *and* the greedy, foul-smelling, fornicating men of Paris who stood in the pissoirs all day long so they wouldn't have to work or go to war.

"One fourteen rue de la Boetie."

Chamay lost another five minutes while Madame Mustachio, as he now thought of her, explained how to find the street. It was to be found not far from the Panthéon. "Follow the rue de Vaugirard to the Théâtre Odéon . . . if you are solicited by women be strong. They are all horribly diseased. Then right along the rue de Medicis—"

The carriage entrance was shut off from the street by tall heavy doors. A small portal door was cut in one side. Chamay opened it and stepped into a cobbled courtyard. Two flanking buildings formed the sides and at the end stood a small baroque house which appeared to be an entity in itself. Chamay smiled. Hélène must have acquired a wealthy friend.

There was her name on the heavy dark green door. Chamay pulled the bell cord and heard a melodic tinkle. He took off his kepi, smacked the rain water off the top and replaced it. He heard footsteps beyond the door and tried to reassure himself that his unscheduled arrival would be a welcome surprise.

The door opened slightly and in the gloom behind it Chamay saw part of a face. He had forgotten how Hélène's eyes were so like Denise's.

The face was suddenly withdrawn.

"Hélène?" What kind of a game was she playing? The door was slowly closing. He stopped it with his foot. "Hélène! It's me. Paul."

He pushed the door open enough to enter. Laughing, he reached around the door for Hélène. He caught her arm and pulled her into the light. And he shouted his pleasure.

"*Denise! What luck!*" He closed her in his arms. "You rascal. Trying to hide from the man who has been starving for you." He kissed her eyes, her mouth and her neck. He lifted her until her feet barely touched the floor, then slowly walked her backward toward an archway framing the salon. "I am drowning in my own luck. Quick! Which way to the nearest bedroom? We must not waste one minute of this glorious, magnificent, God-given rainy afternoon!"

Suddenly he realized she had not responded in any way. He set her down just beneath the arch. "What is this?" He held her a little

181

away from him and tried to read her eyes. "You haven't even said welcome, or why haven't they made me a general, or—"

"Paul. We are not alone."

Her voice was strangely flat. He looked beyond her questioningly and saw a large salon. The dull afternoon light filtered through an arched window and revealed a scattering of furnishings in gilt and brocade. On both sides of the window paneled mirrors extended from floor to ceiling.

He whistled softly. "This is quite a place. But I hope Hélène hasn't been changed by it. She'll understand if we—"

"Hélène is not here."

He had been looking beyond Denise. Now, reflected in the mirror, he noticed a certain chair faced to the window. A uniform tunic was draped over the back of the chair, the arms hanging limp—the four horizontal gold bars of a major, the grenade collar device of the infantry. There were no gold combat chevrons—certainly the tunic of a staff officer. Now he noticed a table just inside the entrance to the salon. It was partially obscured by the tall door. Still holding Denise, he leaned slightly forward and saw a kepi with four gold stripes encircling it. There was a swagger stick beside the kepi and a pair of chamois gloves.

"I see what you mean," he said. "That is, I think I do. It *was* really too much to ask of a single afternoon." When he tried to meet her eyes she averted them. "A friend of Hélène's?"

"No. It was impossible to see you. I was lonely. I didn't want to write you, or couldn't make myself write—I can't remember which. It doesn't matter now. I'm afraid I'm not a very nice person."

He released her slowly, then stood back to look at her.

"Well—well. In the escadrille there are a thousand stories about this sort of thing. It's like being wounded—it's always happening to the other man." He paused, wondering at his lack of anger. It was as if Denise was a stranger and had always been.

"Forgive me, Paul? I meant no harm."

"Oh, you've done a great deal of good. You taught me to love, and now you've taught me to be wary. Now I can concentrate on something more important than us. Thank you for the rich experience. Adieu, Denise."

The door facing on the courtyard was still open. He turned and walked toward it, striving to keep his manner casual. He put on his

182

kepi and stepped into the rain. Looking back into the hallway he saw that Denise had not moved. She stood perfectly still with her hands clasped in front of her. She was crying.

"Stop that nonsense. I want to remember the girl who always laughed."

He closed the door and walked quickly across the courtyard toward the street entrance. He started to look back, then determined not to slow his pace. He must think about anything but Denise. He must lose himself—somehow.

Think about Kupper.

Chapter Ten

May 1917
During a balmy afternoon—

MANY OF THE CHANGES in Kupper's patrol habits were a result of a dramatic improvement in the weather. It had suddenly become much warmer aloft. Except on the early morning patrols, he now wore only a light leather jacket over his uniform tunic and there had been several afternoons when he would have dispensed with the jacket had it not been for the Mercedes' nasty habit of spewing oil vapor into the slip stream. It seemed that spring had at last come to the skies above Champagne, and there had been days when Kupper longed to throw back his head, close his eyes, suck in the soft, balmy air and allow the euphoria to lull him into total security. But it was not to be. Though it appeared that the French attack had been a disaster for their infantry, the enemy airmen had been more than ever anxious to fight. They so recklessly pressed the attacks it was difficult to meet them with anything but the same abandon. Thus Kupper hardly dared think of either the past or future—it was now, this moment, and if it could be survived then another moment might reasonably be expected to follow.

Kupper's eyes were painfully wind burned because he now believed in pulling down his goggles only when actually closing for a fight. During the hunt, which was by far the greater proportion of the time he spent aloft, goggles could be a dangerous handicap. There was just enough metallic rim around the glass to create an area of blindness. Constant turning of the head should presumably diminish the handicap, but the specks of distant airplanes were first recognized in a split-second glance, and if at that instant the area

185

was blocked off, then the petty omission could compound itself and lead straight to a trap. Kupper left the choice of goggles during the hunt to his individual pilots. Steilig, he noticed, wore his up also, but then Steilig was tremendously aggressive and would try anything to increase his victory score. Hochstetter wore his down over his eyes all the time, but then Hochstetter didn't give a damn about victories and pretended not to care about dying. Zimmerman rarely pushed up his goggles. Meyer, who was relatively new to the Jasta and remarkably full of fun, did exactly what his leader did. But not for the same reason, Kupper thought. I do not keep my goggles up because I am so extremely anxious to find an enemy aircraft I can attack—I keep them up because I am afraid one of them will get the jump on me. And every day I am a little more afraid.

Strangely enough the warmer weather had brought on an epidemic of gun-jamming. The splendid record of the Spandaus made them a most reliable air weapon, yet near the end of April they started to behave like temperamental popguns.

Kupper had conferred with the Jasta 76 armorers and with Hildebrandt, his technical officer. They were unable to find the trouble. He had appealed to air staff armament experts for further technical advice and found them only mildly concerned. They were not, after all, he remembered, doing the shooting or being shot at and had no conception how maddening it could be to set up a target and discover oneself sitting behind dead guns. To Kupper's dismay the experts blamed faulty ammunition, which was the easiest solution since one bullet looked exactly like the next and the faulty ones only announced their presence at the least convenient times.

In his disgust Kupper turned his command over to Steilig for one day and set off on a visit to four other Jastas in the vicinity. He was welcomed with honor everywhere, congratulated on his twenty-three victories, and queried at length on the attack by the British triplanes. His day had been fruitful, for he learned that Jasta 82 was experiencing similar gun troubles. Investigation revealed they were lubricating their guns with an identical consignment of winter grease. Apparently it could not sustain its proper lubrication viscosity in warmer temperatures and in both Jastas the jamming seemed to occur after considerable firing. Kupper and the commander of Jasta 82 arranged to borrow grease from the other Jastas and waited for results. At once the occurrence of jamming fell off, but there was still too much of it in Kupper's opinion, and it was all the more dangerous because of the unpredictability. Who knows better than I, he thought, how naked a man can feel without his guns.

As if to balance the gun trouble, spring had brought an important technical innovation of which Kupper approved. A canister of oxygen was now secured behind the seat in each Albatros. A rubber tube led from the canister to a metal clip on the left side of the cockpit. There was a wooden tip at the end of the tube which was held in the pilot's teeth like the stem of a Turkish water pipe. Along with his regular breathing the pilot could suck at the stem and the results were most promising. Although Hochstetter said it made him feel guilty, as if he had reverted to nursing, and others complained of sore lips, stomach gas and vertigo, the fact remained that Jagdstaffel pilots were now able to keep their wits while hunting and fighting higher than five thousand meters. Kupper could not understand why the enemy continued to fly without oxygen.

There were other changes. Since the disastrous attack on Jasta 76 by the English triplanes, which Intelligence had eventually advised Kupper were Sopwiths of a Royal Naval Squadron, Kupper's weight had dropped alarmingly. To those who remarked on his gaunt appearance he would smile and say it was due to simple disgrace. What other Jasta of the entire Luftstreitkraft had taken punishment from the English *Navy!* Kupper alone knew that his uniform drooped about his frame because he had flown too hard and long during the first days of the French offensive and the effect had been cumulative. He had been badly frightened several times both for himself and others of the Jasta and now the unsteadiness about his hands had become impossible to conceal. He could not eat a full meal in spite of his efforts and he rarely managed an hour of full sleep. On the ground any sudden noise startled him. In the air it was worse. After many warnings to himself he found that he could remain efficient and controlled in actual combat, but now he had suddenly become terrified of flak. During all of his previous combat flying he had sneered at it. All one must do, he had told every new arrival at Jasta 76, is fly straight into a flak burst. The hole in the sky which is there will not be hit again. Or, if one wished to play games, or if it was necessary to remain in a heavy flak area, then hold course during the first bursts. Show no evasive action. Almost invariably the gunners below would change range a hundred meters

187

and the poison flowers would start blossoming either above or below one's aircraft. If you then start "jinking" all over the sky, the gunners would be certain they have the range. One could have a very satisfying laugh watching the pyrotechnic display while remembering it is costing the enemy one hundred francs a shot. Kupper no longer took flak so casually.

Recently Jasta 76 had been charged with eliminating four French observation balloons. The ground area around them bristled with flak batteries. Hoping to redeem the Jasta reputation, Kupper had personally led the attacks and pressed them so successfully only one balloon escaped. But the effort had done something to Kupper no orthodox fight had been able to do. He was convinced his ultimate fate lay in a balloon attack—somewhere along the Western Front, some day.

Spring had brought changes even in the fighting methods of the Jagdstaffel. Now the unwieldy formation of a full Jasta was split into elements of three or six airplanes, called *Kettes*. Kupper considered it a great improvement. More area could be covered even if the Kettes remained in sight of each other for mutual support. And the smaller elements could be much more versatile.

On this sparkling afternoon Kupper led a Kette of five Albatroses with his old reliables just off his wing tips—Hochstetter, Steilig, Zimmerman, and Just, stair-stepped upward in a V. It had been almost like a holiday flight thus far without any contact with the enemy. Three of the new French Spads had been spotted far below. While Kupper had been trying to decide if he should lead the Kette down on them they had disappeared behind a candy floss cloud and he could not spot them again. So much for hesitation, he thought. Or was it that I do not *want* to see them again. The new French Spads were to be approached with great respect. An Albatros could outclimb it, but was much slower in level flight. And a Spad was put together with such strength it could dive as the pilot pleased. It would not come apart unless someone shot it to pieces. Kupper had been vastly relieved when the Spads vanished. He had tried to justify his lack of initiative by assuring himself there would be easier game later in the patrol and the Kettes should conserve their ammunition. But nothing had appeared.

Far below, spread out like a soiled carpet beneath the clouds, splotches of the front were visible. It was strangely quiet, more so than it had been for days, and Kupper was grateful. Perhaps the French had finally had enough. The poor sheep! They had not won anything worthwhile for their blood. A few meters of mud. During the investigation of the Royal Navy attack on Jasta 76 Kupper had talked with a Leutnant Buchman whose advance observation post had been captured by the French but held for only two days. In the haste of leaving his threatened post Buchman had been involved in a motorcycle accident and suffered a nasty cut across his forehead. But he was a jaunty fellow and had told Kupper the war was as good as over. The French had completely lost their drive and their troops were mutinying. Good enough!

When he saw Fismes through a hole in the clouds, Kupper banked steeply and set his formation on a course back to the north. There was nothing here this afternoon and it was as well to borrow a hint from the infantry and conserve one's energies when the chance came. He started a gradual descent from five thousand meters. At the end of it they should be over the aerodrome.

Though his eyes never ceased their constant searching of the sky, Kupper's thoughts now turned from the abandoned hunt to matters of less intensity. Jasta 76, he thought, could again afford to hold its head high, for the last week's activity report made solid reading in spite of only two days' fine weather. "Changes in personnel: Lt. Schröder returned to flight duty from base hospital. Six flying days, ninety-five flights, seventy-eight flying hours. Flights: April 27th. Lt. Steilig successful. 1730 hours, near Bruyeres, Nieuport one-seater. Occupant Sgt. Dutil killed. Lt. Hochstetter successful. 0700 hours, between La Fère and Tergnier, this side, F.E. two-seater. Occupants Lts. Moore and McKay both wounded. 11th victory."

He had signed his name to the report with a flourish and then noticed that for the space of time required for the gesture his shaking hand had remained quite steady. Eleven victories for the week. Huzzah!

Laon was on the left horizon now. They were nearly home. There, not five minutes ahead, the aerodrome waited like a sleepy village. Home! Suddenly Kupper remembered two paintings on the wall of his room in Mainz. They had hung side by side all through his boyhood and he supposed they were still there. "Autumn on the Neckar" and "Winter on the Main." *That* was home, not a Frenchman's field and a corrugated iron shack. One could not hang paintings on a hedge-row—

Keep your head turning, you fool, or you will never see home again! More men had been shot down on their final approach to their home base than in any other single situation. Once the aerodrome was in sight the tendency was to sigh gratefully and relax. Just then some ambitious Frenchman or a wandering Englishman down from the north might pounce. You may stop turning your head when the propeller is still and Pilger is holding the ladder so you can step to the ground.

The Kette passed over Liesse at two thousand meters. Kupper led them into a steeper descent to slip beneath an oncoming layer of cloud. As he did so he leaned to his left for a better look at an enormous flock of birds flittering along from south to north. They would migrate, he thought, war or no war. Starlings? They were disappearing beneath his lower wing so he kicked a little right rudder to swing the wing around and uncover the birds. Almost instantly his muscles froze. In the next instant he was looking wildly about the sky. Machine-gun fire. Where?

He looked to the right and left of his tail. There was Steilig. There was Hochstetter. The idiots! Hadn't they heard it?

Kupper looked over the side again. Perhaps the unmistakable sound had come from below. There it was again. A quick burst.

No! It was somewhere behind them.

He hauled the Albatros around in a vertical bank. The Kette followed him, ragged in their surprise. When he straightened out again he glanced at Steilig and Hochstetter. Now their faces were puzzled. Steilig shrugged his shoulders and shook his head.

Kupper was about to reach for the charging bolts of his Spandaus when he decided to look down once more.

As he leaned toward the cockpit rim he again heard machine-gun fire. But it was more distant this time. He shifted his weight to look down from the right side and the firing stopped. Again to the left and the firing resumed. To the left—to the right? This was—? He reached around to the back of his neck and suddenly knew he had become the jumpiest man in the Luftstreitkraft. To protect his neck he still wore a white silk scarf. Now without the weight of a heavy winter coat to bear down on it one end of the scarf had worked itself free. When he skidded slightly or leaned into the slip stream, the end snapped against his leather helmet. It sounded exactly like a machine gun. Even the cadence was right. Exactly right—to a jumpy man, he thought. He banked around for the aerodrome again.

On the ground Steilig came to him and asked, "What kind of fancy maneuvers were those?" His cold eyes were always humorless and now, Kupper thought, they would have looked better in a fish.

"Fancy?"

"That last fandango. The carousel we couldn't get off when I thought we were practically home. You turned so quickly I almost didn't get out of your way."

"I—I just wanted to make sure everyone is on the alert until the very last."

"Is that so?"

He *knows,* Kupper thought. The flat sarcasm in Steilig's voice and the manner in which he sauntered away was indication enough. A good man to have on your side in a fight but don't ask his iron neck to bend in understanding or sympathy. He was the perfect fighter pilot—always cold, always controlled. Yet Kupper doubted that even the disciplined Steilig could conceal his scorn if he knew his commander had gone into a blue funk because of a flapping scarf.

He walked slowly toward his hut, Pilger a few paces behind. He is like a great dog sniffing at my heels, Kupper thought. He will not leave me alone. He was shocked to find himself wishing it had been Pilger instead of Louie stopping an English bullet. How grotesque his desires had become! He would make amends to his decaying morality and to Pilger by using the familiar *du* next time he spoke to him.

"Congratulations, Herr Leutnant," Pilger said as they approached the line of huts. *Herr* Leutnant? It was the first time in days Pilger had employed the formal military address. Kupper was at once suspicious. Was this weird man now reading his thoughts and, disapproving, stuffing them back in his mind?

"Congratulations for what?"

"You have been awarded the *Johanniter Orden.*"

Kupper barely hesitated. He did not look back. "How do you know this, Pilger?"

"Feldwebel Groos told me. The official orders will not be published until tomorrow."

"Then how did Feldwebel Groos learn about it?"

"Groos has many ways of doing many things."

"You might ask him what the *Johanniter Orden* is." And while you're about it, Kupper thought, you might also ask the omniscient Groos whatever happened to my *Pour le mérite,* which according to my score should long ago have been dangling from my throat.

As he entered the hut a great weariness overcame him. He wanted only to lie down on his cot and rest until morning. And most of all he wanted now to be alone.

His energies were quickly revived when he saw two letters on the table. Both were addressed in Maria's hand. Pilger waited in the doorway as he reached for them.

Kupper picked up the letters and held them close to his chest. Now. He must steady his quivering hands. He must fight back this welling of wild anger against the nearest human being. He heard his thoughts yell at Pilger—stay away from me! Go! Leave me!

He stood irresolutely. His breathing, in spite of his efforts to control it, had become a series of quick short gasps. He realized very suddenly that he was choking. He raised one hand to the collar of his tunic and his fingers took forever to find the clips and tear it open. And Pilger was watching, standing there in the doorway without movement or sound, blocking the air, blocking the light, a great hideous blockade of flesh and hair and bone, standing there and saying without sound: You must not for one instant forget me, you cannot ignore me, I am with you during every activity of your present life and I will be with you when you are dead.

Kupper could no longer control his fury. He whirled on Pilger and screamed at him. "Get out of here you wretched swine! Go away and root in the mud! You will not come near me until I call for you again or I'll have you shot. *Raus!*"

The door closed and Pilger vanished. Kupper raised his hands to his eyes, smashing the letters against his cheeks. His face was slippery with sweat. And *tears,* he thought. My God, I am weeping!

He lowered his head and watched his trembling body as if he were viewing it from a distance. What is happening to me? Where is my strength? "O God," he murmured, "O God, O God, O God, help me . . ."

He sank into the wooden chair and, still clutching the letters, buried his face in his arms.

192

After a time his body quieted. Then the exhaustion of his spirit allowed him to sleep.

Somewhere a mouth organ squawled "Spin, Spin, My Little Daughter." The player paused frequently and uncertainly, then switched to "Stolzenfels," which he rendered expertly. That would be Hochstetter in the next hut and his door must be open to bring the sound so clearly. Kupper raised his head and saw that it was dark. He rose stiffly and went to the window. He pulled the canvas curtain across it, then returned to his table and lit a candle. He took up the two letters from Maria and decided to open the thicker envelope first. He sat down and carefully smoothed the pages before he began to read.

. . . if there was a natural German tendency toward fat, all that is changing now. I can see it every day when I pass through the streets. People are gaunt and bony and I can see that many are actually hungry. We in the family are of course quite well for the simple reason that we have money. But riches will not buy cheese these days. Holland is sending her cheese to England and the Swiss price is too high for the average person. So the government has proclaimed no cheese for anyone—the silly things hope to avoid a possible cheese riot if the poor should see the wealthy munching on Bockstein.

I hear more and more disparaging remarks about the Emperor. No one respects him and whatever goes wrong with Germany becomes his fault. Truly I think the man really is a badly advised pinhead, but it is hardly his fault if a tram breaks down, or the porter at the Adlon sprains his back, or the heating fails at the Esplanade.

I forgot to tell you last time that my Uncle Maximilian came up from Strassburg for an Easter visit. He is getting on, although he is still in the Landwehr and he told us about the way people in all the villages have taken to Nailing. They erect a wooden statue of some famous person like Hindenburg in the square, and they sell people nails of different sorts to drive into the image. The money goes for the war effort and I suppose it is a very good idea.

Everyone here has had terrible colds, but now with the warmer weather perhaps at last we may stop sneezing long enough to cure the epidemic of burst water pipes—that is, if there were any plumbers left to play the doctor. With no men to clean the streets and the snow melted away, the city is filthy now. There are almost no taxis to be seen and you are lucky to find an ancient droshky if you must travel any distance. It's a changed Berlin, as you will see next leave. And when will that be, may I ask? Are you the only soldier in the German army who *never* gets leave? I read the story about you in *Der Krieg* and the whole family was marvelously proud that you had even passed through our doorway. But my sole desire in life right now is to see you come through that doorway again. Ten years from now I do not wish to be mooning over a faded picture from *Der Krieg*—I want to be mooning over you.

I cannot decide which is the more fateful for Germany, the revolution in Russia, which must be ghastly if the amount of snow fallen in the Tiergarten this spring is any indication of the Russian weather, or the entry of the Americans into the war. Dr. Berthold from Dresden was our guest last evening and he said the U-boats would stop the Americans and it was of little consequence anyway because the Americans were an undisciplined people who could not be organized into an efficient fighting force. What do you think?

And what of Pilger? Is he still your shadow? I do hope the poor man is looking after you properly. I wonder what he would have thought if he could have seen the Kaiserin openly insulted by workers at one of the big factories here. The labor leader took a decoration she had presented him and hung it around his dog's neck!

I am still laughing over your description of yourself as a clown. Let me tell you there are other clowns to be seen here in Berlin, one of them being me. We now have to present a *Bezugschein,* which is a kind of voucher, before we can buy a scrap of clothing and before we are awarded the *Schein* we must list everything we possess. Since God has given people like us so much, the listing would take longer than the ersatz clothing would wear. So we patch here and mend there and stay in what we have.

I must close now because I have promised to take Mamma for a stroll in the Tiergarten and it is such a nice day we should go before the heavens frown again. I intend to prolong our walk as far as the post office so this word will speed to you. Tomorrow I shall have the entire afternoon to myself and intend to spend it declaring my love for you.

Believe me, my dear sweet Sebastian, you are ever in my thoughts. May God protect you.

Kupper folded the letter and placed it back in the envelope. He took up the second letter and placed it squarely before him. And for a time he sat staring at the candle as if mesmerized. Maria was there before him, a tiny full-skirted figurine just beside the candle. Now he could hear Hochstetter's mouth organ again. He was back at "Spin, Spin, My Little Daughter," and Kupper wished he would at least try something else, because it was obvious he had developed some insurmountable mental hex which made it impossible for him to stay on key. Maria—spin to his music in spite of his mistakes. Spin for me so daintily I will be incapable of any hard thoughts until tomorrow.

Kupper took his time opening the second envelope. When he had read it, he would reread them both again—and then what else remained for this additional day of life? A walk up to the mess for a glass of brandy and bit of supper. A chess game with Schröder, perhaps. A stroll down to the message center to see if anything special had come through, and then back here. The nights lasted forever, yet so far they were at least peaceful. Farther north in Richthofen country the English were keeping them awake with night bombing on Jasta aerodromes.

He had just steadied his hand enough to pull the letter from the envelope when he heard a sharp rapping on the door.

"Pilger! I warned you!"

"It's me, Sebastian. Steilig."

Kupper pushed the letter back in the envelope and went quickly to the door. He opened it and Steilig, in his stiff mechanical way, entered reluctantly and stopped just inside the door. Kupper saw that he was extremely uncomfortable. Now, he was certain, Steilig's Prussian mind was sniffing the scent of weakness. For only on rare occasions did the Jasta officers come to Kupper's hut. In the past it had been with minor personal requests—a few days' leave to visit a sick parent (not to mention the sweet young thing who just happened to live in the same neighborhood), a suggestion for a new fighting

195

tactic which the creator was too shy to present openly in the mess, the transfer of an enlisted man who was annoying or the promotion of one who was deserving, or advice on a proxy marriage.

They come because in their eyes I am old enough to be their father, Kupper thought ruefully.

Not Steilig. He was ever his own man in the air and on the ground. That sculptured jaw, hard mouth and even harder eyes announced his independence at a glance. Steilig now had seventeen victories, every one of them over a tough opponent. He was the only pilot in the Jasta who had shot down a Spad flown by one of the elite Stork Escadrille. If Kupper were put out of action he was expected to assume command. Steilig had everything a professional officer needed, Kupper had long ago decided—except humor, if indeed that was a requisite. He had never seen him smile.

"Welcome to the palace," Kupper said. He offered Steilig a cigar although he knew he would decline. Steilig neither smoked nor drank. He killed.

"I will only be a minute," Steilig began. "Supper should be ready in the mess . . ." He hesitated, and in Steilig it seemed utterly incongruous. "I want to speak with you—about yourself."

"Certainly we should be able to find a more interesting subject." Kupper tried to see behind his guest's cold eyes. How cold Steilig's eyes must appear when viewed from the wrong end of a machine gun!

"Are you feeling all right, Sebastian?"

"Quite."

"Then why are you so nervous? I am not the only one who is worried about you. The others are beginning to notice how your hands shake."

"My friend, you are blunt enough."

"There is no other way to be. Why don't you take a leave?"

"Just like that? I simply ring up the Geschwader Kommandeur and say I am tired of playing soldier and want to go home?"

"Tell him you are worn out. Which is the truth."

Kupper waited, allowing his sudden flash of anger to subside. He must stall, somehow divest Steilig from his conviction.

Kupper said in a voice which he hoped was as cold as Steilig's, "You do presume, Herr Leutnant. I suppose you have considered that if I am not here you would doubtless command the Jasta."

"I have. And it would be better that way. You are dangerous not only to yourself but to the rest of us." Suddenly Steilig's manner changed. The stiffness left him and the eyes that had been so severe tried to express his sincerity. "Sebastian—I beg you! It is not easy for me to come to you like this. You must know we all honor and respect you. But I'm not at all sure we can cover for you much longer. You don't know how many times recently one or the other of us—Hochstetter or Zimmerman or myself—has saved you. You are making mistakes only a neophyte would make. You go down too low on balloons and trenches, you violate your own rules and break away by yourself chasing some poor photo machine while we're looking all over the sky for you—you are spending more time on their side of the lines than ours, which is unnecessary, since they will come to us. You see things in the sky that are not there and miss some that are. Sebastian, apply for leave. We don't want to witness your funeral."

For a moment Kupper held his silence. Then he slowly raised his hands level with his chest. They were trembling. He watched his hands curiously as if they belonged to another person. Then, with a summing of all the will in his body, he compelled them to remain steady. He held his hands absolutely motionless until he raised his head and smiled at Steilig.

"I appreciate your concern but consider it rather premature. Thank you for coming."

Steilig clicked his heels, turned and went out the door.

Kupper slumped into the chair and bent over his table. Steilig was right. He would apply for leave—soon. His hands were still quiet, but commanding their surrender had been exhausting. He must now see if he could safely ignore them.

Deliberately he reached for Maria's second letter and thoughtfully smoothed its pages.

My dearest Sebastian,

I am writing this after my long and I fear rather silly letter about war and politics of which I know so very little.

Forgive me if this reaches you when you are occupied with more important matters than the thoughts of a woman in love. You are so much wiser than I, but don't you agree true love is the bringing of many gifts to each other, the most precious, of course,

197

being oneself? And it is so difficult to express devotion in informal and unrestricted ways—perhaps we should try the Eskimo custom and simply rub noses. Ecstasy!

It requires thousands of small things, and moments of exchanging the gift of each other, to build a love between two people. I am so anxious for our love to endure and not atrophy with separation, time, or the war.

I know you believe in God and the Fatherland, and I am so glad that you do, as I believe in you.

I have heard of love without respect, but I think it is more likely a delusion suffered by men and women who are sick in heart. They profane the concept of love and cheat themselves and each other. What they call love is really pity, and pity in clumsy hands can become the most subtle torture.

What of us who do honor each other? Are we required by our very devotion to consume each other? God forbid! I would forsake our whole relation if I thought that one day I might grow jealous of your time or insist on your exclusive attention. The sharing of you with others must be my joy and not my fear. If I cannot willingly share your qualities, then I ought better remain a spinster.

I hope I shall learn the truth of love one day. Now there are only my own values to tell me. Oh, Sebastian! Does that sound naïve and childish? Even pompous, perhaps? I ask nothing of you except moments you care to give. And yet I ask a great deal. All I want is to give you happiness and make your life a continuous surprise. Always pleasant? Always tranquil? No, most certainly not, for that would be beyond my capacities. You may say, "My poor Maria!—how foolish you are, how stupid, how aggravating, how inept!" But let your voice always complain with a smile so that at other times, when you may be pleased with me, the smile may broaden all the more.

Say, if you like, "My Maria is neither ravishing, nor particularly intelligent, nor learned—but she is mine." Say that the stilted words of love are a refuge for lonely poets and we give only of the truth to each other.

I love you.

Maria

Kupper put the letter down and lit a cigar. How steady his hands were now! It was, after all, something he could accomplish if he forced them to behave. Steilig, he thought, not *quite* yet. If I can master these hands, then I can master my fears, which are the true cause of my deterioration. And I cannot leave here before becoming master of myself again. The sun of many little defeats can be permanent disaster.

He puffed thoughtfully, blowing smoke at the candle. Hochstetter had stopped playing his mouth organ. He had probably gone to mess. For the first time in months Kupper knew peace, and he treasured it. Perhaps tonight he would sleep.

He readjusted Maria's photo so the candlelight better illuminated her features. Then he picked up her letter and began to read once more. ". . . true love is the bringing of many gifts to each other . . ."

Kupper heard the crunch of boots outside, followed almost immediately by a rap on the door.

He looked up, dreading to break the spell of Maria's words.

"Enter!"

The door swung open. It was Feldwebel Groos.

"What do you want?"

"I regret disturbing you, Herr Kommandeur. Pilger said he has been forbidden to come here."

"For the moment that is my order."

"A dispatch rider just brought this from the Flieger Kommando. It is sealed so I decided it must be important." Groos laid a heavy brown envelope on the table. Kupper saw that it was addressed to him. He was about to open it, then paused. It was said Groos could read things upside down from a considerable distance, particularly if it might be something he could make use of in one way or another.

"You are dismissed."

"Perhaps it requires an answer."

"If it does I will make arrangements. Get out."

Groos clicked his heels, saluted and went out the door. It was very satisfying, Kupper thought, to see the disappointment in his eyes.

Kupper broke the seal and pulled out a small crudely made parachute which was attached to a square tobacco can. A note had been wrapped around the can and secured with a rubber band. He pulled off the note.

> This was dropped on our aerodrome at 4 P.M. yesterday afternoon (the 4th May). Am sending it to Flieger Kommand in hope they will know your location and forward it on to you.
> You will forgive my curiosity. I must confess having read the contents.
> Good hunting.
>
> > Ulrich
> > Staffelführer
> > Jasta 85

He shook the can. It rattled. He opened the top and tipped the contents into the pool of light formed by the candle. Three machine-gun bullets slipped out of the can and one rolled off the table to the floor. He picked it up and saw it was not of German manufacture.

Looking down into the can he saw a folded paper. He shook it out and unfolded it. The address on the box was repeated across the paper except that one word had been added: Obr. Leutnant Sebastian Kupper—*Murderer.*

He opened the paper and read the carefully printed German script. "You murdered my friend over Verdun, 15 December 1916. 1000 hours. You continued firing when the Caudron was obviously done for. I will find and kill you if I have to collide. You will realize the moment has come when we meet. You have not many more days."

It was signed "Chamay. 322nd Escadrille."

Kupper groaned. Here it was again. The nightmare returned in a tobacco tin, the one victory he would never forget. The red-haired flaming Frenchman was back to haunt him. How could he explain to anyone that the most difficult act he had done in his thirty-seven years of life was the deliberate turning back on the Frenchman and firing until he was most certainly dead. Someone had to silence those inaudible screams.

As he shoved the note from him he saw his hands start to quiver again.

He rose slowly and stood for a long time looking down at the bullets. Finally he went over to his cot and lay down cradling his face in his arms.

200

Chapter Eleven

May 1917
The business of a rabbit hole—

AT FIRST BABARIN was appalled by the Spad airplane. When Chamay brought it to the escadrille Babarin walked around and around it on tiptoe, posturing now like a toreador and now like an art critic as he exclaimed over its beauty. It was, he pointed out to Sussote, the perfect union of the delicate and the formidable. He bent down to examine the landing gear legs which were carved in one piece from laminated poplar. He caressed them thoughtfully. Afterward he stood for a long time nibbling at the fringe of his mustache while he studied the system of tubular push rods and levers which actuated the ailerons on the upper wing. With Sussote holding a lantern he spent the better part of one night becoming acquainted with the eight-cylinder Hispano engine, the Claudel carburetor, the induction system, and the two magnetos which provided dual ignition. None of his research saved Babarin from near disaster on the following morning.

Sussote sat in the cockpit of the Spad waiting to switch on the ignition and control the throttle. Customarily the mechanics, riggers and armorers reported to their airplanes for duty at least an hour before dawn. All had to be in readiness for the first patrol. A crew responsible for an aborted sortie suffered ridicule from their fellows and, depending on the seriousness of the deficiency, a tongue lashing or worse from Lieutenant Miralle. Both Sussote and Babarin were acutely aware of their special responsibility on this morning, since here in their hands was the escadrille's first Spad about to make its first sortie against the enemy.

202

"A day of honor," Babarin said. "It will be written in the histories of the Three twenty-second."

"They won't spell my name right," Sussote said. "All my life people write only one *s* and two *t*'s."

Even as the stars began to fade it seemed uncertain whether Babarin and Sussote would make a successful rendezvous with history. For after repeated attempts they could not start the Spad's engine.

"You do everything backwards," Babarin said icily. "I am now certain that when I call 'contact' you are switching off."

"On the contrary," Sussote replied, "it is you who are doing things backwards. Any fool can tell from the shape of the propeller that you are pulling it the wrong way."

"You do not understand these new in-line engines, *mon vieux*. At first it is necessary to pull them opposite to the starting direction several times, or risk a hydraulic pressure build-up in the cylinders."

"There is nothing complicated about starting a right-hand-turning engine by pulling it from right to left."

"It is still dark, thank God. From the cockpit you can't tell in which direction I have been pulling. What's more, when viewed from the cockpit this is a left-hand-turning engine."

"Very well." Sussote sighed. "You take over in the cockpit and *I* will spin the propeller."

Sussote climbed down from the cockpit and swaggered purposefully around the wing. After expressing mutual contempt by placing their thumbnails against their upper front teeth and making a flipping gesture in each other's direction, Sussote called out, "Contact!"

"Contact!" Babarin repeated from the cockpit.

Sussote swung the propeller. The results were immediate and multiple.

The Hispano roared to life in a surge of power far too quickly for Babarin. In response to the sudden blast the Spad's tail rose past the horizontal. As Sussote stumbled backward out of the way, the Spad tried to climb over the wheel chocks. In a second the tail rose higher, the nose went down. Just before Babarin managed to cut the power the propeller tips sawed at the ground. After producing a terrible splintering noise, the Spad dropped back into its normal three-point position. There was then a long and awesome silence.

203

"Sacre bleu!" Sussote muttered from a safe distance.

In descending from the cockpit, Babarin burned himself painfully on the exhaust stack which stretched along both sides of the fuselage, but he did not cry out. Far more agonizing was the thought of his place in escadrille history. And Chamay! His first sortie in the first Spad!

"You are a great ace," Sussote said. "You deserve the Iron Cross."

Babarin had not the heart to reply.

There was that morning a new record established in the 322nd Escadrille. Babarin and Sussote changed a propeller in exactly twenty-eight minutes, which was all the more remarkable since the feat involved stealing a new propeller from Lieutenant Miralle's precious hoard.

Later when Chamay roared into the air, Babarin prophesied that the Spad would bring him many victories—a prediction which soon proved to be accurate. For the Spad seemed to fit Chamay as a particular boat suits a particular sailor—its deep cockpit and ruggedlooking profile complemented Chamay so that the whole airplane seemed an extension of himself, and the flight characteristics of the type were an ideal match for his temperament.

"The Spad is not for old ladies," Babarin declared. In a surge of grandiloquence he told Sussote, "A Spad is for those who would kiss death as well as life!"

The Spad landed fast and its angle of glide was much steeper than that of the lighter Nieuports. It climbed well, and it could be dived straight down and pulled out so sharply that a man's eyes wanted to pop out of his face. It could not be thrown about in quite such quick maneuvers as a Nieuport, but it had a far greater feeling of solidity, which made it a better gun platform. All of these qualities appealed to Chamay, and during the first week he demonstrated his appreciation by shooting down an L.V.G. and a Rumpler. The following week he brought down an Albatros, another L.V.G., and a Roland, which splashed into the Aisne just at twilight. Chamay had become officially an ace by French standards, and in the *popotte* there was speculation on how soon it would be before he might expect an invitation to join the Storks.

Soon after Chamay's seventh victory, Jourdan again suggested they take a walk together. He chose the time after their midday meal, when the warmth of the May sun was at its best. "I find it easier to express myself if I am in motion," he began, "curious isn't it?"

"I hadn't thought of it," Chamay replied. Was Jourdan going to launch one of his aimless orations that went round and round and never arrived anywhere? Chamay forced himself to be patient. He was still flushed with the congratulations of his comrades, and even more stimulating was his discovery of a new sense of independence. He had not realized how reliant he had become on Denise and how much it had been his own doing. He had found no bitterness in thinking of Denise—after all, she had never *promised* anything. He had assumed much more than she had ever intended, and in his letters he had created a relationship that must only have surprised her. The first shock had been painful, but now it was over and the sense of freedom was very good indeed. And now, in less than two weeks, he had achieved special recognition among his fellows and there was increasing hope that he might be able to settle the score for Raymonde—for the spring had brought swarms of Germans to the sky sector patrolled by the 322nd. One of them might be Kupper. In addition, the Spad was an airman's dream and so, if one ignored the official news, it was not a bad war at all.

He hoped Jourdan was not going to talk about his younger brother. An oration would require less listening.

"I suppose I should be very proud of you," Jourdan said. There was something about Jourdan's even tone that irritated Chamay. Here stalked the same old hound dog who hadn't knocked down a Boche in months. Jourdan should really be put out to pasture.

"I received a call this morning," Jourdan droned on, "from the Stork group. They inquired if I would object to your transfer to Escadrille Three."

At last, there it was! Three! the home of Dorme, Pinsard—now commanded by the brilliant Heurtaux! The honors were coming fast. For an instant Chamay pictured Babarin painting a stork on his Spad. How excited he would be. Of course, he would not really consider leaving the 322nd and His Excellency, but it intrigued him to consider it. He tried to seem casual when he asked, "And what did you say to that, Capitaine?"

"I said I would not object at all. I would be quite pleased to be rid of you."

Chamay was stunned. He looked quickly at Jourdan's face. "You are amusing yourself?"

"On the contrary. You are riding very high these days. It seems to me you are much too cocky for the Three twenty-second."

"Maybe the escadrille could use a little cockiness." Chamay had not really intended to make such a curt reply, but there it was. He immediately wished he had kept his mouth shut.

"Perhaps. Although I rather think—not your kind." Jourdan kept his pacing absolutely steady. "I had another call last week which may also interest you. It was from a Monsieur Girard. He went to school in Switzerland with my younger brother."

Chamay was relieved. If talking about his younger brother would improve His Excellency's mood, then he would be willing to listen the rest of the afternoon.

"Monsieur Girard is with the International Red Cross and investigates maltreatment of prisoners. Civilians of course are the most usual offenders. Yet it seems two Boche airmen were rather nastily knocked about in a schoolhouse not long ago. They had surrendered and were quite helpless, and the unsavory part is that their attacker was in the uniform of a French airman. Supposedly a soldier! What do you think of a man who would behave like that?"

Chamay was silent. Instinctively, he brought up his hands as if to examine them, then quickly dropped them. He wanted to say the man must have been drunk and then he knew better.

"Now," Jourdan said finally, "if you want to share your cockiness with the Storks I suggest you pack your kit. However—if you want to remain with us you will take your cockiness out to one of the numerous rabbit holes in the aerodrome and bury it."

"And crawl in after it," Chamay said softly.

It seemed that from the very day of their conversation a transformation came over both Chamay and Jourdan. Word of the invitation to join the Storks soon drifted through the escadrille and Chamay was all the more honestly admired for his firm rejection. The other pilots were not sure they could refuse such a chance at glamour and almost certain glory.

As for Jourdan, the warm afternoon seemed to have triggered a secret reservoir of spirit in him—although it was doubtful if Chamay's firm demonstrations of loyalty were even partly responsible. Yet somehow, at a time when he had every excuse for melancholy, when

206

the whole of France seemed bent on its destruction, when all the established customs and institutions available as solace to the military man were threatened by a mere song called the "Internationale" in Russia and repeated now among French troops, when the fickle press appeared determined to down public morale in the hysteria of defeat, Captain Jourdan suddenly began to step out briskly, and his habitual stoop was replaced by the straight back of a St. Cyr cadet. He abandoned his pre-sortie platitudes, smiled frequently, and was on several occasions observed upon the brink of laughter.

"His Excellency has gone daft," Babarin remarked woefully. Babarin had personally assumed an attitude he considered appropriate to the news from Paris and the front, which was all bad. He found Jourdan's new and relatively buoyant acceptance of the facts shocking and decided it was his duty to behave as a counterweight. He must, among the lower ranks, compensate for his chief's irresponsible expedition into optimism. "He gives me the *cafard,*" he moaned to Sussote. "Either he doesn't know what is happening or he is drinking because he does know."

Jourdan's combat tactics changed as completely and radically as his manner. He was much less cautious now, slinging his fighters at the most distant enemy and their fuel reserve be damned. To everyone's surprise his pugnacious policy resulted in a string of victories with not a single loss since its adoption. A new and exhilarating morale swept the escadrille. It compounded as more and more of the pilots made the journey to Orly and returned with Spads. Only Bernhard, Folliet, Vincent and De Rose still flew their Nieuports, and they had been promised that in a matter of days they too would be flying Spads.

The extraordinary rise in escadrille morale was accomplished in the face of an all-pervading gloom along the Western Front which began on the first day of Nivelle's offensive and now spread like a great mantle of putrid gas over the whole of France. The ghastly losses along the Chemin des Dames, the massif of Moronvilliers, and north in the Forest of St. Gobain, were incomprehensible to the French Chamber; and became more so when it was realized that the German boast, "The situation is not good, it is better than good," did for once represent the truth.

A pitiful few meters of ground had been gained at a reported loss of three hundred thousand men, and to the north around Arras, the British had not done much better.

There was a morning Chamay knew he would never forget, when Jourdan stood in the midst of his pilots as if he held the tricolor in one hand and the sword of Roland in the other. He raised his great hound's nose to the red-dawn sky and delivered his valediction. "France will win," he said in a voice ringing with confidence, "because she must!"

On the same day Jourdan made his pronouncement the 21st Division of Colonial Infantry refused duty. Their action was imitated by rebellion of the 120th Infantry Regiment and soon many other divisions in the French line were in open mutiny. Calamity followed upon calamity. An artillery regiment tried to blow up the Schneider-Creusot munitions works. Mangin was removed from command of the First Army, Nivelle soon followed him into disgrace, and Pétain was placed in full command of the desperate situation. An unknown number of mutineers had already been shot. Painlevé, the Minister of War, demonstrated his mathematician's terror of uncertainty by avoiding decisions. As an opiate to their woes, soldiers not actually in the front line were provided enough cheap wine to keep them stupid enough if not flat drunk, so the haranguing of the agitators made little sense.

These were the days when Captain Raoul Jourdan reached down among the tattered, moth-eaten flags bequeathed to him by his illustrious military ancestors and brought forth banners of his own devising. He allowed them to flow in full glory before the men of his miniature command and in so doing raised them to giants.

Chamay's original admiration now approached worship, as did that of the others. If they had had to, they would have given their lives for the man they continued to call "His Excellency," a title they now pronounced with a new and profound tone of honor. Now, as he stood back to the wall, suddenly displaying a nobility they had thought forever lost in him and in themselves, it was awe-inspiring. They flew in triumph and in anger and with complete *élan*. For the seediest, most ineffectual officer they had ever known had taught them what it was to be a soldier for France.

The slow collapse of the offensive left the 322nd Escadrille with greater freedom of action, since the artillery maintained only token barrages, and spotter airplanes requiring protection were not so constantly at work. Most German troops were well protected in deep trenches or concrete blockhouses. The escadrille strafed them anyway. German balloons spotting for their artillery became irresistible in spite of their suicidal circle of ack-ack. Delander destroyed two, Folliet one. Trains, when they could be found, were much easier prey, but the Germans rarely moved them in daytime. Even so Pleven, Dutoit, Bernhard and De Rose working together managed to wreck three. Yet the main energies of the escadrille were directed to German reconnaissance airplanes and particularly their escorts. Very occasionally there were chances at bombers—the Gothas or Friedrichshafens—but their escorts of Albatroses or Fokkers were always so numerous that no one in the escadrille succeeded in making a fair run on them. It was during one of these pursuits that Jourdan himself shot down a Fokker triplane and thus at last became an ace.

His fifth victory was his first in five months.

After the early morning sortie there was no set schedule for the escadrille's flight activities. One morning they might protect a pair of photo-reconnaissance airplanes, the next they might join with another escadrille to pick up a returning flight of Breguet bombers and ease their ponderous way home. The pursuit ships had not sufficient range to provide escort for the full round trip. Pilots of the 322nd Escadrille flew as many as ten sorties a day and as few as two—depending on the weather, the state of their armament or their machine.

Soon after his rejection of the Stork's offer Chamay began a routine which at first caused little comment. While the other pilots were peeling off their bulky flight suits and making for the *popotte,* where cheese and wine would be waiting, Chamay remained at the side of his Spad, smoking a cigarette and talking to Babarin, whose gesticulations became increasingly frustrated as day after day passed. Chamay did not bother to unbutton his flight suit. As soon as Babarin had refueled the Spad and they had finished a discussion which obviously distressed them both, Chamay would flip away his cigarette, pull on his helmet, and climb back into it. A minute later he would be ascending into the evening sky. No one was greatly concerned, since he invariably climbed out to the west and disappeared in that direction. His fellow pilots would have been much more interested if they had thought he had sufficient time to make Paris and return to the aerodrome before dark. But they knew it was impossible and when they asked where he had been until the very last moments of dusk he simply replied, "It's the heating. We can't seem to solve it. No matter what the condition, as soon as I pour full power to the Hispano it overheats, then if I throttle back it becomes much too cool. And"—he would shrug—"you know Babarin."

Babarin's reputation alone was quite enough to confirm Chamay's need for test flights, and it was true the Hispanos were having cooling trouble. There was a system of louvers across the engine face which could be adjusted from the cockpit by the pilot, but it was a trial and error arrangement which resulted in the engine running either too cold or too hot depending on altitude or weather. Babarin, quick to resort to his tin-snips, had fashioned some bizarre scraps of aluminum around the cowling which he claimed would alleviate the trouble if not cure it entirely. Chamay solemnly explained to all critics that it was his obligation to give Babarin every cooperation and perform the necessary tests. The need for a test flight seemed to come at any time when Chamay was free from his regular combat sorties.

One afternoon as Chamay slipped the Spad down for a landing he saw the unmistakable figure of His Excellency waiting beside Babarin and Sussote. At once he took particular pains with his landing and flared out so that his wheels just kissed the new spring grass. Then he taxied most conservatively toward the tall man who stood slapping at his boots with a swagger stick.

When Chamay swung down out of the cockpit he frowned disapprovingly at the Hispano engine. "No," he said to Babarin, "if anything, it is worse than ever. We must try something else." Then he pulled off his helmet and walked to Jourdan.

He spent a great deal of time fishing a packet of Caporals from his flight suit, more time pulling one out and shaking the tobacco down, and as much time as possible in lighting it. Under Jourdan's silent and unrelenting scrutiny he thought he was putting on a fine show of calm.

At last Jourdan broke the embarrassing silence. "You are a most zealous engineer. Perhaps you should transfer to the technical section before you wear out this one poor airplane."

"It is my motor, Captain. I am having great trouble with the cooling."

"Mine seems to operate satisfactorily. So does every other Hispano in the escadrille."

"Ah, but my Hispano was made by Levasseur, while yours was made in Bois-Colombes. Folliet's is made by Chenard Walker, and he too is having difficulties. No matter what they claim, Hispanos are not all the same, Captain. It depends on who manufactures them." His Excellency, Chamay thought, could not argue with fact. While the Spad airplanes were practically identical, licenses to build the Hispano engine were held by several manufacturers and rarely did the parts of one fit the other.

"You have made eleven test flights this week, according to escadrille records. Quite extraordinary."

Chamay glanced at Babarin. He stood with Sussote in front of the Spad. They were staring at the louvers and cursing quietly. Chamay tried to direct Jourdan's attention toward Babarin with a shrug of his shoulders, and an exasperated sigh.

Jourdan did look at Babarin, but not in the way Chamay desired. "Oh don't be blaming Babarin now. The man is not so eleven-fingered as all that. You have been aloft in every pause in our operations and I am quite aware you have made two landings in almost total darkness. Authorization for test flights does not include permission to risk the aircraft or pilot."

"I really had quite sufficient light, besides it is good training."

"If I thought it were necessary training then I would arrange for us all to practice. Meanwhile, what is the trouble with your guns?"

"My guns?" Chamay asked innocently.

"You must also be experimenting with your armament, for if you use only half your ammunition on a sortie with the rest of us, you invariably demand a full belt for one of your solo test flights. I find this rather strange."

"It makes good sense. Supposing I was jumped?"

"Regulations distinctly state that test flights will be conducted only to the west and not more than ten kilometers from base aerodrome. You know as well as I do it is extremely unlikely any Boche would be in our immediate vicinity, particularly near dark."

"It might not be a Boche. Look at Nungesser. He was obliged

to shoot down an Englishman who mistook him for a Boche and wouldn't leave him alone."

"Alone. Exactly, my dear Chamay. I am not so ancient and fuddy-duddy as you take me. All of these theatrics with your precious Babarin have been interesting to observe, but not quite as convincing as you intend. I find your continuous need for test flights difficult to believe. But why aren't you satisfied flying with the rest of us? Why must you go it alone?"

Jourdan paused and cleared his throat. He slapped at his boot a few times with the swagger stick and flipped a tiny pod of mud from one toe. Ever since the business of the rabbit hole a new relationship had existed between them. Chamay knew now that Jourdan would never mention his siege of cockiness—or the German prisoners—again. He stood now as his friend as well as his commander.

Jourdan said, "I will not order you to cease these so-called test flights, but I will ask you to remember that we need you. Therefore I—I would like to invite myself along while you search for whatever it is you are looking for."

Chamay was so unnerved by the sudden offer that he addressed Jourdan as "Your Excellency" and then sought desperately for a refusal that would not offend. Finally he knew that, as always with Jourdan, only the bare truth would do: "This is a war of my own. It is something I must do alone."

Jourdan sighed. He stood for a moment, fingering his stick and flexing it to such an arc Chamay was certain it must snap. Finally he tapped the stick against the side of his kepi. It made a hollow sound.

"Be careful," he said and turned away.

Mocking birds whistled at the soft May evening and in the poplars bordering two sides of the aerodrome there were owls waiting to take over the serenade when the dusk became night. Already there were gossamer patches of fog in the hollows of the surrounding fields where the rivulets joined the stream, and among the dark clumps of trees which had survived at least three wars. For the air was balmy and yet the cold earth had still to recover from the numbing winter.

There was not a cloud in the sky, so that its depths appeared

212

shallow toward the west where the greatest illumination remained, and became deeper and deeper from the cobalt zenith to the thickening purple of the east.

There were many men who could hear this strange tranquillity, although in the vicinity of the aerodrome only a very few human beings were visible. And in other places they were not easy to spy, for they rarely moved except to scratch at their beards or body lice, or lean forward to spit. They were clutched in trenches or squatting in the forests of Champagne or gathered at the entrances of the multitude of caves which riddled the countryside.

Movement, it seemed, had temporarily been halted. As if by common consent Germans and Frenchmen and Englishmen, Belgians and Portuguese, and even the Russians trapped on the Western Front, paused to absorb these precious moments of twilight and reassure themselves that nature still staged such events. Along the Chemin des Dames the total absence of gunfire was impossible for some men to endure, and they became increasingly nervous. Others found the courage to speculate on what it would be like when the war was over, and what it would be like right now if a soldier was as highly paid as the workers in the war factories.

While men and things of the earth were momentarily held in a strangely fixed tableau, only one faint sound insinuated itself. At first hearing it was a suggestion rather than a definable tone, and then to the careful and interested listener it became the distant buzzing of an aircraft engine. Those with sharp eyes could discover the airplane even though it was so high it appeared from one moment to the next not to be there. It was at such an altitude that the wings still caught a reflection of the sun, although it had long since descended behind the horizon. The consequence was a luminous slit in the fading sky which moved slowly toward the west. And those men below who discovered it pushed back their helmets and said, "There—there he goes again." And others, farther back from the lines said, "There!—here he comes again."

Because of its extraordinary height no one of the helmeted men could be sure if the airplane was flown by friend or foe. And they did not really care. In the recent weeks when the weather was at all suitable they could be reasonably certain of spying it. So the single aircraft had become sort of a symbol of their own secret loneliness and they took it to their hearts. It was comforting to depend on something. "See? There!—follow my finger. Now *there!* —see him?"

Those who had come to anticipate the flight of the lone aircraft soon had various explanations for its presence. It was manned by an especially stupid aviator who was always losing his comrades, it was some general reviewing the battle situation, it was a special spy delivery airplane—it was not a real airplane at all but the ghost of one manned by the last aviator killed that day, and who had to make this final transition flight on the way to his reward.

Each evening when Chamay glided down to the shrouded earth Babarin would be waiting for him expectantly. He would come to the side of the Spad as Sussote slipped the chocks in front of the wheels.

As he pulled off his leather helmet, Babarin would ask Chamay, "Well?"

And Chamay would shake his head. "No. It isn't right yet. Not right at all. I will have to fly another test tomorrow."

"Of course, I will make some other adjustments."

Chamay knew and Sussote knew and Jourdan knew, and in time everyone in the escadrille knew, that Babarin would make no adjustments whatever. They eventually realized Babarin's lack of affinity for machinery was not disastrous. They respected him as a sensitive and understanding man who would certainly have no wish to spoil the aim of his lonely hunter.

Chapter Twelve

_____ *May 1917*

EACH MORNING when Kupper accepted the individual greetings of Jasta 76 and took his tea from the great brass samovar, he would look at it on the white-clothed table and value it still more. It gave the Jasta a sense of elegance and helped to erase the persistent memory of turnip marmalade, strange-smelling bread and tripe, which was the constant fare in the mess. Kupper would have liked to invite as his guest anybody who claimed that the officer Luftstreitkraft was the darling of G.H.Q. Soldiers ate nearly as well in the support trenches.

Now in warmer weather the table provided a pleasant gathering place throughout the day. Those officers not actually engaged in the morning patrol chose to linger about it, holding their cups level with the second button on their tunics in the Prussian fashion and discussing all manner of topics from women, which seemed the favorite, or homefront news, which was mixed, or war news as supplied by the Wolff Büro, which was mistrusted. The propagandists had finally come to admitting that Richthofen had been shot down in mid-March.

Most of the news was very good indeed, which accounted for the general atmosphere of ease and confidence about the table. But only in some ways, Kupper mused. And in others, he thought, there was a disturbing lack of appreciation among his officers. They accepted victory all too easily, almost as their right. And the fact that the Jasta had not suffered a single casualty since the raid by the British triplanes contributed to their arrogance. Now, to be sure, all

216

along the Western Front the Luftstreitkräfte were masters of the skies, but the pilots of Jasta 76 were behaving as if *all* of the opposition had been eliminated. Their own victories in a local sector had been fortified by reports from the farthest frontiers, and the cumulative effect was the belief in an early end to the war, with, of course, a German-dictated peace. The revolution in Russia had made a shambles of any resistance on the Eastern Front, and this had already resulted in the release of several German divisions. The U-boats were starving England out of the war, and the Italians were as good as finished. And no propaganda agency needed to tell the pilots of Jasta 76 who flew over the Chemin des Dames every day how obviously the French spring offensive had failed.

Kupper recognized that there was every excuse for optimism yet he wished it could be more controlled. There were still disturbing reports from the homefront and Kupper did not share the general opinion that America was so far away that its entry in the war should not be taken seriously. On occasion, when the talk turned to the new adversary, Kupper reminded his officers that a belligerent was a belligerent and the distant location of the United States made it just as difficult for Germany to carry the war to them.

Though the discussions were always friendly enough Kupper sensed a missing element which he could not at first define. At last he concluded it must be something rarely found in the Teutonic attitude, or was it possible the German mind was simply incapable of clemency? In the army tradition the majority of the Jastas were distinctly regional and were made up of men either entirely from Prussia or from Bavaria. Kupper had always been rather pleased with Jasta 76's uniqueness. Its personnel was a mixture of men from both major provinces of the Fatherland, and thus should have presented a reasonable cross section of the German entity. If it did, Kupper did not like what he saw.

Victory for Germany appeared to be just around the corner—if all went well, perhaps by autumn he would be walking through Maria's front door. He would arrive in civilian clothes if he could still find his English flannel suit, and perhaps if it was raining he would carry an umbrella. This soldier costume would be hung in a closet until the lemon yellow shoulder epaulets turned rust brown —and he wouldn't forget to lock the closet door.

Yet what about the others of Jasta 76 who appeared so permanently at ease in their smartly tailored uniforms—Steilig, Schröder, Zimmerman, Meyer, Just and Hinkmann? Not once had he heard any of them offer an idea about the enemy's future when their defeat was final. Hochstetter alone had once suggested that the rehabilitation of France and England was going to be Germany's responsibility and would present grave problems. His warning brought only flat uninterested laughter and the most puerile speculations on French booty which at once changed the course of the discussion to the happier subject of women. The Jasta daydreaming seemed unanimous and fixed. There they were, each one landing on a lovely French aerodrome and climbing down from his cockpit, medals jangling. There they were, overwhelmed by amorous French girls who were beside themselves in their attempts to express admiration for such noble conquerors. And who was going to pay the bill? The male enemy—or what remained of his numbers—was to be tramped on, and if he became inconvenient, he would be kicked under the bed.

Jasta 76, Kupper thought, at least made one concession to chivalry. They often remarked on the courage of their enemy even though they seemed utterly callous about his immediate or future fate.

On a muggy afternoon in early May Kupper waited near the table with Hochstetter and Pastor, a rosy-cheeked pilot who had replaced the wounded Keim. The three formed a special Kette and were waiting to take off on a "sausage run." Since the recent stagnation of the front, Kupper had been trying a new tactic which had so far been successful in scoring the destruction of five French observation balloons. In spite of the French defeats the sausage-shaped bags were still active in directing artillery fire at German infantry. At some time during the day the Jasta message center was almost certain to receive a telephone call from Staff, or occasionally a direct plea from a forward infantry position: "The French are flying their damned sausages again! Do something!"

The doing something was not easy. If the French spied an approaching airplane they hauled down their precious sausage, and once it was fairly low their protective fire became so concentrated it was almost impossible to attack, pass through it, and survive. So surprise was the best policy, when it could be achieved. Kupper saw no reason to risk more than one airplane in an actual attack, since the element of surprise would certainly be lost to any succeeding airplane. Thus he kept his Kettes for the sausage run small—one pilot to slip in for the kill and the other two as strength should they encounter an enemy patrol. He had chosen three Kettes for balloon duty and appointed two leaders in addition to himself, Steilig and Schröder. It was the leader's task to destroy the balloon, and the Kettes stood alert in daily rotation.

It was Kupper's afternoon.

They waited beneath the budding elm trees, and the brass samovar glistened in the afternoon sun. They sat back in the utmost comfort, tunic collars open, helmet and goggles at one hand, a cooling cup of tea at the other.

Over the end of his cigar Kupper watched the parade of thunderstorms which had ringed the horizon since early afternoon. Between the larger storms there were cavalcades of towering cumulus, many of gigantic proportions. Kupper was pleased with them. They provided excellent concealment before the final jump on a balloon.

Pastor had his eyes closed and his head turned toward the sun which made his rosy cheeks even more inflamed. He was lounged in one of the three canvas deck chairs provided by the infinite resourcefulness of Feldwebel Groos, who claimed to have found them in the greenhouse of a nearby château. The chairs had actually been commandeered by an infantry sergeant with whom Groos had made a business-like proposition. If the infantry sergeant would give Groos the chairs he would tell him the exact whereabouts of a horse killed by an odd shell that very day. Since the infantryman couldn't possibly carry all three chairs to the front by himself, and since he did not share Groos's belief in spoiling officers, and since the infantry lived mainly on turnips and barbed-wire rations in spite of the way things were going, Groos soon had the chairs. He saw no reason to credit the infantry sergeant with even a mention. It had already become Jasta custom that pilots waiting for a sausage run occupied the chairs and their priority was respected.

Without opening his eyes Pastor said dreamily, "I wonder what it will be like when the war is over."

"It depends on who wins," Hochstetter said.

"Is there any question in your mind?"

"There certainly is." It soothed Hochstetter's sense of mischief to bait Pastor. In his opinion the newest member of the Jasta was altogether too damned pompous and he needed a good many more combat hours under his belt before he should have dared say anything. Moreover he was as much of an iron neck as Steilig—a thorough Prussian with a head shaped like the end of a torpedo. Hochstetter loathed him.

"It would not surprise me," Hochstetter continued, "to see the Kaiser running for his life by midsummer and ourselves flying white flags from our wing tips."

"Oh, come now. The French have shot their bolt, and the English are isolated and will have to do the white-flag flying. The war is over except for the cleaning up."

"That's what I'm afraid of—victory."

"*Ours?*" Pastor opened his eyes and looked incredulously at Hochstetter. Kupper also looked down from the clouds, but not in surprise. Hochstetter was likely to say anything.

"Yes—ours. We are great warriors, but poor victors. We can't get it through our heads that even the vanquished can still hate us. 'Now we have won,' we say, 'and let's all be jolly good fellows together. Don't worry, old fellow—we'll see that you don't actually starve, unless' "—Hochstetter lowered his voice to a growl—" 'unless you disobey.' That's the kind of thing that scares me. My God it's going to be an awful world if we win! We don't know the meaning of mercy."

Kupper rose quickly and went to the samovar. Damn that crazy Hochstetter and his half-wisdom! It was as if he had read his most secret thoughts. He had stumbled upon the thought of compassion, of course—or had he? Hochstetter was far more perceptive than many knew. He was like a monkey imitating the follies of his fellow men, yet the spear of his ridicule was all the more sharp because he disguised it behind a careless manner. Mercy! Wasn't that what he himself had tried to show that flaming Frenchman? And with what result, other than a year of nightmares, hands that would not remain still, and now a new and terrible sense of doom which rose like a fever the moment hostile aircraft were sighted. Since his note from a Frenchman whose name Kupper now knew almost as well as his own, every formation of enemy airplanes included a man named Chamay and every French airplane became *the one*. The most skillful fighter could not handle a man who was willing to collide. The prospect of actually meeting Chamay often became so inevitable in his mind he had actually considered having the target device painted over—but then he had rather been damned than be such a poltroon. He told himself he would really never meet Chamay out of a thousand other Frenchmen, and even if it did happen, then Chamay would present no more threat than any of the others.

He mastered his hands momentarily and set his teacup before the orderly. "Another—and add some brandy."

Though he was some distance from the chairs he could still hear Hochstetter's mocking voice.

"We are *barbarians!* The English rightly call us Huns. And why not? A long time ago we did our best to destroy Rome and it wasn't until a few years ago we got around to becoming a nation. We have no long legacy whatever of true civilization, and mark my words, Pastor, if we win this war we'll be at each other's throats in six months."

Kupper heard Pastor's urgent whisper. "Shut up with your nonsense! You've upset the commander."

Kupper strolled back to them. He stopped beside his chair, eying them and sipping from his teacup. He was pleased to see that his hands remained so steady. I am becoming very good at it, he thought. Perhaps in time I will learn to tame them in public and let them loose to fret and tremble only when I am alone.

To Hochstetter and Pastor he said, "I did not leave you gentlemen because I was upset about a few words spoken in jest. I left because I wanted to think for a moment about what might happen to people like us if *they* win."

Pastor rose quickly from his chair. His face was flushed and his blue eyes angry. "Now it is the commander who jests," he said stiffly. He struggled with his tunic collar a moment, clipping it together. "May I have your permission to take a short walk? I will remain in sight."

"Of course." Kupper shrugged his shoulders.

Pastor clicked his heels and turned away. Watching his deliberately casual pace, Kupper said, "I think I have offended our young friend."

Hochstetter yawned at the sun and said, "His little pink ears are hearing a band. Let him enjoy the music while he can. Give him time to live until a bullet bounces off his iron skull and he may win the Order of Despot first class."

The two-hour cruising range of the Spad allowed Chamay a considerable choice of sky before he turned for home. During his earlier flights alone he had occasionally ventured far behind the German lines, hoping wild chance might end his quest. Later he decided that deep penetrations of enemy-dominated sky were a waste of fuel since only once had he even seen any enemy aircraft aloft. He found the hunting much better if he flew a course roughly parallel to the front; then by firmly establishing the farthest limits of his stalk he could turn about and eventually land at his own aerodrome just before darkness.

He always remained high, for he knew very well that his chance of meeting a certain Albatros was the equivalent of putting a bundle of francs on a single roulette number. He wanted to see as much sky area as he could at a glance. Thus he flew at the maximum altitude a German Albatros could achieve, and eliminated the distraction of searching the sky above him. To reduce his oxygen need he remained almost motionless in the cockpit, breathing slowly and deeply. On the ground he deliberately cut his smoking in half.

Before Chamay left on these special flights he vowed he would not be diverted no matter how tempting the bait. He had seen many airplanes marked with the black Maltese cross slithering far below him across the landscape. They were not always escorted and might have been easy kills if he had put the Spad in a long dive. He let all such inviting targets go except on one gray afternoon when the overcast prevented him from flying above two thousand meters. There—three Albatroses escorting an L.V.G. Chamay put the Spad in near vertical dive and stabbed straight through their loose formation. He did not fire a shot because he wanted to look at all three Albatroses before closing in on one. No target device. He had since wondered what the Boche pilots had thought when they suddenly saw a French Spad holding all the advantage slip harmlessly past and keep going.

Another evening he had descended into the twilight and found himself on a collision course with a pair of Fokker triplanes. He instantly shoved the Spad's nose past the vertical and dived for the earth. The Fokkers gave chase but were hopelessly outclassed by the Spad. He lost them over Tergnier and sped westward along the Oise. It was the first time in his flying career he had run away from an enemy. But he intended to do it again if it was necessary. One thing mattered. Kupper. Until that man could be found he must employ every device to stay alive.

Actually the chances of encountering Kupper were not quite so unlikely as he had first supposed. If he was still alive then his experience along the Western Front extended at least back to '16. He was an ace and thus would hardly be transferred to some quiet area—to the Balkans or Austria. Certainly the onslaught of the recent offensive would have kept Kupper within sectors of the hottest action—which would place his Jasta 76 somewhere between St. Caudry and Attigny. From any place in between he could range the front on demand, and there, Chamay told himself again and again, at some hour on some day the demand for Kupper to be in the same piece of sky must eventually coincide with his own regular escadrille sorties or his solitary hunts.

To keep up his spirits during the long and lonely patrols Chamay sometimes sang. He had never been able to carry a tune with any prolonged success—at Pau, Raymonde had once offered to pay their considerable wine bill if he would desist—but in the cockpit, with his vocal sins covered by the steady roar of the slip stream and the Hispano engine, he found he could bellow at the top of his lungs and sound to his own ears like an opera star. Yet he was obliged to confine his singing to the climb and descent. At five thousand meters the lack of oxygen kept him silent.

There were other evenings when Chamay brooded on his purpose aloft and passed the entire flight in a grim review of the day Raymonde had been killed and how the German Kupper had blown his face away. On such days the anger rose in him so fiercely he was compelled to press the triggers of his Vickers guns though there was nothing ahead but sky. After a quick burst his fury would subside and he would go back to searching the sky below. He did not like himself on these days, and when at last he returned to earth he was strangely exhausted. He blamed it on the tension of the hunt and because his movements in the cockpit were so confined. Only his head moved with any degree of regularity. Occasionally he might reach forward to tap his gloved finger on the glass face of the altimeter to make certain he had not slipped down below the fighting limit of an Albatros. Sometimes he would draw his feet away from the rudder pedals and stamp them against the cockpit floor in an attempt to revive his circulation, and sometimes he wiped at his nose with the back of his gloved hand. Otherwise he sat like the mechanical man he had once seen with his father at Tivoli in Copenhagen. He remembered how fascinated he had been to watch his head revolve to a certain limit, stop, then revolve around to the opposite limit, stop, then start the sequence again. Like the man-doll in Tivoli, Chamay seemed perpetually activated by an inner machinery. On such days he discovered that an hour and a half's searching could be a very long time.

At night when he lay staring at the darkness, he would try for a few moments to escape into his private world. Then he would think of Denise, sometimes envisioning her as she had been at Pau, and sometimes as she had been in Monsieur Michaud's little inn. And sometimes he would remember how she had told him, "You will only destroy yourself."

Yet he could not seem to put Kupper out of his thoughts. Some force beyond his comprehension obliged him to enact the same sham every day with Babarin and say to him, "No—you have not found the solution yet. I must make another test flight." Then as if drawn by a powerful celestial magnet, he would mount into the sky, his whole being dedicated to meeting one man.

On the gloomy days he had tried to sing because he also remembered the regret in Denise's voice when she had said, "Revenge is the first step to madness."

And there had been an evening when his throat produced a frightening, high-pitched sound. Not even the thrumming slip stream or the roaring Hispano could make his voice sound like anything but the falsetto whimperings of an imbecile. God, he thought, that cannot be *me!*

Since that evening he made no further attempts to sing, regardless of his altitude. And at last he promised himself that if he did not meet Kupper after ten more sorties he would announce that the Hispano was fixed and abandon the hunt. He pencil marked the actual flights on the fabric inside the Spad's cockpit. When Babarin asked what the seven marks represented he turned on him angrily and told him it was not his affair.

Babarin was worried.

224

A courier came running toward the three deck chairs. After saluting he handed Kupper a slip of paper. He glanced at it and immediately strode toward his Albatros.

A pair of French sausages. Over Suippes. Heavy artillery concentration. The laconic note left much unsaid, Kupper mused, as he pulled on his helmet. The demand of course, was for something to be done about the French balloons, but the how was left to the flier's imagination. There was nothing new about balloons in the vicinity of Suippes. The French had grouped a considerable amount of heavy artillery in the area and as experience had already taught them, they had ringed their heavier guns with hornets' nests of flak batteries. The air above Suippes was a hot place at any altitude. Coming in low brought just that many more guns to bear.

"I hate this sausage business," Kupper grunted as he mounted the short ladder to the cockpit. It was not like a combat aloft between man and man—no special skill was demanded in shooting at a sleeping hippopotamus. If he was close enough a man could close his eyes and still hit the ungainly thing. Which might not be a bad idea, Kupper thought unhappily. Then a man wouldn't see the curtains of smoke and steel he had to penetrate. Hochstetter said that balloons frightened him so he foamed at the mouth. In descending on them, he claimed, his saliva curdled until his lips were flecked with white.

He looked across at Hochstetter now. He was ready, engine running. He flipped a salute and a smile. On the opposite side, Pastor —also ready. A nod. No salute and no smile. The days of *"Hals und Beinbruch"* shouted like an ancient war cry over the thunder of fourteen Mercedes' engines, echoing up and down a full Jasta line of quivering Albatroses, were becoming increasingly rare. The facile Kettes might be more efficient, Kupper thought, but three men could not do the same for one another's morale.

He raised his hand and lowered it. The crews released the lower wing tips of the three Albatroses as the engines snarled in unison. They shielded their eyes against the blown dirt and grass and watched after their charges as they lifted from the earth. They saw them wheel almost immediately toward the west, a trio of mottled birds.

Pilger who had been watching from a distance because Kupper had forbade him near the flight line until he learned how to smile,

225

now smiled. He approved of action and the more the better. He did not like to see men sitting about in deck chairs waiting for the war to come to them.

Chamay was discouraged and was thinking of abandoning his search for the day. During the afternoon he had watched the accumulation of enormous cumulus clouds, some with anvil heads extending for miles and others fat and posturing like overburdened soldiers marching toward the north. The rumble of thunder from every direction gave the impression a great offensive had been launched. Such days were not favorable for Chamay's hunting because too much of the sky area was occupied or obscured by cloud, and his quarry might pass within a few kilometers and not be seen. There were not so many thunderstorms in the direction of Reims, so Chamay set his original climbing course for the torn and crumpled ruins of the city. Once over it he turned south and east, hoping to avoid the principal masses of overhanging cloud.

He saw now that he had been overly stubborn in continuing the flight. He was moving dreamily through an enormous celestial cave, surrounded on every side by pillars and arches and buttresses which seemed to support the few blue patches of sky. There were stalactites of vapor in the cave and little wandering figurines which looked to him as if they had lost their mothers. There were plump and pompous figures, and as he passed these vaporous illusions, Chamay smiled and was reminded of a diplomatic party he had once attended with his father. Everyone in the receiving line was so puffed up with his own importance that no one would say more than a few words to anyone else. *"Bon soir, m'sieur. Bon soir, madame. Enchanté."* For a time he amused himself greeting the more imposing clouds.

There were also creatures in the cave—pythons of trailing mist and immense manta rays squeezed between the arches. There were flowers and insects and every sort of animal—there was all that the mind's eye could see, Chamay thought. And he immediately promised himself that if he saw too much, he would permanently abandon his hunt regardless of the present count.

He looked at the pencil marks on the fabric just below the throttle. There were now seven. Two more to go.

He reached to his flying boot and pulled out a stubby pencil.

Enough for this day. He placed an eighth mark beside the seventh, then carefully replaced the pencil.

Here there were valleys and canyons between the cumulus, but below, the bases had nearly all melted together. There were open shafts and here and there it was possible to see the bottom of the well, but no airplanes of any sort were to be seen. I am alone in the sky, he thought. I am the last boy out of school and there is no one about to play with—or fight. So I am going home before I wander too far and become lost—and anyway I am afraid of the dark. Where am I? Somewhere to the east of Reims. The course then, back to the aerodrome? Say—two hundred and forty degrees. No, two-fifty degrees. There's a north wind here. But thunderstorms everywhere. A minor squall to go around over there—ah! Now a rainbow arching right down to a town that looks familiar. Of course, Betheni-ville. Then you have wandered to the side of the cage where they keep the wild animals. Well they must be all asleep or having late supper, because there is not a sign of any moving thing below. Not even at the bottom of the rainbow.

He reached beneath his thigh and pulled out the small grease-stained chart he had been sitting on. He pushed up his goggles so he could study it better. Betheniville. Good enough for a reference point. Now what was the distance home?

He spread two fingers between Betheniville and the approximate area of his aerodrome. Holding his fingers rigid, he moved them down to the scale of kilometers. Good enough. Twenty—twenty-five minutes' flying time.

He slipped the chart underneath his thigh again, then banked the Spad around toward the sun. He shoved the nose down slightly and heard the thrumming tone of the Spad's flying wires increase in pitch. Oil pressure to the Hispano? Excellent. Revolutions per minute? Excellent, and smooth in the bargain.

Babarin, you are a good mechanic, and at the end, and when this thing is done, then I will make it up to you. I will see that the truth is known and your reputation enhanced. I promise you, Babarin.

He passed down through four thousand meters.

Chapter Thirteen

—————————————— *May 1917*
With a rainbow—

DURING THOSE DREADFUL DAYS when the waves of French splashed against the bulwark of the Chemin des Dames so violently, Leutnant Buchman's church tower had been obliterated. Now he performed his duties from the summit of a hill some fifty-three kilometers to the east of his old sector. While the hill offered a much safer and more stable observation post than the ruined church tower, neither Buchman nor Corporal Stein liked the change. There was relatively little to report except for occasional spasms of fire from the French heavy artillery near Suippes. Furthermore the transfer had deprived Stein of his connections, and without friends to blackmail or steal from, their noon fare was usually barbed-wire rations garnished with a few turnips. Even the artificial separation between officer and noncom provided by the church tower was now denied them. They were obliged to dine in silence not ten paces from each other, and since they were the only men on the top of the hill the situation became increasingly uncomfortable. As a result Buchman often sent Stein away on one pretext or another, hoping he would be gone all day and be damned if the telephone broke down. And he hoped wistfully that somehow, somewhere, during Stein's excursions to the rear, he would discover another cache of wine, and most of all, by some great and glorious miracle, return with another ham from Kempinsky's.

Now Buchman moved to his tripod binoculars and was annoyed to see the French balloons over Suippes still sailing serenely in the last amber light of the sun. His telephone would certainly be buzzing again. The forward positions would be catching a nice dose of French scrap iron and they would want to know where in the hell the Luftstreitkraft was. Well, he could not enlighten them. It had been over half an hour since he had reported the two balloons and they could not have been up more than five minutes prior to his first report because he had faithfully swept his assigned sector every ten minutes just in case. There had been no distractions except the thunderstorms which had crackled and rumbled about him all afternoon. Lightning was everywhere and, inspired by a particularly violent storm, he had pointed it out to Stein and exclaimed, "God's artillery!" And for some time afterward he wondered if the war had not deprived the world of a great German poet.

Suddenly his attention was diverted from the balloons. A brilliant rainbow appeared in his binoculars. It plunged to earth halfway between his position and the balloons! He had never seen a rainbow magnified so extravagantly and he heard himself exclaim, "Ah!"

He could not take his eyes from the spectacle. He was held spellbound by the sunlight shafting almost horizontally across the garish green fields, the veil of the rainbow dragging between the two balloons, and behind it the flashing of artillery.

Finally he said softly to Stein, "Here they come at last—" Now all about the balloons he saw a luminous crosshatching of tracer fire and above them blossomed huge clusters of black and white smoke balls.

A short distance from the explosions he saw three Albatros airplanes. One of them broke away from the others and dived through the flak.

Over the nose of his Albatros Kupper saw two parachutes open, then sail out from beneath the fat brown balloon. The observers. Good! He had no wish to kill them.

The fat brown carcass was looming up at him. In another few seconds it would fill the space between his guns and he would press the triggers. There were men running across the field below the balloon. Many more were clustered around the whirling winch. It was smoking. They were hauling in the cable at full speed.

There was a great yellowish patch on the right ear of the balloon. Kupper swallowed repeatedly to relieve the increasing pressure on his ears. He held only a slight forward pressure on the control stick. A long shallow dive would put more bullets in the gas bag than a steep approach. Explosive bullets. Forbidden, but they got the job done, and so much for the laws of war.

You didn't take all this flak to miss a balloon.

Jesus Christ in heaven, protect me!

Everything to the maximum—everything against the stops. You are not supposed to dive an Albatros at this speed because the wings will come off—first the top fabric and then the rest will depart. So they say. He tried to ignore the sharp explosions all about his wings. Over the roar of the Mercedes and the slip stream they were flat sounds like the smacking of a fist. The nearer explosions made the Albatros jump. Yellow lances were everywhere. Everything this moment was yellow. The sun, his wings, even the black Spandaus were turning yellow. He was flying into a fountain of yellow steel needles. The balloon! Nothing else mattered. Get it and get out fast.

Flak never hurt anyone.

Tracers spewing upward. Spider webs of machine-gun fire. More dangerous than worrying about the wings coming off.

Jink! Jink right, now left. Kick hard rudder, skid—roll the other way.

Steady. Five seconds more—maybe six. Hands, wonderful hands, steady. Maria, say a prayer.

It must be an old balloon. Covered with patches, like a skin disease. One parachute has collapsed over a stream. Men are running away from the balloon. They know it is a goner. Hold for the fat pig, Sebastian! You *will* come out alive! Destroy this gas bag and your day's work is done and you can go home—like a workman in the twilight.

Look to your left. Hochstetter is sliding down on the second balloon. He is catching his share of iron. Brave Hochstetter—the man who plays the clown.

Hold for another two hundred meters. Be sure. God what a fast winch! The sausage is almost on the ground. What a view of the world! A scrofulous balloon between the butts of two guns and crossed with the radiator cooling pipe on the upper wing.

Now! Let go with everything.

He pulled both triggers of his Spandaus. They jumped in response. The entire airplane shook as two long lines of skittering light appeared over the nose. The lines terminated along the top of the balloon.

He pulled back slightly on the stick. The nose of the Albatros rose and the line of tracers raked the fat brown bag. Before the illuminated lines swept back to the thing's ears, there was a tremendous explosion. The Albatros was tossed on its side and Kupper had to use full aileron to keep it from rolling on its back.

He did not remember releasing the gun triggers. He was too busy feeling his airplane and himself. All seemed intact.

A great black glob of shrapnel burst dead ahead. If it had been 155 millimeter the concussion alone would have blown him out of the sky.

Now climb out of here.

He dared to glance back and in an instant saw all he desired. A flamer! The balloon was collapsing in a brilliant ball of smoke and fire. Men were running from the winch.

The flak is easing. Dive down to the treetops now. The flak cannot reach you there. Now along that little valley! Take a chance on the small-arms fire.

Where is Hochstetter? The other balloon is still fat. And nearly on the ground! Hochstetter?

Oh, God!

Hochstetter's Albatros disappeared behind a low rise in the ground. Kupper closed his eyes. Why couldn't it have been that Prussian pig Pastor? And where was *he?*

Kupper searched the few patches of open sky and the cloud bases which were now nearly solid. Where *was* Pastor?

Kupper discovered that he was panting like a dog run a long way. His goggles were steaming up from the great heat of his body.

He pushed his goggles up to his forehead. Where was Pastor? Nothing aloft. Only the dark foundations of gigantic clouds. And a rainbow. He had been too busy to notice it before. Think of the rainbow and not of Hochstetter. You are alive.

Kupper could see the depression which marked the River Suippe. Staying low he could follow it back to Betheniville and then easily to his own aerodrome. He banked steeply left to avoid a clump of French infantry. They began shooting at him, then stopped suddenly. They were waving their arms. They seemed to be cheering. Why? They would butcher you if they found explosive ammunition in the Spandaus. They would not believe it was just for balloons. They would say it could also be used against men, and they would be right.

Where was Pastor?

He glanced back over his tail. At last. All is forgiven, Pastor. You are covering well, though you should be a bit higher. And not so directly behind.

Wait—you are a *Spad!*

Kupper hauled the stick back to his stomach. In response the Albatros rose straight up and rolled over on its back.

Chamay had barely commenced his long descent for home when he saw that his way was barred by crenulated battlements of cloud. Dead ahead there was a series of brilliant lightning flashes. So he turned ten degrees to the left of his original course, thinking to compensate later when he had rounded the southern extremity of the wall. The diversion was complicated by a second flank of cloud which required Chamay to lose altitude quickly. He twisted through the maze of vapor, always seeking the more open places, and when he emerged in the clear found himself over the Suippe. Now he saw the other end of the rainbow!

He leveled off at three thousand meters and passed through a rain squall. The droplets stung his cheeks and for a moment he lowered his head beneath the cockpit coaming. When the hissing on his leather helmet ceased he looked up again. He had emerged from the squall. Only a few seconds later he chanced to look down. He took a deep breath, for there, just behind the trailing edge of his left wing, flew a single Albatros.

Chamay searched the sky all around. There was not another airplane in sight. The Boche was obviously lost. Yet just below the horizon there was Suippes itself quite in the clear. As soon as he recognized it the Boche would certainly turn back for his own lines.

What a pigeon! This one could not be allowed just to fly away.

Chamay eased back on the Spad's throttle for a moment and waited for the Albatros to emerge from the leading edge of his lower wing. When he saw it he shoved the nose of the Spad down until his ring sight centered on the Albatros' cockpit.

He shoved full throttle to the Hispano and dove. In seconds he had closed the distance between himself and the Albatros. He pressed the triggers and it was all over by the time the Vickers had spat thirty times. The lost-lamb Boche never knew what hit him.

Even as Chamay saw him plunge into a marsh near the river his attention was diverted by a display of ack-ack just to the south of Suippes. Then he saw an orange flame against the darkening plain and a biplane pulling away through a screen of tracers.

So his lost lamb had not been alone.

Chamay's alertness returned immediately. He should have known. Where there was one Boche there was another. Now it was he who was alone. He searched the glorious sky, but he found nothing.

He looked down at Suippes again. The ack-ack was diminishing. The Boche was getting away. Also flying an Albatros. Keeping very low. Just on the treetops. Clever fellow.

Chamay made a wide circle. The gunners must be drunk. With all those fireworks something should have stopped the Albatros, but the Boche continued, making fast for his own lines. He was almost directly beneath now, free of the anti-aircraft around Suippes. Only the ground troops were firing at him.

Chamay could not resist such an advantage. He made a final sweep of the sky to make sure the lone Albatros below was not one of many, then he peeled off to the left. He dove straight for a division in the landscape where a valley paralleled the river. There he would slip in behind the Albatros.

Chamay was entirely confident. The Spad was much the faster airplane. And the Boche was preoccupied with ground fire. Imagine Jourdan's pride! Two easily confirmed victories from what was supposed to be a test flight.

The flier's treasure was altitude; it could so easily be exchanged for speed. The flying wires screeched through the long descent and then he was in position. Beyond the propeller blur, rising and sinking with the undulations of the landscape, was the Albatros. Its details were etched against the black base of the same squall Chamay had flown through only moments before.

Even the sun was working for Chamay. He was closing fast now. The Boche had not yet looked back over his tail. He was either a beginner or hopelessly distracted.

The Spad began to bounce slightly in the Albatros' wash. The range was ideal—full wings across the ring sight—tail in the center.

Chamay moved his fingers to the triggers just as he saw the German turn to look back.

He closed the triggers and the Vickers pounded. Smoke and the odor of cordite streaked back to Chamay. Empty shell casings bounced against the guards. But the Albatros was no longer there.

Kupper's cheeks sagged from the pressure of the vertical turn. His whole body was forced down against the seat. The blood drained from his head. He waited for the inevitable. Certainly the wings must give way! The Albatros shuddered like a stricken bird.

Never had he asked so much of an airplane. So instantly, so completely joined in his instant terror.

You fool! Flying in a state of shock because of a little flak. Neglecting your own first dictum—*never* neglect the view over your own tail. This Frenchman owns your life.

He held the control stick back to its limit. The horizon sank. Clouds, then the sky, rolled swiftly past his gun muzzles. Another horizon rolled upward as the blood returned to his head and his cheeks drifted back into position.

And there is the Frenchman. Just over the Spandaus. He was not quick enough and his Spad would not turn so tightly. Aha! Things are now turned inside out.

The Frenchman is turning. He should not. He has more speed. He should dive and come back for another day. If he holds this, I can close the range. I will get him because I must.

You are the greater fool, Frenchman. Run away while you have the chance! Run, little boy—I don't know where you came from, but go home. Little boy, if you hold that climbing turn ten seconds longer—

Kupper pulled the triggers of the Spandaus. The Albatros shuddered for the brief duration of the burst, then smoothed as he released the triggers. Still too far away, of course. Much too far for good deflection shooting. Yet maybe the tracers between his wings would send the little boy scurrying. Better the tracers than explosive bullets.

He is a stubborn Frenchman. He has seen me and knows he will never get away unless he runs. Then why doesn't he?

Suddenly Kupper knew. He was as certain as if the note in the tobacco can had plastered itself across his sights. And his hands began to shake.

Because there was no other open space they climbed into a vast arena with its livid walls and balconies frequently illuminated by inner explosions of lightning. The mighty structure soared full to the evening heavens and against it the two aircraft were like insects.

As he climbed away from the Albatros Chamay raged at himself. While he had sat counting his score the Boche had looped right around him. That man was no beginner! Even so there was no great worry. The Spad could climb at almost twice the rate of the Albatros and at straight and level speed was at least thirty kilometers faster. And there was no comparison in a dive, which was why the Boche dared not run away. I'll be down and underneath him before he can find me—and on my way up in his blind spot.

The smudged green earth revolved more swiftly as Chamay tightened the turn. He looked back. The Albatros was closing a bit. Let him. The poor fellow was valiant. He must do with what he has.

Chamay saw there was only one exit to the arena unless a man chose to be torn to pieces inside a thunderstorm. There was a division in the cloud to the west and the gates were fringed with the gold of the sun. When they reached its level and the sun was right he would dive away.

As they circled, the light changed continuously. At one moment he would lose the Albatros as it passed through the shadow of a cloud. Then it would be revealed as two black lines etched against a lighter cloud, next as two thin slashes of sunlight reflected against a darker cloud. At times the whole arena seemed to whirl around them, and the two airplanes remained fixed in space. They climbed higher and higher until they had surmounted the lowest wall of cloud. They left the vaporous dungeons and sewers and portcullis gates and mounted to the region of arches, towers and horizontal escarpments.

They had made five complete circles of the arena when Chamay saw the glistening lances angling upward past the tip of his right wing.

He glanced back quickly. He had allowed the Boche too much if he had closed enough for even a trial burst. He pushed full throttle to the Hispano and waited until the universe had revolved to the place of his choosing. Then he rolled the Spad over on its back and dove until he slipped out of the sun.

The instant he passed into shadow he hauled back on the controls bringing the nose of the Spad back past the vertical. The pull-out jammed his whole body hard in the seat and his feet slipped down on the rudder bars. But his fingers remained on the triggers waiting for the Albatros to appear in his sights.

Now! He should be just ahead. Certainly he could not have followed through the dive. An Albatros would come to pieces.

Yet the Boche was not in the sights as he should be. And he was not above—or below—or behind. It was impossible, but he had vanished.

Chamay pushed up his goggles and wiped at his eyes. He could not, *must* not, believe them. He studied the wall of clouds. It would be suicide for the Boche to try an escape through such cumulus. Inside there would be heavy rain, hail and violent turbulence.

Then where was he?

Chapter Fourteen

_____ *May 1917*
In the halls of the winds—

FOR A MOMENT Chamay wondered if he had been fighting a ghost. A moment before there had certainly been two airplanes in this relatively confined space. Or had there been? No, he thought, there is just as surely only one, and I am sitting in it.

He shrugged. There was nothing more to be done here. The light was going fast and Jourdan had commanded absolutely no more night flying. And as usual his thinking was sound. The escadrille could ill afford to lose a valuable Spad simply because it was too dark to see a ditch or the top of a tree.

All right, Your Excellency. You've been game enough to look the other way on these test flights. I'll turn for home before it's too late.

He searched the sky once more and turned back toward the northwest. There stood the only gateway leading from the arena. He had been settled on course less than a minute when he became uneasy. He looked back quickly over his shoulder.

The Albatros was so close on his tail he could see the smearing of oil around its engine.

For an instant, for a shattering incredible instant, he knew what it would be like to die. The sight of the Albatros so near studded his reactions so that for the time of a gasp, of five heart pounds, he simply sat and waited for the machine-gun bullets to tear his back and neck to pieces. In this splinter of time he was able to think, What was never going to happen to me—has happened.

There has been plenty of time. How long does it take to press a trigger?

Yet nothing had happened. I am still alive.

He glanced back. The Boche was holding position. But his guns were not firing.

When the sun blinded him Kupper was well aware that this would be the moment the Frenchman might use to his great advantage. Kupper had anticipated his dive and vertical reversement. So the moment he lost the Spad in the sun he also dove the Albatros. His target had been chosen carefully. It was on the outside of their circling perimeter, a long wisp of gray cloud clinging like a parasite to the side of a majestic cumulus. There was a space between the monster and its thin dependent—perhaps two hundred meters. There Kupper thought he could find perfect concealment. As he slipped between the two clouds he looked below and saw the Spad pull out of its dive.

Kupper slowed the Albatros until he barely held flying speed. Then he flew back and forth in a long oval, waiting. At one place in his pattern there was a large tear in the bottom of the parasite cloud. By circling slowly over the gap he could observe the Frenchman less than five hundred meters below. He too was circling,—and looking. In his mind Kupper beseeched him to go away. His hands were calm but he did not want to fight this Frenchman or any other Frenchman or Englishman or American or even a Russian.

"Go away!" he yelled as if he could be heard. "Chamay! Go home before we kill each other! I *know* it is you!"

But the Spad continued to circle within the arena, flying on for a bit, then circling again, then flying straight once more. Searching, seeking me, Kupper thought.

He glanced at his watch. He had been aloft nearly an hour and a half. Maximum fuel duration for an Albatros was two hours. He must allow fifteen minutes to the safety of the German lines and another fifteen to Jasta 76. Even if he planned on a forced landing in an open field he must do something very soon. Go away, Frenchman! I shot up your friend because that was a time long ago when I believed in mercy. I was wrong. It no longer exists in man.

"Go away, Frenchman!"

It was silly of course. Every French airplane was not flown by a man named Chamay. That man below, now so clearly dropping his guard, was undoubtedly a Duval or a Diderot or a Henriot. Well Duval or Diderot or Henriot or Chamay or whatever your name is, you are forcing me. If you will go home now we can both lick our wounds until another day.

Kupper looked at the holes in his lower right wing and saw where shrapnel had torn through the upper left wing. Indeed there were many wounds. From tail to nose. His poor old-new Albatros. But at least the Mercedes seemed to have been spared. At this leisurely speed it hummed sweetly.

You have two minutes to let me out of here, Frenchman. Then there will be no choice.

His eyes swept the whole sky. It was habit. There might still be another airplane, even at this unlikely hour. Friends or foes. But he saw only the great bulging cumulus totally surrounding a vast harbor with a single channel. The red sun shafted through the outer buoys and illuminated the rafts of lenticulars, the jettys, buttresses and piling scattered all around the arena. The visible surfaces of each gigantic cloud were rumpled with bulbs and nodules, grouped humps and wens, old pistules and bubbles, each of which became part of a watching multitude. From the highest cupolas and balconies of the arena, Kupper fancied he heard them beginning to howl.

For it was time. The Frenchman would not go and he could wait no longer. He sighed and wiped his nose with the back of his glove. This was the first time he had ever been able to choose the moment of victory and he did not like it. Without the preceding heat of battle it was more than ever like planned murder. He pulled down his goggles.

He held his concealment until the Spad passed into a position directly below. Then he dropped down on it.

The Spad was flying straight and level. Bound for the exit, Kupper thought. But it was too late now. The Frenchman was looking back. Kupper was so close he saw his mouth open. It must be done. It would at least be quick.

He pulled the triggers of his Spandaus. They remained still. He pulled again. Dead! He grabbed the right charging bolt. It would not move. The left. He could move it only a few millimeters back and forth. A double jam! And the Frenchman was diving away.

Kupper followed the Spad down. He must pretend he could shoot even if he was helpless. He must stay on the back of this Spad, worrying at him until he could free his guns.

The Albatros shook horribly with the speed. The flying wires screeched in protest. Kupper did not care or hear. He pounded and yanked at the Spandau charging bolts with his right hand while he flew with his left. He leaned far forward trying to jerk at the ammunition belts. God damn all guns!

He bit the end of his glove, pulled it from his hand, and threw it into the slip stream. He tried to release the cartridge gate with his bare fingers and in his concentration on the greasy mechanism nearly lost sight of the Spad.

The Frenchman was leveling out and turning. He must not allow it. He pounded alternately on the charging bolts and pulled at the triggers until his bare hand was covered with blood. But there was not a sound from his guns.

After a thousand meters straight descent Chamay knew something had gone wrong with the Boche. Why hadn't he fired?

He looked back. The Albatros was still coming—not more than fifty meters behind. But he was still not firing. Chamay's mind spun in the hurricane of noise. Instinct—reflex—*think!* The Boche must be crazy. If he tries to stay on my tail when I pull out of this dive his wings will fold. His Albatros won't take the punishment. He will have to ease out gently. While he is saving the pieces I can jump on his back.

He ventured a moment's glance over his tail. The Boche was beating on his guns. So! You will not die today, Chamay.

Chamay pulled slowly back on the Spad's stick to ease its wild trembling, then eased in left aileron and rudder. There is no hurry now. I will set him up as I please. I will keep him so busy throwing the Albatros around the sky he will never have a chance to break his jam.

The Spad rose steeply and fell away in a graceful *chandelle*. The Albatros, following, was caught for a moment in hesitation. Chamay glanced back and was satisfied. What could be more difficult than trying to fly and clear a gun at the same time! It made a man curse God, his mother and the fine day he first left the ground.

The moment of hesitation broke their identical maneuvers. They passed, and for an instant Chamay thought the German would ram him. He rolled away to avoid a certain collision. Looking back in amazement he saw the profile of the Albatros for the first time.

A shout escaped him. A savage shout which rose straight and clear from the depths of his soul. For the Albatros bore a painted target on its fuselage.

Chamay hauled the Spad around, slammed full power to the Hispano, and climbed for the extra altitude he needed. At last! *Kupper!*

Turning, he looked down to see the miniature leather-clad figure still struggling with his guns. He had abandoned the chase, knowing his guns were his only hope. Or was this a trick, Chamay wondered.

Now above the Albatros he eased back on the Hispano and slowed until the Spad nearly stalled. Kupper could simply raise his nose and fire a burst if his guns were actually working.

Chamay saw him look up, then go back to his guns.

Cunning—or was it the truth? Kupper, the old hand, would have many ways to an ambuscade, but he had already had his chance.

This was not right. He did not want Kupper this way. Then he thought of Raymonde.

He cut back the throttle, and pushed the nose of the Spad over until the cowling of the Hispano seemed to slice the distant Albatros in half. With the reduction of power the descent of the Spad became an easy glide.

Chamay watched the Albatros slowly enlarge. It was as if he saw it in a secret dream—every twist and turn was matched by his own so that the relationship between the two airplanes remained constant.

Only the distance between them lessened gradually—as it pleases me, Chamay thought. Kupper must know there is no escape and the longer the inevitable can be postponed the better. Be damned to him! He is getting what he deserves.

They swirled about the arena. Time and again the Albatros made for the concealment of the clouds. Every attempt was thwarted by a line of tracers directly across his path. Chamay was herding the Albatros. He would allow him to turn toward the center of the arena if he wished, but not toward the outside.

At last Chamay was so close upon the tail of the Albatros he could see the yellow epaulets on Kupper's shoulders. In a very tight turn he saw him look back. He was still struggling with his guns.

The time had come. His torture had lasted approximately as long as Raymonde's.

Chamay's mouth became a hard line as he maneuvered until the Albatros filled his ring sight. His fingers moved to the triggers, but he restrained them until Kupper's helmeted head swam into the cross of the ring.

Hold another second. Be sure. So close—so easy.

He saw Kupper look back a second time. I can see his eyes, Chamay thought. I can see the rotten bastard's *eyes!*

Gradually, a few meters at a time, he lessened the distance between the tail of the Albatros and the Spad's propeller. When he was nearly upon it he slipped up and to the right so that he flew less than ten meters from the Albatros. He could see down into the Albatros cockpit and every detail of Kupper's jacket and uniform was plainly visible. He appeared to be a much smaller man than Chamay had pictured.

Kupper was no longer trying evasive maneuvers. He was flying in almost a straight line and had apparently given up struggling with his guns. For a moment Chamay wondered if he was about to raise his hands in surrender. If he does, I won't see it, Chamay decided.

Do it now. Have it over with. Slip back a little and blow him right out of the sky. Just as he started to pull away, he saw Kupper raise his hands. He *is* going to quit!

But Kupper only pushed his goggles up on his forehead. He dropped his hands at once and turned to look directly up at Chamay.

He is so old, Chamay thought. He has no right to be so old! And his eyes? They are waiting for me to do it—not challenging, just waiting. How can he sit there like a cornered animal?

Suddenly Chamay knew he must break away from those questioning eyes. They were not begging for quarter as he would have preferred. They clearly asked—when? *Eh bien,* Kupper. When was now.

He eased the Spad's throttle and slowly slipped past the tail of the Albatros. He was aware that Kupper's eyes followed him for a moment, then he saw him turn into the cockpit. Your wait is over, Kupper. Don't look back again.

The Albatros slid into his ring sight. Since Kupper was flying in a straight line it remained fixed against the gray mass beyond. The cross in the sighting ring bisected the fuselage of the Albatros.

Chamay saw that Kupper's head seemed to be bent forward. Why

244

didn't he move? Why didn't he try a turn or chop his engine suddenly—a collision might very well be the end of both of us.

"Kupper! Don't quit on me! Fight with what you have!"

Chamay's fingers crept slowly across the triggers.

"Kupper! God damn you—do something!" To Chamay's astonishment he found that he was yelling at the top of his lungs. As if Kupper could hear him, as if Raymonde and Jourdan could hear him, as if Denise and Nungesser and all the world could hear him.

"Kupper! Move! Quick! You are making a murderer out of me!"

His fingers were posed on the triggers. His will commanded them to press against the metal, but they would not move. And he knew he had waited too long. The tail of the Albatros, the back of Kupper's leather helmet—they were all still full in the right sight, but suddenly his wrath faded before the memory of two frightened faces in a schoolhouse.

He deliberately moved his fingers from the triggers.

He took a deep breath and shook his head as if to spin away the vision of what Kupper could have looked like this second. A hundred-odd thirty-caliber bullets did terrible things when concentrated on a single human body. And at this range he would almost certainly have become a flamer.

I am going to let you live, Kupper. For this day. Perhaps another time we will meet—perhaps never. Now I do not really care. Something has happened to me I do not understand. I know now what it is to make a helpless man a gift of his life. But where is the man who seconds ago would have denied it?

Chamay slammed full throttle to the Hispano, climbing up and away from the Albatros. It was the maneuver of triumph, a signal usually performed over the base aerodrome to signify a victory over the foe. As he rolled off the top of the steep *chandelle,* he looked down to see Kupper's upturned face. He cut the Hispano all the way back, let the Spad's nose fall, and dove at an easy angle until he was once more alongside the Albatros. He eased in slightly, matching his power to Kupper's and for a long moment they flew in formation.

Chamay pushed up his own goggles. Their eyes met, and for the first time since he had seen an enemy aircraft Chamay realized he was looking at just another man.

He raised his hand to his helmet and flipped a salute toward

245

Kupper. He saw Kupper raise his hand more slowly and exactly repeat the gesture.

Then he dived away.

And he knew he would never forget Kupper's eyes.

Chamay found that he lacked enough fuel to make his own aerodrome, so just at darkness he landed at Mareuil, a temporary base for the 24th Escadrille. After his explanations to the commander of the 24th he was allowed to telephone His Excellency. *"Mon Capitaine*—Chamay here."

"Ah? You are alive. That is something at least. And where are you?"

"At Mareuil with the Twenty-fourth."

"Indeed?" Chamay heard His Excellency's voice grow cold. "Is your Spad damaged?"

"No. It is quite all right."

"A good thing for you. If we didn't need your valuable airplane it would not distress me if you stayed there permanently. I ordered you not to fly at night—"

"I did not. I landed just before dark."

"Then why didn't you return here?"

"I went hunting—a long hunt."

"Chamay, you have pressed my patience too far. You will not be permitted any more of your so-called test flights without my special order."

"Very good, *Capitaine*. Further test flights will not be necessary."

"What was that? What did you say?" In spite of the wretched connection Chamay was certain that Jourdan had understood. He smiled because he was so certain His Excellency was stalling while he mastered his curiosity.

"I said it is a poor man who would shoot a helpless pig."

"What was that? I do not follow you at all, Chamay. Ah—but perhaps I *do!*" There was such a long pause Chamay thought the connection had been broken. Then he heard His Excellency's voice clearly, and all the annoyance had gone out of it. "Yes. It is quite clear to me now. I rather think I know what has happened. You sound like a changed man. May you sleep well tonight."

"Better than I have in a long time. Good night, Your Excellency."

Feldwebel Groos stepped into Pilger's tent. He placed his fists on his hips and looked down at the giant who lay writhing on the cot. A single guttering candle illuminated his pale eyes though they were nearly closed in pain.

"You have reported sick. What is the matter with you?" Groos asked.

"I have a bellyache."

"So? Have you been eating something you would not share with your comrades? Have you stolen another ham?"

"Did you see Kupper's face when he climbed down from his airplane?"

"His face looked all right to me. There was some blood on his hand, but from the holes in his craft I should say he was lucky. And what has Kupper's face to do with your belly?"

"He has quit fighting. I knew it when I saw him—right away. Then instead of going to his quarters he went to the message center and sent an application for leave."

"That's bad, I agree. Steilig will take over and he is a fire eater. We will all be working our asses off. So that's the cause of the rumpus in your belly. You are already establishing an alibi."

Pilger groaned and clutched at his service belt. He unbuckled it and threw it at Groos's boots. He clawed at his hair and his mouth became alternately taut and slack. He muttered and mumbled and Groos could only make out a part of what he was saying.

"You're acting delirious, Pilger, and I don't like it. I warn you if you go dippy on me I'll call the medics and they'll probably ram you with an enema."

"God damn you, Feldwebel Groos! Didn't you see his *hands?* They were *quiet!* Didn't you see! They weren't shaking, I tell you! Even when he wrote the message they were quiet—and under control. That's what gives me the bellyache!"

Groos dropped his fists to his sides. He stood for a moment looking down at Pilger's perspiring face. "I don't understand you, Pilger. There are many things about you I have never understood."

He shuddered. Then he turned and walked out of the tent.